These Wicked Delights

JESSI ELLIOTT

For Mom—
your endless love and support means the world

PLAYLIST

America by XYLO
High by Dua Lipa and Whether
Heaven by Julia Michaels
Holding a Heart by Toby Lightman
Little Deschutes by Laura Veirs
Unbreakable by Jamie Scott
Hearts by Jessie Ware
Electricity by Sam Pinkerton
Darkside by [SEBELL]
Can I Exist by MISSIO
Fangs by Little Red Lung
Give Us a Little Love by Fallulah
Waiting Game by BANKS
Medicine by Daughter
Eyes on Fire by Blue Foundation
Piano in the Sky by Winona Oak
Here with Me by Susie Suh and Robert Koch
Hell to the Liars by London Grammar
Heavy in Your Arms by Florence + The Machine

Tessa by Steve Jablonsky
Suns and Stars by Really Slow Motion
Revolution by UNSECRET and Ruelle

CHAPTER ONE

S pending my eighteenth birthday working late on a school
project is hopefully not a sneak peek into what my year
is going to look like.

Stifling a yawn, I reach for my peppermint tea and take a sip,
wrinkling my nose at its lukewarm temperature.

"We're almost done," Lana says with a sympathetic smile as
she ties back her red wine-colored hair.

I wave her off and move to push my tea aside. My fingers
hover around the outside of the paper cup, and I frown. It's radi-
ating heat. *What the—*

"Emery?" Jessa says, pulling my attention away from
the cup.

I shake my head, flipping the page in my notebook. *I need
sleep.* "It's fine. We need to get it done." The assignment is due
in a few days, and with the girls' opposite work schedules,
tonight was the only time we were all available to finish it.

"We should be out partying, not stuck in this musty library,"
Jessa whines, picking at her chipped manicure.

I shrug, glancing around to find we're the only ones left in
the building.

We finish the assignment an hour later. As we walk out of the school, Lana and Jessa link their arms through mine, the wind whipping around us, shaking leaves off the trees lining the lot. It's already dark, and the temperature has dropped. It's only the second week of November, but it feels more like the middle of December.

"Come on," Jessa says with a grin, "let's grab some food."

"Can't," I say. "I need to get home."

Lana pouts. "We have to do something to celebrate you getting old. Where do you want to go?" When I open my mouth, she quickly adds, "I'm not taking 'no' for an answer. Holly can scold me later." As if my mom would ever yell at her.

"Old?" I laugh, elbowing her side. "Fine. Let's go to Bread and Butter. But only for a little while." As much as I'd rather go home, I can't deny the desire for a latte and a massive piece of chocolate cake.

I send Mom a text to let her know I'll be a little late.

"Excellent choice," Jessa says, tugging us along toward Lana's car, where we pile in and head for the café.

Lana drops Jessa off before we head to my place. We take a right onto my road and drive for a while, gravel crunching under the car until Lana slows to a stop in front of my two-story farmhouse. The lights on either side of the door cast a warm glow on the covered porch where I've spent many summer afternoons reading until dark. The black shutters on the windows are a stark contrast to the white siding, but it gives the place character. Most of the house is obscured from view by massive trees anyway, which makes it feel private and secluded. The house belonged to my dad's parents and their parents before that. I often picture myself living here for the rest of my life and passing it down to my own child someday.

"Thanks for the ride," I say, shooting Lana a wink, "and the cake."

She grins at me, her pale green eyes glimmering. "Of course. Hey, before I forget, I'm going shopping in Augusta this weekend. You want to come?"

I grab my bag off the floor. I've lived in Covington my entire life; I've never been anywhere. My heart longs for the adventure of getting away from this town, but I've never been able to bring myself to leave. Even for a day of shopping a couple hours away. "Let me make sure my mom doesn't have anything planned. I'll text you later."

"Perfect." She glances toward the house and arches a brow. "Whose car is that?"

"Huh?" I turn to look, and excitement bubbles in my chest. I'm grinning like a kid on Christmas morning when I say, "Nova's here."

"This a secret boyfriend of yours I don't know about?"

I smack her arm. "No. Gross. I've told you about him. He was my dad's best friend. He comes around a few times a year and always visits on my birthday. Has for as long as I can remember."

"Oh yeah! The silver fox that brings you presents. Huh. He's kinda like a sexy Santa, but for your birthday."

I roll my eyes, shaking my head. "Are you done?"

"Yeah, yeah. Happy birthday, Em."

"Thanks." I shoulder my bag before closing the door, then hurry up the gravel driveway and the steps, the harsh wind making my hair fly in every direction. A hurricane of burnt orange curls obscures my view as I fumble to get my key in the lock.

Lana honks before backing out of the driveway and disappearing down the dark road.

Once inside, I drop my bag onto the bench and flip the lock over before hanging my key on the little hook next to the door.

Then I kick off my shoes and toss them into the coat closet. The scent of cinnamon and apples tickles my nose; Mom always has at least one candle burning in the house, and she tries to coordinate them with the seasons.

Muffled voices float through the warm house, and I follow the sound down the hall, the old wood floors creaking under my stocking feet. I run my fingers through my hair, attempting to untangle it as I step into the kitchen and find Mom at the stove. My eyes quickly land on Donovan—or Nova as I've called him since I was old enough to talk—who is sitting at the kitchen table. His brown hair is a bit grayer than when I saw him over the summer; longer, too, curling slightly at the ends.

"Hey, Nova." A grin spreads across my lips as he gets up, opening his arms just in time for me to run into them.

"Happy birthday, Emery," he says, wrapping his arms around me. There's a fondness in his tone that makes my heart swell.

Donovan is the closest thing I've ever had to a father. My dad died a few months after I was born from a brain aneurysm. Mom says it was completely random. He was fit and healthy, but none of that mattered. For eighteen years, I've missed someone I never really knew, someone I have no memory of. It's a weirdly unexplainable grief that I'm still learning to live with.

Nova made it a point to become a part of my life after his death, and I look forward to each visit. Maybe it helps me feel connected to my dad, and maybe that's weird, but I don't care.

And when my birth mom died in a car accident while on a business trip in Savannah when I was five, her sister Holly took me in and raised me. She never married or had kids, but from the moment she adopted me, we became the only family the other needed.

"Hi, honey." Mom smiles once I detach myself from Nova, who leans against the table. She pushes the pin-straight light brown hair away from her face with the back of her hand and wipes her palms on her worn jeans. "Did you have a good day?"

I take a seat at the table. "Same old." I look to Nova. "What have you been up to?"

"Same old," he says with a smile. It's the kind of smile that makes the skin around his eyes crinkle.

"I ordered burgers from that barbecue place you love." Mom glances at the silver watch on her wrist; I gave it to her for her fortieth birthday a few months ago. "Should be here soon."

I try to catch her gaze, but her eyes won't meet mine. "Did you get fries?"

She finally looks at me for a brief moment, forcing a smile. "And onion rings."

I nod along because I'm not sure what else to do. If something is wrong, I don't want to bring it up in front of Nova. "Great," I say instead.

"I'll be right back," Nova chimes in. "I left Emery's gift in the car."

That catches my attention. "You didn't have to get me anything."

He waves me off, grabbing his navy jacket from the back of the chair and shrugging it on as he leaves the kitchen.

"Is everything okay?" I ask after hearing the front door shut. We don't have long before Nova comes back, but I need to know what's going on. Maybe she had a bad day at work. She's a nurse at one of the hospitals in Atlanta, and as she's told me on more than one occasion, some days are harder than others.

Mom nods, again forcing a smile.

I can't help but frown. "Why don't I believe you?"

She presses her lips into a firm line. "It's your birthday, Em—"

"I don't care. Talk to me." I want to be there for her like she's always been there for me.

There's a moment of heavy silence, then she sighs. "There's a lot you don't know about this family, and I'm not sure how to tell you."

Uh, where did that *come from?*

I cross my arms. "Wait, what?" That is *not* the direction I was expecting this conversation to go. "What are you talking about?"

"Oh, Emery, I—"

The front door opens and closes. "Food's here," Nova hollers, coming back into the kitchen with a brown paper bag in one hand and a purple gift bag in the other. He glances between us. "Everything okay?" He sets the gift bag on the counter and the food on the table.

"Of course," Mom says as she turns to the cupboard and pulls out plates. "Let's eat while it's hot."

We sit around the table. I chew and swallow, but my burger tastes like dust. My stomach is twisted in knots and my mind is racing. Mom didn't have a chance to elaborate before Nova came back, so my brain has resorted to coming up with impossible answers. I have a long lost sibling. Mom was in the CIA, which is why she was always away on business trips. My inheritance was stolen and now I have no way to pay for college.

This is ridiculous. I shove those thoughts away. *I need real answers.*

I glance up from my plate at the exact moment Nova and Mom seem to be exchanging a worried glance. I drop the fry in my hand and exhale a heavy breath. "Okay, that's it. Someone needs to tell me what's going on. You're both acting super weird, and I'm freaking out over here." I shove my plate away and turn to my mom. "What were you going to tell me?"

Her face pales as her bright blue eyes go wide, and she looks at Nova as she wraps her beige cardigan tighter around herself.

"Emery," he starts, his voice level and calm, which only makes my pulse race.

My attention snaps to him. "You know something about this?"

He nods. "It's why I'm here."

For some reason, my stomach sinks. Something like betrayal flickers through me, but I don't have time to question it. "I don't understand," I whisper. Nova comes every year on my birthday.

"There are things you need to know." There's a subtle urgency in his tone that I definitely don't like. "You're eighteen now," he continues. "Things are going to change quickly. You need to be prepared for that, or it could be very dangerous for you and those around you."

The food in my stomach feels like concrete. "What are you talking about?"

He hesitates before saying, "I understand what I'm about to say is going to sound crazy. You've known me forever, so I hope you can trust that I want to make sure you're safe. It's what your parents wanted."

My vision blurs as tears gather in my eyes. I swallow hard, but can't bring myself to speak.

Donovan's face is filled with a gut-wrenching mix of concern and guilt. "You're a Wielder, Emery. Someone with the ability to call on the elements of nature and use them. And now that you're of age, your magic has been awakened. You may not sense it now, but you will soon. It could take days, or weeks . . . even months for some Wielders, but it's important you start learning how to use and control it early on."

I stare at the man I've known my entire life who suddenly feels like a stranger. I open and close my mouth twice before turning to Mom and shaking my head. "Is this some sort of joke? Because it's not funny." It sounds absolutely ridiculous. *Wielder. Magic. Awakened.* What the hell am I supposed to do with that?

She glances down, exhaling a shaky breath. "It's not a joke, honey." She lifts her head and meets my gaze, her eyes glassy with unshed tears. "He's telling the truth. Your father's family . . . they had power—"

"No," I snap. "I don't believe any of this." And I don't want to hear about it.

"I'm so sorry, Emery," she says. "I wanted to tell you. I should have years ago, to prepare you for what's coming. But I was scared. I didn't know how to tell you or how'd you react."

I'm waiting for one of them to laugh, to let me in on the joke, but their expressions remain serious.

My head spins as I try to rationalize what I've been told. Nope. It's not happening. This is crazy. It's not . . . This isn't real.

I push my chair back, and it scrapes across the linoleum floor. "You're lying." I'm not sure which of them I'm directing the accusation at. Both, I guess. Hot tears burn my eyes, and I try to blink them away. "Why are you doing this?"

"I know this is a lot to take in," Nova says, his voice soft and filled with sympathy. "I'm here to help you, Emery. I have a place you can stay. It's a safe environment where you can learn and explore what abilities you have. There are other Wielders who live there. Spending time with them will help you adjust as your magic grows stronger."

He's insane. I need to get out of here. No. *He* does.

"Stop." My voice cracks as I back away from the table. "You need to leave." I press my hand against my chest as if that will help stop my heart from cracking in two. I've looked up to this man my entire life, and now . . . I don't even know what's happening, or *why*.

"Emery, please," Mom says, getting up and coming toward me.

"No," I say through the tears. "He's lying. He has to be. My dad—"

"Was one of the strongest Wielders in history," Nova says, still sitting at the table.

Mom reaches for me, but I pull my arm back and retreat another few steps until I bump into the counter.

"Mom . . ." My voice is thick with tears.

Her expression crumbles. "Your father didn't die from what you think he did," she says.

I freeze. "What?"

Nova gets up now. "His magic consumed him. He pushed his power away, refused to work with it. He wanted to live a normal life, to be a normal husband. Simon didn't want his magic, so he pretended it didn't exist. And it worked for a while—until it didn't. His power went unchecked and it destroyed him, Emery, and if you don't come with me and let me help you, the same thing will happen to you."

My vision blurs with tears, and my throat feels so tight I don't think I can speak.

"Honey—" Mom starts.

"Get. Out." I manage those venom-filled words and swallow past the lump in my throat.

Mom shakes her head, panic flashing across her features. "Nova—"

"It's all right, Holly," he assures her in a soft tone.

"Get out!" I scream until my throat is raw.

Mom closes her eyes, tears rolling down her cheeks. "You need to go with him, Emery." Her voice is steady.

I shake my head. "You can't be serious. Mom, he's crazy. There's no—"

She sniffles, opening her eyes to meet my gaze. "I started packing your bag while you were at school."

Betrayal whips through me like a smack to the face. "What?"

She wipes under her eyes, but tears continue to fall. "I can't help you with this, but Nova can. Please, *please* let him." She reaches for me again, and this time I let her wrap her fingers around my wrists. "Because I-I can't lose you too."

"I can't just leave. I'm in school. I have a life." It sounds like a weak argument even to me, but it's all I can come up with. I don't believe anything I've been told. I can't. Because if it's true

—if I somehow have magical abilities—everything I've ever known about my family, my life, it all comes into question. And I'm not sure how to live with that.

CHAPTER TWO

"Please don't make me go," I beg my mom, my bottom lip trembling as I watch her continue to pack some of my things into a duffle bag.

She stops moving around my room and guides me to the end of my bed, where we both sit. She holds my hands in hers, squeezing them almost to the point of pain. "I don't have a choice, honey. I am so sorry."

I stare out the window, watching the trees sway in the heavy wind. "None of this makes any sense, Mom. I don't . . . have magical abilities." I turn to her, shaking my head. "There must be some mistake."

"Emery—"

"I think I would know if there was magic inside me," I snap, and she flinches. I pull my hands back and stand. "I don't know what angle he's playing or what he wants . . ." My voice trails off when Mom starts packing again. "Are you really going to force me to go?"

She stops filling the bag with my clothes, keeping her back to me. "You'll be grateful for it someday." She sniffles. "I only hope you can forgive me."

"So I don't have a choice." My voice is barely above a whisper.

"You have no idea how much I wish I could help you, but what you need to learn should be taught by someone who has experienced this change and understands it."

"There hasn't been a change," I shoot back in a defensive tone. I feel exactly like I did yesterday and the day before that. Nothing is different.

With a sigh, she zips the bag shut and faces me. "I know you don't believe anything we've told you. It will take some time, but you'll understand more once you accept this. Please let Nova help you. Listen to him. Allow him to show you how to figure this out. Okay?"

I stay silent because no, it's not okay. Everyone is lying to me and has been for years. I don't know what to believe anymore. Which of the stories I've grown up hearing about my parents are true? How can I be sure?

She stands in front of me in silence for a moment longer before she nods. "I love you, Emery. Nothing will change that, not ever. Please remember that." After glancing around the room, she walks out, leaving me staring at the bag on my bed all ready to go. And the only family I have left packed it for me.

Hushed voices travel up the stairs; they must be standing at the front door waiting for me. I look toward the window, briefly considering trying to escape through it. Where would I go? Not to mention I'm on the second floor, with nothing to scale down to reach the ground safely.

With a sigh, I shoulder my bag and walk out of my bedroom, not knowing when I'll return. My stomach is a mess of nerves, but there's an odd tinge of excitement. For the first time in my life, I'm leaving Covington. *Against your will*, I remind myself. This isn't a vacation—it's a freaking nightmare. My feet stop moving a couple steps away from the top of the stairs as it becomes increasingly difficult to pull air into my lungs.

I can't leave. I can't do this. If I leave, something bad will happen just like it did when my biological mom left.

I shake my head, trying to push the thoughts away, but they still linger at the surface.

Forcing a few deep breaths, I put one foot in front of the other, counting my steps until I'm standing at the base of the stairs, looking between my mom and Nova.

"I love you so much," Mom says, her voice cracking as she throws her arms around me and hugs me tight.

"I love you," I say, pulling away.

She wipes the tears from her cheeks and turns her gaze to Nova. "Take care of my baby, Donovan."

He nods, taking my bag while I put on my jacket and dark brown hiking boots.

Before long, we're in his SUV heading toward . . . I have no idea where. I reach into my purse to pull out my phone only to find it missing.

"Holly thought it might be best if you didn't have any distractions for a while."

My head whips in his direction as my pulse kicks up, and I grit my teeth. "You can't be serious."

"I think it will help," he adds, keeping his eyes on the road as we get on the I-20. "Don't worry, you won't have time to miss it."

I glare out the windshield. "What about school? My friends? You can't just disappear me without people asking questions."

He nods. "It's being handled."

"How?" I push.

"Your mom will contact the school and let them know you've transferred out of town for the remainder of the year. Your friends will be told you're staying with family."

"Hold on. The entire school year? It's November! You're saying I'm going to be stuck wherever you're taking me for seven months?" The panic in my voice makes it sound screechy, but I can't help it. The thought of being away for that long has tears gathering in my eyes again.

"Emery—"

"I don't want this, Nova," I whisper, my voice thick with tears.

He frowns. "I know. I'm sorry, but it's the safest thing for you."

"That is total crap," I snap. "Something else is going on here, it must be. There's no way—"

"Everything your mother and I have told you tonight is the truth. I understand it's difficult, I do, but you need to start accepting it."

"Like hell I do." I haven't felt such anger since my mom died. Even as a child, when something that traumatic happens, you remember it years later as if it was yesterday. "You crashed my birthday and told me I have magic that will kill me if I don't learn to use it and you expect me to just be okay with that? You want me to be excited that you're going to teach me how to use these abilities you claim I have?"

"I won't be teaching you," he says. "I don't have Wielder abilities. However, I have been studying them for many years in order to facilitate this process for people like you who are coming into their power."

I stare at him, but he keeps his focus forward. "You sound like you should be locked in a padded room," I tell him. I've never experienced carsickness, but this conversation is starting to make me feel queasy.

"I know you're not ready to hear everything. I'll let your mentor explain the basics tomorrow."

Mentor? This almost sounds legit. Great. I'm going to a house full of crazy people who think magic is real.

"You can sleep for a while if you want. We're about an hour and a half away."

Yeah, right. I need to keep my eyes open, to see where we're going so when I make my escape I know the route. I yawn despite that. My eyelids are heavy, and staring out the window is only adding to the nausea rolling through me like a tidal wave. Maybe closing my eyes for a few minutes will help.

I curl onto my side as best I can in a seatbelt, leaning my head against the window. The cool glass feels nice on my skin, and it doesn't take long for me to doze off.

The bedroom I wake in is not mine. Confusion floods through me as I try to remember what happened. When it all comes rushing back like a speeding train, I sit up in a flash. My eyes take a second to adjust to the dim light from the lamp next to me, and I hold my breath as my gaze moves around the small, pale blue room. There's nothing but the twin bed I'm on, the table next to it, and a dresser against the opposite wall. The small window across from the bed is dark, and the leaves on the trees outside dance in the wind.

Did Nova carry me into the house?

I find my bag hanging on a hook on the back of the door and rummage through it for . . . what? My phone isn't here; all I have is clothing and toiletries.

I fight to swallow as my chest tightens with panic. Even as my head remains fuzzy, the rest of my body goes into flight mode. *I need to get out of here.*

I press my ear against the closed door and am met with silence. I reach for my bag, then stop myself. It'll be easier to get away if I don't have to carry anything. I manage to squeeze my wallet into my jacket pocket. I don't exactly have a solid plan— or *any* plan—but I'll need money to get anywhere.

My fingers shake as I reach for the knob, turning it slowly as if any tiny sound will alert Nova that I'm awake.

I pull the door open and cringe when it creaks. I freeze for a good thirty seconds before opening it enough to slip into the hallway. My stockinged feet are met with plush carpet, and I frown. *Where are my shoes?* I look back into the bedroom but don't see them. That could be a problem if I have to make a break for it outside. I push that worry aside. I'll run barefoot if I have to—I can't stay here.

The hallway isn't long. There are two closed doors on either side, and it opens into the kitchen at the end. There are no pictures or art on the soft gray walls, and I'm not sure what to think of that.

I come to an abrupt stop when voices reach me. I press my back against the wall, my jaw clenching. *Crap.* So much for an easy getaway.

My eyes land on what looks to be a side door off the kitchen, but I'll have to make it past a wide doorway without being seen. It's unlikely, but really the only shot I have.

"This is ridiculous," a sharp feminine voice mutters.

"Relax, Zoe," a new male voice says. It's warm and soft like melted caramel, and I hate it. "No one is asking you to train with her. Just be nice."

She scoffs. "Whatever."

A few seconds later, a door slams, and I flinch. *Don't worry*, I want to say, *I'm not staying.*

There's a small stretch of silence before a male voice speaks again. "How did she handle it? I'm sorry I couldn't be there."

That is met with a sigh. Nova. "As well as can be expected, Kit. She had no idea about her lineage. She doesn't believe anything I told her, which of course is partially my fault. Her mother and I didn't want to put her through this until it absolutely had to be done."

I lean against the wall, my knees a little unsteady. What he's saying . . . He truly believes it. Which means I'm in worse trouble than I thought.

"You did what you had to do. You're taking care of Simon's daughter just like you promised him you would."

"All I can do is hope that's enough," Nova says.

"We'll figure it out. In the meantime, how would you like me to approach the situation?"

"With caution."

The other guy—Kit, I guess—chuckles. "Noted."

One last deep breath, and I bolt. My sight is set on the door; the space between where I am and where it is blurs, as if the world has sped up. I don't have time to question it as I reach the door, flip the lock over, and turn the knob. Forget shoes, I'm getting out of here *now*.

The cold night air chills my face when I pull on the door, but before I can open it wide enough to get out, an arm reaches past me and pushes it shut.

My heart crashes against my ribcage as my stomach plummets. I let go of the doorknob, my hands balling into fists at my sides. "I shouldn't be here," I say in an uneven tone, still facing the door. I don't want to turn around.

The hand pressed against the dark wood flexes before pulling back. "You're scared. I understand that, but you need to be here." I recognize his voice as the guy Nova was speaking to in the other room.

I whip around, then stumble back into the door as my eyes lift from Kit's black T-shirt to his blue-gray eyes. The expression in them is soft, empathetic. It only fuels the fire in my chest.

"I need to go home," I say, desperation creeping into my voice.

Nova approaches from behind Kit. "Please hear us out. I think you'll find that once you have more information, you won't feel so . . . caged."

My eyes narrow on him. "I trusted you."

He frowns. "I'm doing this to protect you."

I shake my head. "I don't need protection from anything but *you*."

Kit cracks a smile so faint I almost miss it. Almost.

"What are you smiling at?" I growl.

"You are going to be one interesting Wielder," he says.

His easygoing demeanor makes me scoff, and I cross my arms over my chest. "I'm not going to be *anything*. I want to leave."

"Em—"

"I've got it, Nova. Just give us a few minutes," Kit says, without taking his eyes off me.

I hold his gaze out of spite more than anything, as if looking away would give him some sort of satisfaction. It doesn't make sense, but I keep staring regardless.

Nova walks past the kitchen table and disappears down the hall I came from, stepping into one of the rooms and closing the door.

I look back at Kit. "I'm not staying here." My voice is firm. I don't want him getting any ideas that he can somehow convince me otherwise.

Kit blows out a breath and shoves a hand through his dirty blond hair. It's short on the sides and longer on top, and I hate that I notice that. With the way it keeps falling into his face, it could probably use a trim.

"Will you sit and talk with me?" he asks after a moment of silence between us.

"Do I have a choice?" I fire back.

He presses his lips together. "Sure. Nova's gone. You want to leave, I won't stop you. But I will tell you that leaving is the worst possible thing you could do. Your magic may not be dangerous tonight—hell, you may not even have tapped into it yet—but it can become that way very quickly if you don't learn how to wield it. You think your life is upside down now? Imagine trying to live a normal life, go to class or out with your friends when your magic is consuming you from the inside out. You have the potential to be one of the most powerful Wielders of our time, but left untrained, you also have the potential to hurt a lot of people—yourself included."

I close my eyes, letting his words sink in as tears clog my throat. *I'm not seriously considering believing this guy, am I?* I take a moment to rein in my tears before opening my eyes. "Fine," I finally say. Because no, I don't believe I have a treasure chest full of magic inside of me, but the idea that I *could* has me absolutely terrified.

He smiles and extends his hand. "I'm Kit, by the way. I know you don't want to be here, but I'm glad you are. It's nice to meet you, Emery."

After a moment of hesitation, I shake his hand. It's warm and firm. "Um, thanks. You too?"

Kit's smile morphs into a full-blown grin, and I can't help but stare at it. "You sound so sure," he says in a teasing tone. "I'm hoping we can turn that into something that doesn't sound like a question."

We backtrack the way I came and into a living room. A wood fireplace heats the cozy space as I follow Kit over to a couch that looks as though it's seen better days, and we sit on opposite ends.

I press my lips together before blurting, "None of this makes sense."

Kit nods. "That's fair. What did Nova tell you?"

I give him the lowdown, which isn't much considering I didn't exactly give my mom or Nova an opportunity to elaborate.

"Why don't we start with the most basic question?" he offers.

"Okay then. What the hell is a Wielder?"

The corner of his mouth tugs up into a lopsided smile. "Once upon a time—"

I cut him off with a dark look. I'm not in the mood for jokes.

"Wielders are inhuman people with the ability to harness one of the elements in most cases, sometimes two depending on their lineage. Air, earth, water, and fire. We are descended from angels, which sounds, well, just about as crazy as everything else you've learned so far."

"Angels?" I blink at him, processing the information. "That's . . . All right then. So Wielders come here to learn how to use their element?"

"Yes. We're one of a handful of houses in the area that train newbies." He shoots me a wink and continues, "Most come, learn about their abilities—and themselves—and then move on."

"So, what, you're still learning? How long have you been here?"

He purses his lips. "My parents brought me to Nova just before my eighteenth birthday. They knew about my power, though it skipped my mother's generation as it sometimes does —magic isn't always predictable—and they'd heard about Nova's home for 'gifted individuals.'" He uses air quotes and rolls his eyes. "At first, I thought it was a joke—much like I'm sure you did. But I couldn't explain the changes I was feeling."

"What changed? I don't feel any different, so I really have no idea what you're talking about."

"Everyone is a little different, but for me, it was a building pressure in my chest and in my veins. It made my skin tingle, but it also made me feel as if I was going to explode from the inside."

My eyes go wide; I don't want that to happen to me.

"So when my parents told me everything and about this place, I didn't fight them. I packed a bag and came here."

I nod, fixating on a loose thread in the couch cushion I'm sitting on. "How long have you been here?"

"Two years," he answers.

My stomach plummets. "You expect me to stay here for *two years*?"

Kit laughs, shaking his head. "I could've left a long time ago, but I decided to stay and help Nova run the place. To help new Wielders like you to navigate the changes that are coming."

I wet my lips. "Really? Why?"

His brows knit as he regards me thoughtfully. "Because it makes me happy, helping others. I remember what it was like when my entire life changed." He leans in a little and lowers his voice. "I've been where you are, so please, let me help you."

I stare into his eyes, and his gaze remains sincere. Everything about him makes me feel as though I should trust him. Either I'm right in believing I can, or my gut is seriously wrong—and he's got a damn good poker face.

"Okay," I finally say, not because of what he or Nova said to me, but because of what I heard them say when they didn't know I was listening. If there's even a tiny chance this magic stuff is real, maybe I owe it to my dad to stick around and find out.

***

I toss and turn for the rest of the night, unable to find a position comfortable enough to fall asleep. This mattress is too firm. I miss my mountain of pillows and my heated blanket. *I miss home*. I crack the window open and close my eyes, listening to the soft chirp of crickets outside.

Eventually, I doze off, and the darkness is a welcome reprieve.

"Please," my mom begs in a cracked voice, tears rolling down her cheeks. "My beautiful girl, this isn't you."

My jaw clenches as energy ripples through me. The shadows are closing in, but I am not afraid. In fact, I welcome them. Their embrace is all that I've been searching for. All those years of being misunderstood—they don't matter now. I twist my wrist, and the tendrils of darkness wrap around my mom's throat.

"You lied to me." My lips shape the words, but the voice isn't mine. It's deeper and far more menacing than I could ever be,

especially toward the woman who took me in after I lost everything.

She gasps, clawing at the darkness around her throat. "Pl— please. I'm so sorry. Please don't do this . . ."

"Emery, no!"

I whirl around and find Lana and Jessa running toward the clearing, panic etched into their features as the dark air fogs with their heavy breaths.

My chest tightens. "What are you doing here?"

The girls glance at each other before looking back at me. "Holly told us everything. We know what you're going through, Em. We want to help."

I bark out a cold laugh. "Help? How could you possibly help me? Do you all of a sudden have magical abilities I'm unaware of?"

Jessa frowns, her eyes welling with tears as she looks past me to where Holly is pinned to a thick tree trunk. "Emery, you're going to kill her."

I roll my eyes, focusing my magic on Jessa. "Actually," I say as the darkness spreads toward my friends, "I'm going to kill all of you."

The clearing fills with shrieks of terror as my focus shifts to a guy dressed in black standing at the tree line, untouched by the chaos of my magic.

I wake with a gasp, then start coughing from the dryness of my throat.

What the hell was that?

Trying to shake off the chilling remnants of my dream, I peek out the window to find a hint of the sunrise. I tug on my favorite black hoodie and wander down the hall into the kitchen. I grab a glass and fill it with water from the tap, downing it as my eyes catch the time on the microwave. It's just after six. With a sigh, I glance around the small kitchen. Oak cupboards line the room and the appliances are definitely dated.

My gaze halts on the espresso machine in the corner. *Thank god.*

"I'm not used to anyone else being awake at this time."

I whirl around, clutching my chest in surprise, and my eyes land on a short girl who looks to be around my age. She has dark skin and curly brunette hair, which is piled on top of her head in a messy bun.

"Sorry. I didn't mean to frighten you." She smiles. "I'm Lydia. It's nice to meet you. Emery, right?"

My hand lowers back to my side as I glance at the oversized band T-shirt she's wearing over a pair of black leggings. "Right. Uh, hi."

"Are you hungry?" she asks.

I shake my head. Something about this girl makes it impossible to be angry around her, which is kind of annoying considering I've been clinging to my anger with every fiber of my being since I arrived—and for good reason. "Coffee would be good, though."

"Caffeine for breakfast?" Her brown eyes seem to sparkle. "I like you already."

While the machine heats up, Lydia grabs two mugs and sets them on the counter.

"So, you're a Wielder?" I ask.

Lydia presses her lips together, clearly trying to hide a smile. "Yes. We all are. Well, aside from Nova."

"Oh, right."

She touches my shoulder as if to offer me comfort. "How much has Kit told you?"

"Some, but I'm sure not even close to everything. I think he's afraid of overwhelming me." To be fair, I am most definitely overwhelmed.

She nods, grabbing a glass from the cupboard behind me and filling it with water from the sink. "It was terrifying for me. Both of my parents are Wielders, so my power was stronger than someone with only one Wielder parent to inherit magic from. It got pretty intense." She takes a drink and sighs, leaning against the counter. "Things spiralled out of control fast—as in, I flooded my family home. I couldn't figure out how to work my magic, and because your emotions are tied closely to your magic, the frustration and panic I was feeling only made things worse. Until I came here. Nova saved my life." Lydia smiles. "And now look," she says, dropping her gaze to the glass in her hand. She stares at the water inside, and a second later, it's funnelling around the glass as if she's stirring it.

Holy crap.

I blink, waiting for her to reveal some hidden, non-magic cause, but she only smiles at me again before setting the glass in the sink.

"It's a neat trick, but my point is, once you gain control over your abilities, it will change your life for the better. I didn't believe it until it happened to me, and I have Nova to thank for that."

"That seems to be a theme around here," I comment, recalling Kit's story earlier.

"He's one of the good guys."

I nod, wondering if she knows he's been a part of my life since I was a baby. Something in me decides to keep that to myself.

Once the espresso is done dripping, Lydia divides it into the mugs and turns to the fridge. She grabs the milk and scoots past me, steaming it before pouring it into our mugs.

"Hold on," she says, reaching into the upper cupboard and pulling down a spice tin. She sprinkles cinnamon on top of both lattes before handing me one.

"Thanks." I lift it to my nose and inhale slowly, savoring the aroma.

Lydia and I sit on the porch at the front of the house, our legs covered in a heavy blanket.

"How are you settling in?" she asks, taking a sip from her steaming mug.

I bite the inside of my cheek, staring out at the front yard. The grass is covered in a layer of frost, and massive oak trees line the property. I can't see another house on either side, just trees. There's a gravel driveway where Nova's SUV is parked in front of a smaller car, and the smoky scent of burning wood permeates the cold air.

I turn my attention to Lydia. She's being nice; I don't want to sit here and tell her that I hate it and want to go home, but that's the truth. "Honestly, I don't know that I am."

She nods. "I know it's hard. I mean, I tried for weeks to get out of this place, but every time I did, I wound up coming back."

My eyes widen. "You left?"

She cracks a smile. "A couple of times in the first month I was here. It's overwhelming, finding out your life isn't what you thought it was." She pats my knee. "I get it, Emery. Believe it or not, we all do."

I tap my fingers against the side of my mug. "Why did you come back?"

"I tried to learn and practice the magic on my own, but I was too new. I didn't understand how to work with it. I was also too ashamed of what I did to my family home to return there, and too afraid to stay with any of my friends."

I feel the urge to reach over and squeeze her hand. The pained expression that flickers across her face makes my chest ache, and despite hating pretty much everything about the situation I'm in, I like Lydia.

"I spent a few days feeling completely lost. Sleeping in bus terminals or on park benches. Nova sent Kit after me, and when he found me and offered to bring me back here, I didn't hesitate."

"I'm sorry you went through that," I tell her.

"We all have different stories, but the magic we share ties us together in a sense."

I sigh, sipping my latte. "So, basically you're telling me to give it a shot. Wait it out even though all I want to do is hightail it out of here and bury my head in the sand."

She's smiling behind her mug when she says, "Basically."

I look out at the property again before asking, "Where exactly are we?"

Lydia rests her mug on her knee. "About an hour and a half outside Atlanta."

"Which is where?" My eyes travel the length of the front of the house. I was passed out when I arrived, so this is the first time I'm seeing the wooden cabin-style bungalow.

"A small town called Helen. There's not much around, which works well for learning magic."

I nod. At least I know the name of the place I've been taken to.

We watch the sunrise for a while, and it's nice. It's the only splash of normalcy I've experienced in the last twelve hours.

With our empty mugs and flushed cheeks, we head back into the warmth of the house. In the kitchen, Lydia starts pulling out things for breakfast.

"You want to help?" she asks, cracking an egg into a large bowl.

"Uh," I say with a short laugh, "I don't think you want me to help. That is, if you want the result to be edible."

Lydia grins. "Gotcha. Feel free to hang out and watch. You may learn a thing or two."

CHAPTER THREE

ydia and I chat while she cooks enough eggs, bacon, sausage, and hash browns for an army. Or a house of Wielders.

"How many people live here?" I ask her.

She glances at the massive amount of food and chuckles. "Six, including you and me. We're all around the same age—aside from Nova. Mason's the oldest at twenty-two, and you're the new youngest. I'm nineteen, so not much ahead of you there." She loads the toaster with bread and glances over her shoulder at me. "The guys eat like it's their last meal, so I always cook a ton," she explains.

"Fair enough."

I make a pot of coffee and offer her a mug as she finishes flipping the pan of sizzling bacon. "Thanks."

I manage a small smile, and my stomach growls at the smell of everything. I wasn't expecting to be hungry, but I can't deny it. Lydia can cook.

"I smell bacon," a deep voice grumbles.

I turn and lean against the counter as another unfamiliar face enters the room, shuffling as he stifles a yawn and shoves a hand through a mess of dark brown hair. This guy is more muscular than Kit, but a little shorter. He's pulling off the hipster look with gray sweatpants and a plain white T-shirt under a red plaid flannel.

"Good morning, Mason," Lydia says, waving with the spatula in her hand.

"Morning." His deep brown eyes shift to me. "New girl," he says with a nod.

Lydia props her free hand on her hip. "Her name is Emery."

He shrugs, walking into the kitchen and shifting past me for the coffee machine. "I'll learn her name if she's still here next week." He glances at me over his shoulder. "No offense."

Before I can say anything, Lydia says, "Don't mind him. He's grumpy before coffee."

Mason snorts, sliding his arm around Lydia's waist and tugging her toward him before smacking a kiss to her cheek. "I'm grumpy all the time, and you know it."

She elbows him in the side. "True. Now help or get out of my kitchen."

He takes his coffee and slips away, leaving us to finish breakfast.

"So you two are . . . ?"

Lydia sighs, dishing the scrambled eggs into a large bowl. "He's a pain in my ass, but yeah. I sort of love him."

I can't help but smile at that.

While Lydia finishes cooking, I set the table in the dining room just off the kitchen and start carrying dishes of steaming food out. Nova is coming down the hallway as I'm walking back into the kitchen. It's barely seven-thirty on a Saturday, but he's already dressed in dark jeans and a gray sweater.

"Good morning," he says with a smile, and I catch the concern that lingers in the way he looks at me. It tugs at my heart, but I shove the feeling away. I can't think about it right now.

"Morning," I say in a low voice. "Lydia made breakfast, and there's coffee in the pot."

He nods. "How did you sleep?"

"Fine," I lie without hesitation. I'd forgotten about the nightmare I had . . . until now. And I'm not ready to talk about it—especially not with him. I'm still struggling to trust him after yesterday. I want to—I have my whole life—but there are still too many secrets, too many things I don't know. *I still don't want to know them.*

Sitting around a large table with five almost-strangers is weird. I take a sip of my coffee, keeping my gaze on my plate while the others have a conversation about a party next weekend a few towns over. Kit sits at the head of the table to my left, with Nova taking the opposite end, and Lydia is next to me on the right. Across from her is Mason, and I can only assume the blond girl shooting daggers at me from beside him is Zoe.

"Are we just going to ignore the new girl?" Zoe says during a lull in their conversation.

My fork stops halfway to my mouth, and I glance across the table at her. "That's okay with me," I tell her.

She snorts. "Right. You've got Kit's attention, so you're probably just fine."

"Zoe," Kit warns.

"What?" she snaps at him, narrowing her ice-blue eyes.

He pauses mid-chew, pointing his fork in her direction. "Be nice."

"Yeah, quit being jealous," Mason cuts in. "It's not a cute look on you."

She smiles as she flips him off and then picks up her plate, standing and leaving the room, taking most of the tension with her.

"She doesn't like me," I comment, pushing a pile of scrambled eggs around my plate. I've never had to deal with someone who dislikes me before they even know me. And what on earth does she have to be jealous of?

"Don't worry about it," Kit says from beside me. "She doesn't like to share attention."

I try to smile and brush it off. I'm pretty sure a mean girl is the least of my problems right now. "So," I say to the rest of the table, "magic, huh?"

"We each have our own specialties," Lydia says. "You already know I have water magic. I dabble a bit with earth magic as well, but I suck at it."

I glance between Kit and Mason. "And what about you guys?"

"Air," Mason says with a yawn, "which is very boring for the most part, by the way."

Kit chuckles. "I work with fire magic."

"It's why he's so hot," Mason says, winking at Kit.

Kit arches a brow at him. "You want a piece of this?"

Mason tears a piece of bacon off and tosses it in his mouth. "Bring it, fire boy."

"Like you could handle me."

Lydia rolls her eyes. "See what I have to deal with?" she says to me.

I find myself laughing, feeling as if I'm a part of something even as that little voice in the back of my head reminds me how badly I want to leave. Shifting my gaze to Nova, I ask, "Do you know which element I supposedly have?"

He takes a drink of his coffee and sets the mug on the table before answering. "You'll work with Kit to figure that out. He'll be your mentor from here on out."

"I'll be here for you as long as you need me," Kit adds before downing half a glass of orange juice.

"Okay," I mumble, not knowing what else to say. "And what about school? I don't want to graduate late because I had to go off to some *Cabin in the Woods* version of Hogwarts."

Kit chuckles. "Don't worry, you'll be able to complete the school year online. Nova has connections."

I let out a breath. Of course I'd rather be at school with Lana and Jessa, but at least I'm not going to lose the entire school year.

Once breakfast is over, Kit pulls me aside after we carry our plates to the kitchen. "Take a walk with me?" he asks. "I want to show you something."

"What?" I ask, following him to the side door I tried to escape through last night.

He grabs a jacket off the rack of hooks on the wall next to the door. "I know you're struggling to accept everything being thrown at you since you arrived, which is completely understandable."

I nod without saying anything, sliding my feet into my hiking boots.

"I thought it could help you to see what we're all talking about. So you know we aren't making this up. What do you think?"

I press my lips together. "You're . . . inviting me to a spur-of-the-moment magic show?" I don't bother telling him that Lydia already gave me a peek at her magic. I can't help it. I'm curious to see what Kit can do.

He grins at me as he pulls on his shoes. "Okay, smartass. Make it sound lame. I'm trying to help you understand who you are."

I tug at a loose thread on my sweater, focusing on that stupid piece of material instead of Kit's face. "I know who I am," I mutter.

"No, you know who you *were*," he corrects. "You have so much to learn about who you're becoming."

"Because magic," I say.

He laughs, nodding. "Because magic."

I take a deep breath and exhale heavily as we step outside. "Okay," I finally say. "Bring on the show."

We walk around to the back of the property. It's a huge lot with a stream near the back of the yard and a firepit with logs set around it as seating.

I shiver against the cold mid-morning air, and Kit has his jacket off and around my shoulders before I can protest. "Thanks," I murmur, holding it. "Aren't you going to get cold?"

The corner of his mouth kicks up. "Fire magic, remember?"

I arch a brow. "So what? You never get cold?"

"Never."

"Well, that's . . . kind of cool, actually," I say, and he grins. "Clearly that's not my specialty, because I'm freezing my ass off out here."

"Here, this should help." He focuses on the firepit. His lips move, but I can't hear anything he's whispering under his breath. A few seconds later, flames surge to life in front of us.

I jump back even though they aren't close enough to reach me, although heat radiates from the firepit. "Whoa," I breathe, swinging my gaze toward him.

"Want to try something?" he asks.

I shake my head, taking a healthy step back from the fire—and from Kit. "I don't know."

He offers a sympathetic look. "It's not scary. I'm just curious what your element might be."

"You think I have fire magic?" I ask in an uneven tone.

"We won't know until you try it."

Fire magic would be cool, I guess. The whole never-getting-cold thing could come in handy. I watch the flames for several beats before saying, "What do you want me to do?"

"Use the water from the stream to put out the fire."

"Uhhh." I flick my gaze between the stream and the fire. "How am I supposed to do that?"

"Focus on what you want to do. You can close your eyes if you want. Sometimes that helps with concentration."

"Right. Um, okay." I try to relax my muscles as I close my eyes. I can feel Kit's warmth as he comes to stand behind me.

His voice is soft in my ear. "Visualize the water flowing from the stream toward the flame. The heat calls to the water. You're just the vessel to allow it to get there."

I do what he says and wait for the sound of the fire sizzling out, but it doesn't come. I open my eyes and turn to face him, frowning. *What did I expect would happen?* I try not to dwell on the heaviness in my chest, but I can't stop myself from asking, "What am I doing wrong?"

He smiles. "Nothing. You've never practiced magic before. You can't expect to get it on your first try."

"Is there a spell or something? You were speaking something when the fire ignited."

He nods. "There are certain incantations, yes. But spells are the lazy way to do magic. I don't want you learning that way first."

I prop my hands on my hips. "Then why'd you do it?"

Kit grins at me. "Do as I say, not as I do."

Rolling my eyes, I turn back and focus on the fire. Instead of closing my eyes this time, I focus on the flames. The way they move and flicker in the air. I let my gaze unfocus as I stare into the warm colors, imagining the air around me suffocating the flames.

Instead of putting the fire out, somehow it flares higher. Kit yanks me back, and I gasp.

"What was that?" I demand.

He shakes his head. "I don't—"

"I thought I didn't have fire magic." My voice shakes.

Kit squeezes my shoulders before slowly letting go. "Breathe, Emery. It's okay. You're all right."

I blink at him, my chest rising and falling quickly. "I don't understand."

He offers a reassuring smile. "It's okay," he repeats. "You have plenty of time to learn. Magic is tricky, and it's definitely not mastered in a matter of minutes. This is going to take time, so you'll have to try and be patient with yourself."

I inhale slowly as my pulse returns to a normal pace. "Stupid fire," I mutter.

Kit laughs. "What exactly were you trying to do?"

I press my lips together, shaking my head.

"I'm here to help you," he reminds me.

"Fine. I was trying to suffocate it. I thought maybe air magic was worth a shot, but evidently not." Whatever *that* was, it didn't feel natural. My hands shake at my sides even as Kit appears unconcerned.

"Interesting," he muses. "It was a good idea to try."

I don't want to listen to him try to make me feel better. This whole situation . . . I need a pause on the magic stuff. "Can we go back inside? I'm going to lose a toe to frostbite if we stay out here much longer."

"Sure." He turns to head back to the house.

I go to do the same, but pause a few steps in. "What about the fire?"

"What about it?" he asks without turning around.

I look back at the firepit only to find it almost empty, save for a couple charred logs barely giving off enough smoke to fog the air. Kit extinguished the fire without any visible effort.

"All right then," I mumble under my breath, following him across the yard. Trees line the outskirts just like in the front yard, and it looks as if there aren't any houses within walking distance.

Kit's jacket starts to fall off my shoulder, but he lifts it back up before I can reach for it.

"Thank you," I say as we keep walking at a comfortable pace.

"Can I ask you something?"

I turn my face toward Kit's voice. "Yeah."

"Will you promise to give this place a chance? To give me a chance to help you?"

I stop walking and stare at him. "You understand why I don't want to, right? This is all kind of insane. I've been here less than twenty-four hours and I miss my normal life, my friends, my bedroom at my own home."

His soft gaze is filled with understanding. "I do. But you staying here isn't forever, and it will ensure your life—and those around you—aren't in jeopardy because of your magic when you leave."

I press my lips together, holding my breath for a few seconds before I exhale heavily. This whole magic thing is becoming more and more difficult to deny. I mean, how many times can you see something and still pretend it isn't real? Finally, I say, "Okay."

He searches my eyes as if looking for some untruth in my answer. "Yeah?" he checks.

I crack a smile. "I said yes, Kit. Teach me all of the things so I can be a badass Wielder or whatever. And so I can go home." A gust of wind makes me shiver, and I hug Kit's jacket closer.

He steps in and touches my shoulder. My body quickly fills with warmth all the way to my toes, which tingle in response to the sudden temperature change.

I suck in a breath. "Oh. That's handy."

He shoots me a wink. "Come on. Let's get you settled in."

CHAPTER FOUR

fter lunch, I curl up on the beaten-down L-shaped couch in the living room with a steaming vanilla latte on the glass coffee table in front of me. My eyes keep wandering to the wood fireplace in the corner of the room to watch the flames dance.

"Do you think you have fire magic?" Zoe asks, pushing away from the doorway to the front hallway and walking into the room.

I try to mask my surprise that she's speaking to me. "Honestly, I'm not so sure I have *any* magic."

She arches a brow, her eyes flicking toward the large bay window that looks out into the front yard. "If that was true, you wouldn't be here."

"I think you'd prefer that," I comment without thinking.

Zoe smirks. "You picked up on that, huh?"

No point in lying now. "Just a little."

Her gaze shifts back to me, and she says, "It's nothing personal."

Right. I choose to let that go by without comment; nothing good can come out of that conversation. Plus, I'm not here to be her best friend. I *have* best friends. "How long have you been here?" I ask, mostly to fill the silence.

She purses her lips in thought. "Five months. I was practicing on my own when I heard about this place. Did some digging, but Nova found me before I found him."

My brows lift. "That didn't freak you out?"

Zoe shrugs. "At the time, sure. Nova's got connections, though. In order to keep our abilities a secret from the humans, there's a secret branch of the local government that monitors the situation."

The pit in my stomach suddenly feels heavier. "We're a situation?"

"We have the ability to burn down forests with a flick of a wrist. Or cause floods. Droughts. Severe wind storms that could wipe out complete infrastructures."

"So they think we're weapons of mass destruction?"

She blinks at me. "We very well could be, new girl. Keep up."

Dread fills me at an alarming rate. "If the government knows all of this, why do they let—"

"Sorry to interrupt," Nova says as he walks into the room. "Emery, I was hoping we could chat."

I glance at him. "About what?"

"Just want to check in."

"Um, okay." I get up and look to where Zoe is now perched on the arm at the far end of the couch. "Can we talk later?" I still have questions, and based on what I've seen of Zoe, she'll be the one to give it to me straight.

She shrugs, turning her attention to the phone in her hand.

With a sigh, I follow Nova out of the living room. We pass the front door and continue down the hallway that runs parallel to where my bedroom is. This hallway is shorter and only has two doors. We pass the first one and end up in an office that looks more like a library.

Bookshelves line the walls from floor to ceiling, save for the wall behind the giant oak desk, which instead features large windows that look out to the front yard and the side of the house, which is a sea of green—trees as far as the eye can see.

Everything is made of dark wood, and the air smells like old books. To some it would be musty, but I could spend all day in a place like this.

Nova gestures to a small seating area in the corner of the room, and I follow him, sitting in one of the faded red chairs and tucking my legs under me.

He crosses one leg over the other and folds his hands in his lap. "How are you doing?"

I have his complete attention, and it makes me squirmy. Instead of meeting his gaze, I focus on the gray peeking through the brown in his hair. "I'm okay. I mean, considering. Everyone has been welcoming." Aside from Zoe, really, but I don't think there's much I can do about that. She has her thoughts and feelings about me being here, and I don't have the energy to try and change them.

"That's good. Is there anything we can do to help you feel more at home here?"

I pick at a hangnail on my thumb. "I don't know. How long am I going to be here?"

"That depends on you. It could take longer than you may expect—or like—to get a grip on your abilities. Simply put, you have a lot to learn. Kit will work with you for as long as you need, and I of course will assist in any way I can."

"What exactly is expected of me here?"

"The only expectation I have is that you try. Put the time in with Kit, observe the others, and keep an open mind. There are many different ways to measure progress, and this isn't something you can rush through."

"I . . ." I finally meet his gaze, and something inside of me cracks open, letting doubt rush in. "What if I can't do it, Nova?"

"You've been here one day," he says in a soft tone. "Give it time, and give yourself some grace. You *can* do it. I've known you since you were a baby, and to this day, you're one of the most strong-willed and determined people I know."

His words render me speechless. They tug at my heart and make me want to believe him.

"I know you have a lot of questions. About how this all works and about your father. We can talk about those things, but I would like to see what you can do on your own before outside influences are brought in."

"That's your way of saying you're not going to tell me which element my father used, right?"

"Let's wait and see which one calls to you."

I try not to feel irritated by that, but I shift in my seat, not wanting to sit still. Instead of pushing it, though, I bring up the conversation I was having with Zoe before Nova pulled me away. "So the government knows I'm a—a Wielder?" It's the first time I've said it out loud. The words feel foreign on my tongue, but at least my entire body doesn't fill with dread as I thought I might.

Nova nods. "I'm under oath to report any incoming Wielders to this facility."

I blink at him. "You realize how creepy that makes this sound, right?"

He chuckles. "I'm sure it does, but I assure you, it's better this way. It's an added layer of protection for you."

Doubt unfurls in my chest. "What if one day the government decides they want to use the abilities that Wielders have against another country? Surely they've considered us ideal weapons of war."

A muscle feathers along his shadowed jaw. "You're safe here, Emery."

I push back. "You're not answering my question."

He sighs, moving to rest his hands on the arms of his chair.

"It won't happen. Decades ago, the Elders signed Accords with the Capitol. For the protection of all parties involved."

My eyes widen. "The Elders? Accords? You're saying a lot of things that are making this whole thing way more confusing."

He presses his lips together to hide a smile. "I apologize. The Elders are the first known Wielders in history. They aren't exactly immortal, but they age slowly enough that most live at least five hundred years or so. You can think of them as the royals or the leaders of the Wielders. They exist to ensure the protection of their people, which includes you."

I nod, though I'm not sure I fully comprehend everything I'm being told. "I still don't understand why my mom kept this whole part of my life from me. I understand she was scared of what would happen once I found out, but wouldn't this have been easier if I'd known about Wielders and the Elders and magic as I was growing up?"

Nova nods. "She didn't want to alter your life in such an extreme way after you went through the loss of your parents."

My parents.

Swallowing past the lump in my throat, I say, "So where does that leave me?"

"In a place where you can learn about who you are," Nova says, and something in the soft tone of his voice cracks through the walls I've spent my whole life building.

I float in and out of restless sleep. It's the middle of the day, but I'd much rather sleep and risk another nightmare than face anyone in this house right now.

Eventually, though, I pull myself out of bed. I grab my bag off the back of the door, dumping my clothes and toiletry bag onto the bed and glancing toward the dresser. The idea of putting my things inside seems so final, as if I've accepted that I'll be here for a while. I don't want to do it, but living out of a duffle bag isn't ideal either.

With a defeated sigh, I drop the empty duffle bag onto the floor, frowning when it hits the hardwood with a *thud*. I pick it back up and feel around inside, finding a tear in the inside lining. My brows knit as I reach inside and touch something solid. Pulling it out, my interest is piqued when I see it's a black leather-bound book. *Why would Mom hide it in the lining of the bag?* I push my clothes aside and sit on the end of the bed, flipping it open. I start from the beginning, letting out a little gasp when my gaze falls on a message written on the inside cover.

To my beautiful daughter—

I don't know when you'll read this, but it is my hope that if I'm not around when you do, it will help you gain a better understanding of who you are. I have the utmost confidence that you will handle your magic beautifully. Remember, my sweet girl, trust yourself over anyone else. You will learn very quickly that nothing is as it seems. Trust your gut and be strong.

Forever and always,

Dad

I blink back tears and hug the book to my chest, sniffling as I curl onto my side.

I spend the rest of the day in the bedroom, putting my clothes into the dresser before going back to my dad's book. The pages are textured and worn, so I take care in thumbing through them. The same handwriting from the passage at the beginning is carried throughout. A lot of the entries are in French, but I can pick out bits and pieces of each paragraph where he talks about power and fear and protecting his family.

My brows tug closer as I turn the pages. Some have abstract sketches that cover the entire page, others have poem-like verses that I can't help but think could be spells. I'm torn between wanting to show Kit to get his take on it and keeping it to myself, the only thing I have that connects me to my dad.

I read one verse in my head a few times as pressure builds in my chest. It talks about light—taking it away. Whatever that means, I want to find out. I open my mouth to speak the verse aloud, but quickly clamp it shut as fear races through my veins like ice. I have no idea what this could do, if anything. Everything in me wants to try it, to see if it helps me connect with my magic, but not knowing what will happen if I do makes me swallow that urge. For now.

I keep reading for a while until the smell of garlic wafts into my room, and my stomach grumbles in response. As much as I would prefer to hide in here, I need to eat something, and whatever is cooking out there smells too good to deny myself.

After tucking the book in between two pairs of sweatpants in the dresser, I tug on a pair of fuzzy socks and step into the hallway. Voices from the kitchen float down the hall, but they're too quiet for me to decipher. I walk toward the sound and recognize Kit and Lydia's voices. They're chatting about some hiking trail they want to explore, and the conversation fades when I step into the room.

"Oh, hey," Lydia says with a warm smile. "I'm making fettuccine alfredo and garlic bread for dinner. It'll be ready soon, so I hope you're hungry."

I press my lips together, inhaling deeply. "It smells amazing."

Kit makes his way around the counter and approaches me, touching my arm as his gaze holds mine. "You okay?"

I nod, but I can't form the words. They wouldn't be true. I keep going back to the book, to my sense of urgency to try the magic my dad wrote about. Something about it called to me; it felt right. But my fear stood in the way of what felt like a step in the right direction to figure out my magic.

He searches my eyes. "We'll talk after dinner."

"No, I'm—"

"You're not," he murmurs, his thumb tracing back and forth across the delicate skin at my wrist. "And that's okay."

I clamp my jaw shut as my eyes burn. Blinking away the tears threatening to gather, I pull back and turn my attention to Lydia. "Can I help?"

"Didn't we already establish that wouldn't be a good idea?" she teases, stirring the creamy sauce on the stove.

I crack a smile. "Yeah, definitely. I could set the table?"

"Kit already did."

"Sorry," he says, leaning against the counter beside the fridge. "It's my true calling."

Lydia snorts. "Please. You can barely fold a napkin properly, Harris."

He slaps his chest, over his heart. "You're so *mean* to me."

Watching the two of them get along like, well, siblings makes my chest ache. I'm an only child, and I really only had my mom growing up, so my friends became my family—and now I'm not even able to see them for who knows how long.

Lydia scoots out of the way while Kit slides in and picks up the giant pot of noodles, draining the water into the sink. After he sets the pot back on the stove, he picks up the spoon Lydia was using to stir the sauce and tastes it.

"Hey," she scolds, smacking his arm. "Other people are going to be eating that."

He drops the spoon into the sink and backs away with his hands up. "Had to do a quality control check."

"Out."

Kit chuckles on his way out of the kitchen.

"You two seem close," I comment as Lydia pulls the baking sheet lined with bread out of the oven, filling the air with warmth and the delicious smell of garlic.

She pulls off her oven mitts and grins. "Yeah. He's pretty much my brother at this point. We're all kind of family here, but Kit is special to me."

I nod. "Is he your mentor too?"

"He wasn't at first. Nova paired me with Mason, but that

didn't really work out when we spent training sessions making out instead of practicing magic."

A surprised laugh escapes me. "Makes sense."

"Kit replaced him as my mentor, and it worked out for the better. He knows pretty much everything there is to know about our abilities. He made learning to wield a lot easier for me than I was expecting. Plus, he's not bad to look at, in case you haven't noticed."

I press my lips together as warmth floods my cheeks. "Ha. Yeah. Kind of hard not to notice."

"Notice what?" Mason says, waltzing into the room and kissing Lydia before ducking into the fridge to grab a can of Coke.

Lydia and I exchange a grin before she says, "Nothing. Dinner's ready."

"Amazing. I'll grab the others."

After dinner, Kit tells me he wants to chat. He grabs the heavy wool blanket off the back of the couch and we walk outside, heading down to the firepit.

He hands me the blanket, and I wrap it around myself as we sit on one of the massive logs. Kit ignites the fire, and the flames crackle in the cold night air for several beats before he says, "I'd like to officially start your training tomorrow."

Something in my chest flutters. I'm not sure if it's nerves, but part of me thinks it could be a tinge of excitement as well. "Sure."

"It's okay to feel nervous about it. I can't promise any sort of outcome, but I'm very good at what I do. I'm confident you'll benefit from training with me." He lowers his voice as a grin curls his lips. "Some people even say I'm not bad to look at."

My eyes widen, and I fight the urge to cover my face. "You heard us?" I squeak.

He laughs deeply. "Every word."

"Great," I grumble, "that's just . . . great."

"Don't worry about it, Emery. Really, I'm flattered that you noticed."

"Uh-huh." I bury my face in the blanket. "You're killing me over here."

"I'm enjoying this immensely." The amusement is clear in his tone.

I groan and shove his shoulder. "I'm so glad my embarrassment is entertaining for you."

"Hey." He bumps my shoulder with his, and I look at him. "You never have to be embarrassed. Not about that, and certainly not with me."

I grip the blanket around me, having the sudden urge to close the little distance there is between us and taste his lips. My cheeks flush at the thought, and I turn my face away. I can't do it. It wouldn't be smart to start anything with him, not here and not now. I barely know the guy. Though he's been nothing but kind and welcoming to me, I have to remind myself that it's his job. That's literally why he's here. And I'm probably reading way too far into it because I'm lonely and scared and have pretty much no experience in the realm of guys or dating.

"I can see those wheels turning. What are you thinking about?"

"I . . ." I stop myself with a dry laugh. "I should go, uh, clean the dinner dishes."

Kit gives me a knowing look and chuckles under his breath. "I'll walk with you."

I stand and drop the blanket into his lap. "I think I can manage."

"You sure?"

"If I get lost from here to the house, you've got a much bigger problem than teaching me how to wield magic."

I hurry away before he can respond, and before I can say anything else that I'll immediately regret. I have a feeling there will be plenty of time for me to do that during my training.

CHAPTER FIVE

K it wakes me up at five in the morning. Five. In the freaking morning. He gets points for bringing coffee, but still. He's lucky I don't dump it on him for getting me out of bed at this ungodly hour.

"Why do you hate me?" I grumble as he stands outside my room while I get dressed. I grab a loose-fitting beige sweater and black cotton leggings to keep warm.

Kit laughs through the door. "I know you don't believe this, but I'm actually trying to help you."

"What is it about Wielder magic that makes us have to train before the sun comes up?"

"Nothing."

I yank the door open and glower at him. "*What?*" I whisper-yell because the rest of the house is probably still asleep.

"Your mind is most open right when you wake up," he explains. "I want to have the best chance of this working."

"This," I echo, grabbing my coffee off the nightstand and following him down the hall. "Oh, you mean my ability to use magic. Right. How could I forget?"

"You're not a morning person, huh?" he asks in a teasing

tone.

I glare at the back of his head. "You're really asking for a coffee shower, Kit."

"You'll get used to the early mornings, I promise. And it'll be well worth it once you see how well the method works with your abilities."

"Uh-huh," I mutter. "Sure thing, Professor."

Kit grins at me over his shoulder. He holds the side door open for me, and we wander around to the backyard. My breath fogs the air, and I grip the mug tighter, willing it to warm me up.

Small lamps light the yard just enough to cast a silhouette on our faces. I take a gulp of my coffee, closing my eyes momentarily as it warms my insides. I open my eyes when Kit speaks.

"Yesterday, we played a bit with fire magic, and that didn't seem to call to you. Water magic, either. I didn't want to overwhelm you with all of them at once, so today we're going see if you connect with the others."

"That leaves me with air or earth, right?"

"Potentially," he answers, vague as ever.

"What does that mean? I could have different magic?"

"Elemental magic isn't as straightforward as you may think. You could have the ability to wield multiple elements. Those abilities may come and go, and one may be stronger than the other."

I take another sip of coffee. I'm nowhere near awake enough for this conversation. "Why?"

Kit laughs. "We don't know *everything* about our abilities. We're constantly learning—all of us."

"Okay," I say, dragging out the word. "Where are we going to start today?"

"I want to keep it light and easy. Nova is planning to go over your online school stuff in a bit, so I don't want to overwhelm you too much."

I exhale with a dry laugh. "Awesome."

"You'll train with me and do schoolwork pretty much every day. Class isn't on a set schedule like you're used to."

"School on the weekends," I mutter. "Great."

He offers a sympathetic smile. "Let's try to focus on this for now, okay?"

I nod. "Teach me all the things." The quicker I catch on, the sooner I can go home. If nothing else, that's at least motivating. I also can't help but think about my dad. The words he left me in his book. Maybe there's a part of me that wants to figure this out, to make him proud of me. To escape the fate he met when his magic spiralled out of control.

As we walk around the yard, Kit tells me to focus my senses on the nature around us. "Take my hand and close your eyes. It'll help you concentrate, and I'll make sure you don't trip or walk into anything."

We stop walking, and I set my empty mug in the grass, shooting him a look. "Smooth. You just want to hold my hand."

The corner of his mouth twitches as he shakes his head. "Come on. Quit being difficult and focus."

Exhaling heavily, I slap my hand into his and grumble, "There. Happy now?"

His expression is smooth, focused. "Close your eyes," he instructs, and I do, suddenly not cold from the frigid temperatures thanks to Kit's hand surrounding mine. "Good. Now try to open yourself to the world around you. What do you feel, smell, hear? Take your time."

I take a deep breath in an attempt to center myself and follow Kit's guidance. The faint chirp of crickets fills my ears and the grass smells damp, earthy, as if it rained last night. My tongue is still coated with the bitter aftertaste of my coffee, but oddly enough, I think I can smell the fresh pot of coffee—in the kitchen.

"What do you feel?"

"Nothing," I say with a sigh.

"Keep trying. You might be thinking about it too hard."

"Me? Overthink? Never."

Kit doesn't know me well enough for the joke to land where it should. That, and he's only concerned with teaching at the moment.

I take a second to get back into the zone. This time, I focus on the air, on the way the wind is blowing through the trees and making my hair fall into my face. I try to visualize slowing the wind to a gentle breeze.

"Slow down." The words fall from my lips in a whisper.

Kit gasps softly, and my eyes fly open. The world seems darker somehow, but it quickly returns to normal once I blink a few times.

"Did I do it?" I didn't feel a difference, but maybe I missed it.

Kit just stares at me for a moment. Finally, he blinks, shaking his head.

I grimace, confused by his response, and tilt my chin down. "I don't know how to make this work."

"Don't you worry about that," he says, rubbing his hands up and down my arms. "That's my job. You figure it out on your own, and Nova won't need me anymore."

I try to smile, but the result is weak. "How long does it usually take a new Wielder to figure it out? To actually use magic?"

He pulls his hands away, slides them into his jean pockets, and shrugs. "Everyone is different."

"Can you give me a ballpark?" I push.

"It doesn't matter. I don't want to upset you."

I look away. "Because I should be figuring it out by now."

"No, that's not what I'm saying. I just don't want you to have expectations that don't work out for you. Playing the comparison game won't help you. It will only ever hurt you."

"Maybe that's the problem. My expectations are misguided

because I don't really have any idea what I *can* do. Or can't for that matter."

His head tilts to the side. "That's a good point. All magic has limitations. The older the Wielder, the more powerful they are, but we aren't invincible. We have mortal lifespans and can be hurt just like any human."

"So I shouldn't expect to be able to move mountains on day two, is what you're saying?"

He offers a bemused smile. "I'm saying to be kind to yourself. In the grand scheme of things, you're handling this exceptionally well."

"Yeah, me trying to escape on foot the other night was super level-headed," I joke, surprising myself with how easily it came. Maybe I'm more comfortable here than I thought—or than I want to be.

We go through a few more exercises with no success before calling it a day. Heading back inside, Kit goes for a shower while I stop in the kitchen and pour myself a giant bowl of Fruit Loops. I skip the milk and spoon, eating it like popcorn as I sit cross-legged on the couch.

Slowly, the rest of the house gets up and starts moving around. Lydia is the first one to join me in the living room, coffee in hand.

"How'd it go this morning?" she asks with bright eyes and a barely concealed smile.

"I'm eating a huge bowl of cereal that's more sugar than anything else, and without a spoon. How do you think it went?"

She arches a brow. "What do you mean? I eat my Loops like that all the time. I've even got a stash in the back of my closet."

I can't help but laugh. Despite how awful I feel, talking to Lydia makes me feel more grounded, which seems more and more important these days as I explore this whole part of my life I had no idea existed until my birthday. "It didn't really go anywhere."

She frowns. "That sucks. Sorry, Emery. You'll get it, though. Took me a few days to break through that mental block before I accepted the whole thing. Once I got over that mountain, the magic stuff became a lot easier."

"You think I might be blocking myself from my magic?"

Lydia takes a drink of her coffee, setting the mug on the table in front of the couch. "Maybe. I'm sure Kit has given you the *everyone is different* speech, so I won't bore you with it again. He's right, though. I know it can be ridiculously disheartening at the beginning, but once you have that breakthrough, everything will fall into place."

I glance at the bowl in my lap. "You sound so sure."

"Of course I do." She tosses her dark brown curls over her shoulder dramatically. "I'm speaking from experience here."

"Well, I appreciate it."

She nods. "Hey, you've got a friend in me, Em. I want to see you succeed here. Same as Nova and Kit."

When tears spring in my eyes, I turn my face away in surprise. "Thanks, Lydia."

"Anytime." She pats my knee. "I'll catch you later. I've got training with Zoe and Kit, but I'll be around this afternoon once you're done with class. I think Nova's waiting for you in his study."

Oh, right. I still have to deal with high school classes on top of all the life-changing stuff going on. Fantastic. "Sounds good," I tell her, smiling as she gets off the couch and leaves the room.

I finish my cereal and put the bowl in the dishwasher before meeting Nova in the study. He stands from the chair behind his desk.

"Before you ask, I really don't want to talk about this morning, so can we please just focus on the mundane stuff for a while?"

Nova smiles softly. "Of course." He gestures toward the chair on the other side of the desk, and I walk over, dropping into it.

"How does this work, exactly? Am I going to have a video feed of a live class or something?"

He lowers himself back into his chair. "You have access to all of the course material you would have received at your old school." He leans back and opens one of the desk drawers, pulling out a laptop—*my* laptop. He sets it on the desk in front of me along with the charger. "You'll go through learning modules and assignments on an individual basis. However, I'll be here to assist if you need."

I was under the impression before coming here that Nova was a teacher, so this is one of the few things that doesn't surprise me and that I feel confident won't be a total disaster.

"Uh, okay. So I work with Kit at the ass crack of dawn and then have schoolwork for the rest of the day?"

Nova's lips twitch. "Yes."

"His whole *practicing magic in the morning helps* thing. Is there any truth to that, or is he just trying to torment me?"

He laughs. "It has been proven to help other Wielders."

"Great," I deadpan.

"If it doesn't work for you, let him know. He's here to help you, Emery."

"You keep saying that," I tell him. "I'm just wondering when I'm going to believe it." I lean back in the chair. "I thought I did believe it or that I was at least starting to, but—I don't know. Lydia suggested that maybe I'm still blocked and that's why the magic isn't coming to me."

Nova nods. "Possibly."

"Possibly?" I echo. "That's it? That's all you've got for me?"

His smile is faint. "You said you didn't want to talk about this morning."

My eyes narrow slightly, but I can't say anything, because he's right. "Okay. Can I have my lesson for today?"

"Emery?" he asks.

"Yeah?"

"Do you want to talk about it?"

"I really don't."

"All right." He turns his attention to the computer on his desk, typing quickly for a few moments before looking at me again. "I've sent a link with your materials to your student email."

I arch a brow. "How'd you get that?"

He gets up and walks around the desk, coming to stand beside me. "I have connections with a lot of the schools in the area."

"Right," I say as I flip open my computer and connect to the Internet. "I'm surprised you can even get Wi-Fi out here in the middle of freaking nowhere," I mutter under my breath.

Nova's brows rise, making his forehead crease, but there's amusement in his eyes. "Yes. Electricity and running water too. It's mind-boggling." His tone is light and teasing, and for a moment, I see the Nova I knew growing up. The one who always made me smile. I let myself remember that feeling, the warmth and comfort. For a split second, I forget the reason I'm here.

When everything comes rushing back, it punches a hole in my chest, and I shift in the chair, dropping my gaze to my lap. "I should probably get to work."

"You can work in here for today," he says. "I have some things to attend to in town, so I'll be gone until later. My cell number is on the fridge if you need to get in touch."

"I don't have my—"

Nova sets my cell phone on the desk beside my laptop. "I've asked you to trust me," he says in a low voice, and my eyes lift to his. "Now I'm going to trust you to be careful with this." Meaning I won't use it to contact my friends or call a cab to get the hell out of here? Of course those thoughts cross my mind, but the longer I'm here, the more I understand how important it is to keep what I'm experiencing from my friends. As much as that kills me, there's a part of me that gets it.

I reach for it. "I will. Thanks, Nova."

Once Nova is gone, I lose myself in something I at least understand and can work with. Plain old high school English.

It's dark outside by the time I close my laptop after three pre-recorded lectures and a short paper. I wander into the living room to find Kit and Mason watching a football game on the TV above the fireplace.

"How was class?" Kit asks, turning his attention toward me while Mason keeps his eyes glued to the TV.

I shrug. "Good. Pretty boring, though I guess it's nice to have some semblance of normal in my life. Something I actually know how to do."

He smiles. "Fair enough."

Glancing around, I ask, "Where are the others?"

"Nova's still out, and the girls are on their way back from a hike. They should be back any minute."

I pull at the sleeve of my sweater as I lean against the door-frame. "Should I start something for dinner?" My tone wavers, not wanting to step on any toes.

"Nah," Mason chimes in now that the game has switched to a commercial. "Nova's picking up wings and pizza."

My stomach grumbles at that. "Oh, cool." I glance toward Kit. "Do you have some time? I was hoping to try again before dinner."

His smile grows. "Yeah? Let's do it."

"Dude, the game," Mason says.

Kit rolls his eyes as he gets off the couch and walks toward me. "I'm glad this morning didn't scare you off," he says as we walk outside. "I know slow progress is frustrating, but consistency is key here, so I need you to keep working with me. I'm good at what I do, but that only means so much. If someone doesn't want to learn, like really deep down suppresses their abilities, then I can't help."

I frown. "Do you think that's what I'm doing?"

Kit doesn't hesitate. "No, I don't think so at all."

"You sound so sure," I mumble, wanting to look away. His certainty in my ability to figure this out has put an uncomfortable amount of pressure on me. I don't want to let him down. I don't want to let *me* down.

The nightmare I had where I hurt the people I cared about lingers at the back of my mind, almost like a warning. Or a reminder of why I'm here. I need to figure this magic thing out so I don't hurt someone I care about. And so it doesn't hurt *me*.

The corner of Kit's mouth kicks up and his blue eyes—which look more gray than blue right now—sparkle. "You're still here, aren't you?"

I press my lips together. "I've thought about leaving more than once," I admit.

"But you're here," he repeats, "because you made the decision to stay. There's a reason for that, and we both know it. Lean into it. You know you're supposed to be here, which is exactly why you haven't left."

"Well, that, and the fact I have no idea how to get anywhere from here." I try to laugh to show him I'm only kidding, but it comes out high-pitched and weird.

"That didn't seem to be a concern when you tried to make a break for it," he teases, his gaze dropping to my lips, making me blush.

I cross my arms over my chest, pinning him with a half-hearted glare. "Oh, and what would you have done in my position?"

Kit shrugs. "I'd have been a lot faster, that's for sure." He shoots me a wink, and I reach out and shove him. His deep laughter fills the air, and I end up joining in, laughing until my belly aches.

"Hey!"

We both turn toward the house and find Lydia sticking her head out the window. "Dinner's here! Get your asses in here before Mason inhales it all."

Kit and I look at each other, and I say, "So much for extra practice. Maybe later?"

He scratches the back of his head. "If you're up for it. Or we can pick it up tomorrow morning."

I sigh. "Sounds good, but how about we let the sun rise before you drag me out of bed?"

Kit shakes his head as we walk back to the house. "You're really not a morning person, are you?"

"I think we established that today," I shoot back, hurrying inside to the warmth—and the pizza.

Once I've successfully taken down four slices of pizza, Lydia pulls me aside, grinning as if she's got some secret she's barely holding in.

"What's up?" I ask, not completely sure I want to know.

"I'm taking you out tonight, and we're going to party like it's your birthday."

"Uh, hard pass. I'm not the partying type. Plus, my birthday is over."

She frowns. "Well, too bad. I didn't know you on your birthday, so I'm forcing you to celebrate now."

"Why does that sound like more of a gift for you than for me?"

Lydia bats her lashes at me. "Oh, come on! It'll be fun, I promise. Mason and I know this great spot. It's a little ways away, but Zoe agreed to be our DD."

"But we're not—"

"Don't worry. This place is on the smaller side, and Mason knows the door guy."

I look back at her, hesitating. "Okay," I finally say, and she squeals. "But I have pretty much nothing to wear."

Lydia purses her lips, looking me over. "I've got the perfect outfit for you."

The music is thunder in my ears. It's so loud I can't hear myself think. *Why did I let them bring me here?* Even with what feels like fifty layers of makeup on my face and a black cocktail dress hugging every curve on my body, I feel wildly out of place. I appreciate Lydia's intentions with this whole girls-night-out thing —though Mason is around here somewhere—but this really isn't my scene, and I'm kind of hoping we don't stay long. I try to enjoy it, though. I sip the rum and Coke in my hand, swaying my hips with the beat. It vibrates through my entire body as the haze of perfume and alcohol and body heat makes my head spin. People scream over the music while others belt out the words, and I get a strong whiff of pot as a group of women teetering on insanely high heels rush past where Lydia and I are dancing. Strobe lights flash around the room, and the crowd hoots and hollers with excitement as the song changes to one of the current chart-toppers.

We laugh and dance, and I let myself get lost in it. To forget what brought me to this moment and all of the unknowns waiting for me when we go back to Nova's.

Closing my eyes for a moment, I allow the sound to drown me.

When I open them a few moments later, my entire world narrows on the guy leaning against the bar across the room, surrounded by moving and dancing bodies.

His hair is so dark it appears black and sweeps across his olive-toned face. He's dressed head to toe in black, and his blue eyes are locked on me, blazing with an intensity that makes my knees lock.

Everything about him is hauntingly familiar.

Panic is ice in my veins, freezing me in place as the world moves on without me.

It's him.

But it can't be. He's not real. It . . . it was just a dream. A horrifically scarring nightmare wherein my magic hurt the people I care about while this guy—this stranger—stood by and watched, but it wasn't *real*.

"Emery?" Lydia's voice is muted by the music, but I feel her at my side.

I can't stop looking at him. He's watching me with recognition in his eyes, and fear clamps down on my chest. "I need some air," I choke out, pushing through the crowd toward the neon red EXIT sign. I slam my shoulder into the door and sigh when the cold night air seeps into my skin. I appear to be in an alleyway between the club and another building, surrounded by brick exteriors. I work on getting my pulse back to a normal speed as I step away from the building, taking a long gulp of my drink. I don't know how I'm going to explain myself to Lydia. I could probably blame it on the combination of the alcohol and the temperature of the club getting to my head.

"Are you all right?"

I whirl around, the glass slipping from my fingers and shattering against the concrete. "Crap," I mutter before my eyes shift in the direction of that deep, smooth voice. And then my heart slams against my chest. It's the guy from my nightmare. The only person my magic didn't touch. Everyone else was destroyed, but not him.

"Wh-what . . . ?" I shake my head, my breath fogging the air. "No. I mean, yes. I'm fine."

He arches a dark brow, regarding me curiously.

My mouth goes dry, and swallowing only makes it worse. "Do I know you?"

The guy smiles, and that small act makes my stomach flip-flop. Maybe it's the rum . . . though most of it ended up on the ground.

"Our families go way back," he finally says.

My brows scrunch up even as my chest tightens. "Um. I think you have me mistaken for someone else."

"Nope. I don't."

I suddenly feel very defensive. "I'm adopted," I say, in hopes he'll realize his mistake and leave me alone.

He leans against the brick, rubbing his jaw. "Of course you are," he says under his breath.

"Who are you?" I demand, standing straighter as if that'll somehow help me feel less freaked out. Or appear it, anyway. But with the way I'm shivering, I probably look ridiculous.

The corner of his mouth kicks up, and he lifts his gaze to my face, taking his time doing so. "Remington Henstridge."

"That's quite the mouthful."

"Indeed I am," he says without missing a beat.

"Has that line worked for you? Ever?"

He smirks. "You'd be surprised, little bird."

My eyes narrow as I cross my arms across my flushed chest. "Why did you follow me out here?"

Remington purses his lips before shrugging. "I enjoy a good chase." His eyes flash with mischief, and my breath catches. There's something going on here, and my gut tells me I need to remove myself from the situation.

"Well, I don't enjoy being chased, so feel free to get the hell away from me." Anger bubbles in me, and if my arms weren't crossed over my chest, they'd be balled into fists, ready to take a swing at his stupidly attractive face if necessary. He can't be much older than me, but the guy radiates confidence as if nothing can touch him.

He pushes away from the wall, closing the distance between us as his eyes flick across my face. "You have no idea what you're in for."

I stand frozen, staring into his eyes. I can't bring myself to move, because even as my heart pounds in my chest, something in his pale blue gaze draws me in. It doesn't make a lick of sense, and before I can think anything of it, the door to the club swings open, slamming against the brick as Kit storms out.

"How wonderful," Remington says, his voice dripping with sarcasm, "the fun police have arrived."

Confusion floods through me. "Kit, what are you—"

"Get away from her, Henstridge," Kit barks.

My eyes widen at his tone. *Kit knows this guy?*

Remington chuckles. "We both know it's only a matter of time before I get what I want."

"What?" I cut in, my eyes bouncing between Kit and the guy I've had the misfortune of meeting tonight. "What does that mean?"

"Forget it," Kit says without taking his eyes off Remington, then grabs my hand to guide me back inside.

"She deserves to know," Remington says.

My head swings back toward him at the same moment he reaches for my wrist. The second our skin touches, tingles shoot through me. I gasp, pulling away from him. It didn't hurt. If anything, it was energizing. Like a jolt of caffeine.

My eyes snap to his, but there isn't shock or surprise there like I was expecting. Just a mix of amusement and something darker.

Lydia and Mason appear in the doorway just as Kit and I hurry back inside the club.

Kit's hand goes to my back and guides me out the front of the club into a waiting car. Zoe is behind the wheel, shuffling through her music. Mason slips into the passenger seat while Kit, Lydia, and I slide into the back.

Once we're on the road heading home, I break the silence.

"Someone care to explain what just happened?"

"What were you thinking?" Kit demands, and Zoe turns off the music at that point.

"I'm sorry," Lydia says, shaking her head. "I just wanted to let Emery have a night out. She's been wrapped up in training and school for the last couple of days. She deserved a fun time after everything she's been through."

"And you thought taking her to some shady club was a good idea?" Zoe chimes in.

Mason scowls at her. "Relax, Zoe. Nothing even happened."

"What are you talking about?" I cut in. "Of course nothing happened! Why would it?" When the car goes eerily silent, it's my turn to scowl. "Oh no. You're not allowed to be secretive now." I look at Kit's over Lydia's head. "Who was that guy?"

"Here we go," Zoe mutters under her breath, pulling onto a main road.

"Kit—" Lydia starts.

"Who is Remington?" I ask.

Kit sighs, raking his fingers through his hair. "We'll talk about this at home. Once I have a chance to discuss it with Nova."

I glare at him. "Seriously? What does Nova have to do with this?"

Kit shakes his head but doesn't answer me. "I can't believe you went there," he grumbles under his breath.

"Chill out, Kit, okay?" Lydia snaps. "I'm sorry. I didn't know he'd be there."

"He lives above the club," Zoe says in a dry tone.

"So? That doesn't mean he's always there." She sighs. "He probably saw Emery there with us and just wanted to mess with you."

Confusion floods through me as I try to piece the events of tonight together. No luck. All I can figure is there has to be some connection between Remington and the Wielders. He must be one, but if that's the case, why do they seem to hate him?

CHAPTER SIX

T he minute we pull into the driveway and Zoe puts the car in park, Kit is out the door, storming toward the house.

"What the hell?" I whisper to Lydia.

She frowns at me. "I'm sorry, Em. I wanted to take you out for a fun night to celebrate your birthday.

"We better get inside," Zoe mutters from the driver's seat, pulling the keys out of the ignition. "Nova's going to want to talk to you," she says, glancing in the rearview mirror at me.

That's fine. I have some questions for him.

The four of us walk in the front door at the same moment another door slams shut. Kit's voice booms through the house, but the words are muffled through the walls.

"I don't understand," I say to no one in particular. "Why is he so upset?"

Zoe and Lydia look at each other, and Mason flat-out ignores me, walking toward the kitchen.

"I think it's best if Nova explains," Lydia finally says.

Despite the pounding in my chest, I square my shoulders and march toward Nova's study. Standing outside the door, the voices are a bit clearer. Nova's voice is calm and steady—a stark contrast to Kit's venom-filled shouting. It makes me pause. I had no idea this side of Kit existed, and while I don't know the circumstances that caused this reaction, hearing him like this makes me suddenly unsure of my opinion of him.

I hesitate before closing my hand into a fist and knocking on the door. The room falls silent for a moment before footsteps echo from the other side. The door opens, and Nova stands in front of me.

"What's going on?" I ask before he can speak.

"Kit and I were just having a conversation about what happened this evening." He opens the door wider, inviting me in.

When I step inside, my eyes immediately go to where Kit is pacing in front of the wall of bookshelves. "Why are you so pissed?" I demand. "Someone needs to tell me what's going on." I turn my attention to Nova. "I want to know who Remington is and how he knew who I was. I need the truth, or I'm out of here. I've lived in the shadows of this part of me for my entire life. I'm not going to put up with more secrets."

"Kit, perhaps you should get some air while I talk to Emery," Nova suggests, though his stern expression and dark eyes make me believe it's not as much a suggestion as it is a thinly veiled order.

After one final tired look in my direction, Kit leaves; I'm half-surprised he doesn't slam the door behind him.

"I'm so confused," I tell Nova. "This guy from the club knew who I was, and Kit obviously knows him too. You should have seen him when he found Remington and me together." As much as I hate admitting it, Kit's reaction scared me more than the random guy following me into the alley.

Nova gestures toward the sitting area, and we each take one of the chairs. "Kit feels responsible for you. He is your mentor, and the idea of you being in harm's way, well, it set him off. He's always been protective over his mentees."

"He barely knows me," I mutter.

"Even still. And Remington is . . . not someone you want to associate yourself with. Kit was right in that he is dangerous."

I blink at him, swallowing past the dryness in my throat. "But that doesn't tell me why or how he knew who I was. He said something about our families knowing each other?"

"That very well could be true. Remington is a Wielder, too." Great. That isn't exactly groundbreaking information; I assumed as much.

"He said some really weird things," I continue, "but I didn't have a chance to press him for information because Kit appeared and went ballistic." I shake my head, shivering at the memory. "Remington said something about getting what he wants. Does that have something to do with me?"

Nova frowns, glancing at where his hands are folded in his lap. "Remington is a troubled young man. He has little care for anyone and an utter disregard for the rules put in place to protect Wielders from discovery. Kit saw the danger of the situation with Remington and was likely upset he wasn't there to stop it from happening."

I pick at my thumbnail while I stare at the soft dimple in Nova's cheek. "So Kit was all uptight because he's protective over me?"

"Essentially."

My stomach flutters. "He doesn't need to be. I—I can take care of myself." I always have. Well, Mom and I took care of each other. I don't need anyone else.

Nova smiles. "We look out for our own, Emery. No matter how you feel, you are not alone here."

I open my mouth to tell him about the nightmare I had. Having met Remington tonight, I have to believe the dream is connected to my magic, but I'm not sure what to do with that. I want to tell Nova, but something stops me. No words come out.

He's keeping secrets from me. Maybe there's a part of me

that needs to hang onto something for myself. If I can't get answers here, I'll find them elsewhere. Even if that means seeing Remington again.

"Emery?"

I shake my head, refocusing on him. "It's late. I should . . ." I let my words trail off as I stand. "Good night, Nova," I say on my way to the door, my temples aching with tension. The longer I'm here, the more I learn, and I'm beginning to wonder if that's such a good thing.

***

Kit is late for our training session the next morning, and when he does arrive, I'm not greeted by his normal friendly demeanor.

"Are we going to talk about last night?" I ask, my arms crossed over my chest. I'm not digging his cold behavior, and I'm not about to spend the next two hours with him if he's going to be acting like there's a giant stick up his ass. I'm having a difficult enough time learning magic as it is.

"There's nothing to say," he tells me as he zips up his gray hoodie. "Besides, you already spoke to Nova about it."

I kick at the grass. "Yeah, but Nova has this great ability to answer questions without actually answering them."

Kit chuckles, but it lacks his usual warmth. "That's probably because the answer isn't something you're ready to hear."

I pin him with a glare. "And who is he—or you, for that matter—to decide that?"

His gaze collides with mine, and the coolness there makes my breath catch. "You don't know anything, Emery, so watch your mouth."

I scowl. "Why are you being such an asshole? Do you hate Remington so much you're going to let him control your emotions?"

He shoves his hands inside his black jean pockets. "Emery—"

"Nothing happened last night, so please, get your head out of your ass so we can have a productive session. Pretend that guy doesn't exist. He isn't here, I am. Focus on me."

His gaze softens as he steps closer. "You're right," he says. "I'm sorry. Remington and I have history. I'm not proud of it, and every time I see him, it's an unfortunate reminder."

I lick the dryness from my lips. "Do you want to talk about it?"

He smiles, but it doesn't reach his eyes like it usually does. "No. Thank you, though. As you said, we need to focus on you." He winks at me, warming my cheeks.

"All right. Let's get to it, then."

He pulls his hands out of his pockets and starts walking toward the tree line.

"Uh, where are you going?"

He pauses and looks at me over his shoulder. "I'd like to see if a change of scenery might help. Come on, it's not far."

I jog to catch up to him. "What isn't far?"

"Do you trust me?" he asks as we walk next to each other, our steps muffled by the wet leaves beneath us.

"I've known you less than a week," I say instead of telling him no, because I don't want to hurt his feelings when he's trying his best to work with me.

We walk in silence for a few minutes, through fallen branches and over the stream that cuts through the trees. The air is damp and earthy, and if I weren't on edge following Kit through these woods, the smell would put me at ease.

When we reach a clearing, I scan the space, the headstones scattered across the ground obscured by debris from the trees surrounding them, and land on a stone structure. It's crumbling in places, but still standing. There are stone steps that descend to a dark entryway.

Kit starts toward the building, but my feet are rooted in place.

"No way," I tell him, my pulse thrumming beneath my skin. "I am not going down there."

He stops and turns back to me, trying to hide a grin by pressing his lips together. "It's perfectly safe, Emery. The others and I come here all the time."

"Our magic is based on the elements. Don't you think it's a little messed up to be practicing among the dead?" I wrap my arms around myself against the cold air.

Kit regards me with a thoughtful expression. "Death is the balance of nature." When he sees the doubtful look on my face, he smiles and offers me his hand. "Just try. Please?"

My eyes drop to his outstretched hand. I go back and forth over whether I should turn around and go back to the house or give this thing a shot. I want to figure out my magic, but I'm finding it difficult to do that when I suspect I still don't have the whole story. And I'm not giving up on getting it.

I walk toward Kit and slide my hand into his. Warmth spreads through me, and I fight the urge to close my eyes against the pleasantness of it. It's different from the way I responded to Remington. This is warm and safe, whereas Remington's touch stole the breath from my lungs. I still feel it against my skin like a brand when I think about the moment his fingers wrapped around my wrist, and it sends shivers through me all over again.

I give my head a shake to refocus and walk with Kit toward the mausoleum. Our steps echo on the stone, and my breath catches when Kit holds his other hand out in front of us, conjuring a burst of fire from his palm to light the space.

"I don't know if I'll ever get used to that," I tell him, a little breathless.

He grins as he uses his foot to push the metal gate open. "You haven't seen anything yet."

The room is smaller than I thought it would be. There is one full wall of casket drawers sealed in the stone, and four large marble tombs spread around the room. Vases are scattered around the space as well, though by the cracks and dust covering them, it's safe to say it's been a while since there were flowers down here. The candles around the room, however, look new. Melted wax has hardened down the sides of them, but they seem to be the only thing in this place not covered in cobwebs or dust.

The flame from Kit's hand blows out, drowning the room in darkness for a moment before it's blanketed in soft, flickering light from the candles.

"Did you just decide you wanted the candles lit and voilà?"

Kit laughs. "Something like that."

I punch him lightly in the chest. "Come on. You want me to learn. Even if fire magic isn't my specialty, I think learning about it would be beneficial."

He arches a brow at me, leaning against one of the tombs. "Do you now?"

"Tell me I'm wrong," I challenge.

Kit shakes his head. "It's not a bad idea."

"Great," I beam, "so how did you light an entire room of candles simultaneously in the time it took me to blink?"

"Lots of practice," he says. "When I first started out, I could barely light a single candle. For the longest time, I could only spark a tiny flame and it would burn out seconds later."

"Hmm, so the great Kit Harris wasn't always a badass Wielder." I gasp in mock surprise.

"Poke fun all you want. This is good news for you."

"Because it means I won't always suck?" I offer.

"For lack of a better phrase, yes." He pushes away from the tomb and circles me slowly. "I want you to extinguish the candles whatever way seems most natural to you."

I arch a brow at him, leaning over to the candle closest to me and blowing it out. "Ta-da."

Kit shoots me a dry look. "Try leaning into one of the elements this time."

I exhale heavily and close my eyes. With a slow, deep inhale, I try to focus on the earthy smell lingering from the forest. It's a little difficult in this musty old place, but I'm able to get nodes of it through the overwhelming amount of dust.

I dig into my memory and picture the camping trips my mom used to take me on when I was younger. We didn't want to waste the jug of water we'd brought to put out the fire, so we'd smother it with dirt. It was usually damp and heavy enough to do the trick.

My pulse races as the rich scent of dirt overtakes the dust. The stone walls rumble, and my eyes fly wide open just in time to watch the dirt floating from the stone floor fall back into place while the candles remain lit.

"I . . . Did I do that?" I whisper, my hands shaking.

Kit is grinning. "You sure did."

"But it didn't work. The candles are still lit."

His grin remains. "I'm fairly confident it would have worked if you hadn't scared yourself into losing your concentration."

I blink at him. "Does that mean I have earth magic?"

"It's possible. Do you want to try again?"

I nod. "Which did my father have? Maybe we're the same. I mean, does it work that way? Or could he have specialized in a different element?" I suck in a breath after my slew of rapid-fire questions.

"Slow down," Kit says with a laugh. "I don't want you to focus too heavily on one area. I think we should continue to explore the different elements as well."

"Can you learn new ones even if you were born without them as a specialty?" My pulse has returned to a normal pace, but my stomach is filled with nerves and excitement; I'm unable to differentiate the two at the moment. Having a taste of success in practicing magic makes me want to keep going, to learn more, and I'm not sure how I feel about it.

"It's possible, yes, though very difficult."

"Have you?"

"I've dabbled," he answers.

I roll my eyes. "Of course you have."

"Hey, you asked."

"Is there anything you're not good at?" I mutter.

"Folding napkins, apparently."

I stifle a laugh, recalling Lydia's teasing dig at Kit before dinner last night.

Kit glances at his watch, then at me. "We should head back so you can start class."

The walk back through the forest is more comfortable. We chat about our favorite movies, and just as we reach the property line, I ask him about Thanksgiving.

"Do you think Nova will let me go home?" I can't imagine not spending the holiday with my mom.

"I think it's worth having a discussion with him."

"Are you confident enough I won't implode from my magic if I leave here for a few days?" My tone is teasing, but he doesn't so much as crack a smile.

"You need to be careful, Emery. Today went well, but this isn't a game."

I swallow past the sudden tightness in my throat. "I know that. I was just . . . never mind."

Back inside the house, I grab my laptop from Nova's study and settle in on the couch with the fire crackling. The house is quiet, save for soft music coming from one of the bedrooms. Kit disappeared when we got back, and I try not to read too much into that. I scroll through my lesson for the day and start taking notes just as a light rain falls outside. The sky is overcast and gray, the perfect weather to curl up on the couch with a hot drink and read the day away. Unfortunately, I still have twenty pages of this history lesson to get through and an assignment to start.

A few hours later, I take a break for lunch. I find the things to make a tossed salad and a ham sandwich and start putting everything together. I glance at where I left my phone charging and debate texting Lana and Jessa. I haven't spoken to them since I left and have ignored the messages they sent to our group chat mainly because I have no idea what to say. They know I left town, and I owe them an apology for leaving without saying goodbye—not that it was by choice, but they don't know that.

I shake my head, turning away from my phone and walking to the fridge. I'm not ready to face them yet.

Mason and Lydia come into the kitchen as I'm pouring a glass of orange juice.

"Hey, Em," Lydia says with a smile. "How are you?"

"Not bad," I tell her, taking a drink. "What have you two been up to?"

"We had class this morning and went for a little field trip to do some research."

"That sounds—"

"It was incredibly boring," Mason cuts in, and Lydia rolls her eyes. "How'd your training go?" he asks.

A flutter of excitement builds in my chest. "It actually went really well. I mean, I'm not an expert yet or anything, but I managed to use a little bit of magic."

Lydia squeals. "That's amazing! What did you use?"

I purse my lips before they curl into a smile. "Earth."

Her eyes widen. "No way! That's so cool. We should definitely practice together. I need to work on my earth magic a lot more."

"Yeah, for sure. That would be great."

"Have you told Nova? He'll be so pleased."

"Not yet. I was going to chat with him after lunch." My stomach is in knots over what he's going to say about me going to Covington for Thanksgiving, but I'm not going to take no for an answer. I deserve to spend the holiday with the only family I have, and my mom shouldn't be alone, either.

"We won't keep you then," Mason says, snaking his arm around Lydia's waist and pulling her away. "Catch you later."

I'm still smiling after they're gone. I shove the sandwich in my mouth and take a bite so I don't look like a weirdo smiling at an empty room.

CHAPTER SEVEN

I knock on the door to Nova's study shortly after lunch and step inside after hearing his muffled invitation.

"Emery," he says with a smile from behind his desk. "I hear congratulations are in order."

I smile a little, closing the door and walking over to him. Sitting in one of the chairs at his desk, I say, "Kit told you then?"

"He did. He was very proud to report how well you did."

"It didn't really seem like a lot, but I guess progress is progress."

"That's right. And your schooling is going well?"

"No issues so far." I glance down at the worn fabric on the arm of my chair. "I wanted to talk to you about Thanksgiving."

Nova folds his hands in his lap and offers me his attention. "What would you like to discuss?"

"I want to go home for the weekend." Before he can immediately say no, I add, "I haven't seen or spoken to my mom in almost a week. She doesn't deserve to be alone on Thanksgiving because I all of a sudden have the ability to wield magic." As much as I'm still struggling with her keeping said magical ability from me, I want to see her.

Nova rubs at his jaw, nodding. "I understand, and I would like nothing more than to allow it."

"So allow it," I cut in.

He tilts his head. "I'm not sure you're ready."

"What? It's not like I'm going to have the urge to destroy a bunch of things with magic. I made some dirt float for a few seconds today. Not sure how you could see that as threatening. And I'm not trying to suppress it either, so there's no chance of it consuming me or whatever. Nova, please. I need this."

He watches me for a few moments before sighing. "I'm not sure."

"I'll take Kit with me," I blurt without thinking.

Nova blinks, leaning back in his chair. "Have you spoken to him about this?"

"Uh, no. But if he agrees, will you consider letting me go for a few days?"

His brows knit, and he places his hands on the desk. "I suppose that would be all right. However, you can't stay for long. You need to stay on track with your training."

"Of course," I say quickly, overcome with the excitement of seeing my mom. I'll have to let Jessa and Lana know I'll be in town. I should see them—after I've figured out my non-Wielder story for leaving in the first place. I know what my mom told them, but I'll have to build on it if they're actually going to believe it.

Slow down, Emery, I tell myself.

"Talk it over with Kit. If he says yes, you can go. I'll let your mom know."

"Thank you, Nova."

I'm wearing the biggest smile as I walk out of his study and head right for Kit's room. I knock on the door, but there's no answer.

"He went out about an hour ago for some meeting with one of the Elders."

I turn and find Zoe leaning against the wall. "Oh, okay." I want to ask more about the Elders, but from what I've been told so far, they kind of scare me. The idea of them anyway. Just another thing I'll have to get used to—leaders of this magical population I've joined.

Zoe crosses her arms, looking me over. "Earth magic, huh?"

"Yeah," I say, though the confirmation makes my chest feel tight. *News travels fast around here.*

Her red-stained lips twitch. "I suppose that's better than nothing."

"Is it?" I cringe and quickly add, "I guess."

"I'm assuming that means you're staying?"

"Um, yeah. Now that we've figured out which element I can wield, I have to figure out how to actually use it."

"Right." She stands there, just staring at me.

"Can I ask you something?"

Zoe sighs. "Be my guest."

"Why don't you like me? Is it because of Kit?"

Her eyes narrow and she barks out a laugh. "Please. Kit is—"

"Is what?" The guy in question rounds the corner from the front hallway and stops in front of us, raking his fingers through his windswept hair. He's changed since this morning, now wearing a gray knit sweater and dark navy jeans. "There a reason you're both hanging out in front of my door?" His gaze flicks between us.

"No. I mean, yes. I need to talk to you," I say.

Kit opens his bedroom door and walks in, leaving it open. "What's up?"

I dare to look back at Zoe, who just rolls her eyes and walks in the other direction. *So much for making progress with her.* "I talked to Nova about going home for Thanksgiving next week."

I linger in the doorway, looking around the room. It's slightly bigger than mine, with a double bed and night tables on each side. The walls are dark blue and free of any pictures or art.

Interesting. I definitely took Kit for a superhero poster type of guy, but this space is tidy and organized. No clothes on the floor, a bookshelf full of different-sized books, and a desk with a laptop sitting open.

"What did he say?" Kit walks over to his bed and sits on the end, kicking off his boots before looking up at me.

I lean against the doorframe. "Well, at first he said no." I bite my bottom lip, rolling it between my teeth for a second before I continue. "He said I could go if you go with me."

He pauses. "He suggested that?"

"Not exactly." I sigh, taking a couple steps into his room. "I'm sorry, I wasn't even thinking when I asked him if you could take me. I figured it would make him feel better if you were there to help me in case my magic decides to start going all, I don't know—" I wave my arms around, then cringe. "I should have talked to you about it first, but the idea came to me while I was talking to him. If you don't want to go, I completely understand. I know these people are your family, or maybe you want to spend it with your actual family, I have no idea. But I shouldn't have assumed that you would be willing to take me to Covington, so I'm sorry."

Kit chuckles softly while I catch my breath. "I don't mind taking you."

My heart races as I sit next to him, grabbing his arm without thinking. "Are you serious?"

"Yeah." He peers down to where my fingers are wrapped around his forearm. "My family never really celebrated holidays. It was something I started doing when I came here. So, I would be happy to celebrate with you and your mom."

I blink to keep the tears back and let go of his arm. "I'm so happy right now I could kiss you." The words are out of my mouth before I can clamp it shut. *Oh my god. I did not just—*

His brow rises. "Go for it."

"What?" I squeak.

"What?" he echoes with a grin.

"Oh, ha ha. You're very funny." He gives my side a playful nudge with his elbow, and I grumble, "How am I constantly making a fool out of myself in front of you?"

"I think it's cute," he tells me.

"I'm so glad," I remark dryly.

He's still grinning when he asks, "When are we going?"

"Next Thursday. I'd like to stay until Sunday, but Nova's concerned about me falling behind with training."

Kit nods. "That makes sense. Why don't we head out Thursday morning and come back Saturday night?"

"Sounds good," I say. At this point, I'm just relieved he's agreed to go with me. Otherwise, I wouldn't be going at all. "You're going to love it. Mom always goes all out for holidays. You'll be full for days after, and I'm sure she'll send us back here with plenty of leftovers."

Kit smiles. "I look forward to it."

"You're the first guy I've ever brought home," I muse aloud. "You'd better be on your best behavior."

He laughs. "Scout's honor."

I just shake my head at him and walk backward to the door. "Seriously, though, I really appreciate this, Kit. Thank you."

His cheeky grin turns into a genuine smile. "You're welcome."

As I walk out of his room and head toward mine, I have the fleeting thought that the flush in my cheeks and fluttering in my stomach might have something to do with Kit.

In the few days leading up to Thanksgiving, Kit and I train every morning for at least two hours. I'm frustrated with how slowly things are progressing, and by *slowly*, I mean the progress is pretty much nonexistent. The little earth magic trick I managed a few days ago doesn't work today, which makes it hard to focus when I can't help but feel as if I'm moving backwards.

Kit doesn't seem the least bit concerned. He's as patient and encouraging as he's been since I arrived. At this point, if I were in his shoes, I would have given up on me.

"What about trying a different element?" Kit suggests.

"If you think that will help," I say. I'll try anything right now. I just want *something* to work. I've been at this for over a week now. Sure, the first couple of days were essentially a write-off because of my own stubbornness to accept what I was, but now that I'm actively trying to work with magic, I was hoping things would come a bit easier. No such luck. *I must be doing something wrong.*

"The first time you tried magic, you talked about suffocating the flame to put it out."

"Yeah, but it didn't work."

He nods. "Things have changed since then. You've decided to accept the truth, which was a huge step. I think you should try it again. The theory was solid. Now let's see if you can bring the magic aspect into it."

"All right." My voice is filled with uncertainty, but I close my eyes and breathe deeply, in and out, until I shut out the rest of the world.

Candles flicker around the room. Their warmth surrounds me, and the light plays against my eyelids. I visualize the air around each flame as a physical thing. A heavy blanket that blocks out the oxygen needed to keep the fire lit. In my mind, I drop that blanket onto the candles and wait for the warmth to seep out of the room.

When nothing happens, I open my eyes to find Kit watching me closely. With a sigh, I shrug. "Oh, well."

He smiles. "Hey, it was worth a shot."

I try to smile back even as anger blossoms in my chest, making it difficult to breathe steadily. I'm not used to failure, and

I certainly don't like it. Or the feeling that I'm wasting Kit's time when he could be helping someone else.

"We'll try again tomorrow, okay?" he says.

"Sure." I don't move when he starts toward the stairs. "I'll catch up with you back at the house. I want to try it again."

"And you want me to leave?" he asks, grinning faintly. "Am I distracting you?"

I roll my eyes. "Yes, Kit, your dashing good looks are the reason I can't make my magic work. I'm so distracted by your face, I can't focus on my abilities."

"Thought so," he teases, though he doesn't make a move to leave. "But I don't think leaving you alone while you're working with magic is safe at this point."

"You've seen what I can do, Kit. Or, I should say, *can't* do. I'll be careful, I just want try it myself. Please?"

"You realize if I leave you here alone and something happens, I could get in serious trouble? The Elders are very strict about supervision during training."

"How are they going to know unless you tell them? Are they spying on us?" It's a joke, but the thought of that makes my skin tingle with goosebumps. That would seriously add to their creepy factor. And I'm already picturing them as cloaked, face-less figures.

"You are very stubborn," he comments.

"Most people find it endearing."

"I doubt that," he says dryly. He crosses his arms, then exhales a heavy sigh. "Fine. Just this once. You have five minutes, and I'm waiting right outside." Kit waits for me to nod before heading out of the mausoleum.

Once he's gone, I tug my shirt up and pull my father's book out of the waistband of my jeans. I flip through the pages, looking for the verse about light I wanted to try the other day. I figure fire is a form of light, so it should work. Kit didn't want me to learn to use my abilities with spells at first, but I can't ignore the pull to try the magic my dad wrote about in his book.

I take a deep breath and recite the words under my breath, and my voice shakes as if I'm afraid someone will overhear me. Nothing happens. The flames don't even waver. I try it again, louder, but again—nothing. On my third try, I close my eyes and recite the words in my head instead of out loud.

There's a whoosh of air that makes me shiver, and when my eyes spring open, I suck in a sharp breath. The flames . . . they're *black*. In the space of a heartbeat, they return to normal and sizzle out completely, leaving the room in a smoky haze.

Something isn't right.

I shove the book back into the waistband of my jeans and hurry up the stone steps, almost knocking into Kit when my feet hit the ground. My heart is pounding in my chest, and my head is spinning.

Kit catches me, steadying me with his arms on my shoulders. "Whoa, slow down." His eyes are like deep pools of blue, searching mine. "What happened?"

I pull in a breath, shaking my head. "It didn't work," I force out, breaking free of his grasp. I want to put as much distance between me and that mausoleum as possible. "Let's just go." I start toward the house with Kit quick on my heels.

"You want to tell me why you're so upset?"

"I'm just frustrated," I lie, and I don't even know why. Kit is here to help me, but I can't risk telling him about my dad's book and him taking it away.

"Take a breath," he says in a soft voice as I slow my steps to a more normal pace. "You're doing great, Emery. Earth magic can be tricky, but you'll figure it out, I know you will."

I have no idea what I just did, but it sure as hell didn't feel like earth magic.

Kit and I stop for coffee and croissants at the local café on our way out of Helen on Thanksgiving morning. I'm surprised it's even open, but the place is packed with people picking up pies and other fresh-baked desserts.

"You've been quiet this morning," Kit comments once we're back on the road heading toward Covington.

I stare out the window, looking at nothing in particular. "I'm just tired." It's been three days since the incident in the mausoleum, and the pit in my stomach hasn't left.

He nods, keeping his eyes on the road as he switches lanes to pass a slow-moving car. "You must be excited to see your mom."

More like desperate to ask her about the book. Did she know what was in it when she gave it to me, or did she just want me to have a piece of my dad? I have so many questions, and while I'm terrified of the answers, I need them. I can only hope they'll bring me some semblance of clarity.

"Definitely," I say. "I'm hoping to see my friends too." I still haven't contacted them since I *moved* to Helen—it's time to break the silence. It's either that or risk losing my best friends.

"Do I get to meet these friends?" he asks with a little grin.

I take a sip of my coffee, having already devoured my croissant while we were waiting in line to pay. "I don't know if that's a good idea. They'll have questions. Like why you're here. What would I tell them?"

Kit glances sideways at me. "You could tell them I'm your boyfriend."

I almost choke on my coffee, returning it to the cupholder before facing him. "The fake dating story? Really?"

He shrugs, tapping his fingers against the steering wheel, but I don't miss the tinge of pink in his cheeks. "It's just a suggestion."

I press my lips together. I can't say I haven't thought about Kit *that* way. He's attractive and nice, and it would be nearly impossible *not* to think about that when his attention has been focused on me since I got to Nova's. Not that I'm going to act on that attraction, but I'd be lying if I said it was non-existent.

"Fine," I say, "but be prepared for a tsunami of questions." I laugh and stare out the windshield, glad that he has to focus on the road and can't see me blushing like crazy right now. "You're going to regret this so fast, and I can't wait."

We spend the rest of the drive chatting about what we're having for dinner and other holiday traditions Mom and I have made over the years. Talking with Kit is easy. He listens and asks questions that tell me he's genuinely interested in the conversation. It's . . . nice. Maybe pretending to be his girlfriend in front of Jessa and Lana won't be the worst thing in the world.

We arrive at my house just after ten. Kit grabs our bags while I rush to the door, grinning the second I step into the warmth. Christmas music is blasting, and the house smells of rosemary and thyme.

"We're here!" I holler as Kit steps inside behind me, setting our bags on the bench adjacent to the door.

Mom rushes out of the kitchen, her hair tied messily in a bun on the top of her head. She's wearing an apron and the deep green cashmere sweater I gave her for Christmas last year. "Honey!" Tears fill her eyes as she throws her arms around me, hugging me tightly.

I wrap my arms around her, and we rock back and forth, sniffling. When we finally break apart, she takes my face in her hands, staring into my eyes.

"I am so happy you're here. I've missed you every single day." She pulls her hands away from my face and wipes the dampness from her cheeks before glancing past me at Kit. "Thank you for bringing her home."

He nods, stepping forward and extending his hand. "Kit Harris. It's very nice to meet you, Ms. Marcus, and it's my pleasure. I'm happy Emery is able to be home for the holidays."

She shakes his hand. "Likewise, and please, call me Holly." Her eyes flit across his face. "Nova was right. You are charming."

Kit blushes, and I struggle not to burst into laughter. "Ah, thanks," he says before reaching for our bags again. "Where do you want these?"

"Upstairs," I tell him. "Last door on your left."

Kit nods. "I'll let Nova know we're here."

"Cool," I say, watching him carry our bags upstairs before turning to Mom. "I'm so happy to be home. Even just for a few days."

She wraps her arm around my shoulders as we walk into the kitchen. "I know I have a lot of explaining to do. I'll be honest, when Nova called and told me you were coming, I was surprised. After what happened on your birthday, I was worried you'd never want to see me again. I've checked in with Nova every day, but I knew I needed to give you space to work through everything. I had to remind myself that even if you hated me for making you go, you were safe, and that's what mattered."

I blink back more tears. "I could never hate you."

She offers me a watery smile. "You have no idea how

relieved I am to hear that." She leans in and kisses the side of my head. "I'm making all of your favorites. There's going to be way too much food, but I wanted to make sure we had everything you love."

"You didn't have to do that," I tell her, leaning against the counter, but my stomach grumbles anyway.

"Of course I did." She walks over to the oven and peeks inside before turning back to me. "Now. Tell me everything. You've only been gone a couple weeks, but it feels like a year."

Wiping my hands on my thighs, I say, "I know." Then, without taking a breath, I add, "I will, but first I need you to tell me where the book came from. The one you sent with my things."

Her brows draw together, and she glances toward the doorway. "You've read it, then?"

My heart is thunder in my chest. "Some of it. It's all very confusing. I thought I was an earth Wielder, but I'm not connecting with the magic like it seems I should be."

She lowers her voice, and when she looks back at me, her face is several shades paler. "Have you told Kit about this? Nova?"

I shake my head. "Things have just started to feel a tiny bit normal, and I'm scared that this will throw a wrench into that."

She stops in front of me and wraps her fingers around my arms. "I know things are scary, honey. But you're doing everything right."

The urgency in her voice makes me frown. "I feel like I don't know anything. And the second I figure something out, a million other things happen that prove that to be true." I shake my head. "When does it stop? Will it ever?"

She squeezes my arms. "Of course it will. You'll figure this out, and you won't be alone while you do. There are people who care about you that aren't going anywhere."

Kit pops his head into the kitchen. "Can I help with anything?"

"Speaking of," Mom says with a little wink at me. "Sure, hon. You can chop up the potatoes and yams." She points to the paper bags on the counter. "Everything's in there."

"Great," Kit says with a smile, walking toward his newly appointed station at the kitchen counter.

"Do you mind if I steal my daughter for a few minutes?" she asks Kit as she undoes her apron, draping it over the back of a chair at the table. "We have some catching up to do."

"Not at all," he tells her before sending me a smile that warms my cheeks. "I'll be right here if you need anything."

Mom and I sit on the back porch overlooking the bit of land attached to our property. It's got nothing on Nova's place, but his place isn't home—this is.

"I know you probably have a million questions. I'll do my best to answer them, but—"

"Mom, something isn't right."

She angles herself toward me. "I know it feels that way."

Before she can say anything else, I shake my head. "I'm not connecting with the magic. I've tried it all, and even when I thought I'd figured out how to wield earth magic, something didn't feel right. Nothing worked the way Kit was trying to teach it to me."

Her lips are pressed in a thin line. "Nova told me you were able to use it."

"I don't think . . ." I stop myself, because what I was about to say scares me more than finding out about my abilities did.

"Emery?"

I try to take a breath, but it gets stuck in my throat as panic clamps down on my chest. "Something is wrong with me," I whisper as hot tears blur my vision. "My magic—nothing about what I've been able to do feels like it's connected to nature, and I know that doesn't make sense, and I haven't told anyone because

I have no idea why." I ball my hands into fists until my nails bite into the skin of my palms.

Mom's face drains of color. "Oh, honey—"

"But that's not possible, right? Because it has to be tied to one of the elements." Even as I say the words, something inside me knows I'm wrong. That I've been betrayed and lied to. Again.

"No." Her voice cracks on that one word.

"I don't understand. You're saying my magic isn't elemental?"

Her eyes widen and whip around as if she's worried about being overheard. "Don't. You can't . . . You need to keep trying."

My brows rise as the wind chime over our heads fills the air with a soft tune. "Trying what?"

"Earth magic. Air, fire, whatever. It doesn't matter."

"What are you saying right now?"

She grabs my wrists and pulls me in. "Listen to me. Your magic isn't safe."

"I get it," I say. "You've all been telling me that since my birthday. That's why I'm at Nova's."

"No, that's not—" She cuts herself off. "Just please, keep trying the magic Kit is showing you."

My eyes narrow. "Why?"

Her grip tightens. "Sometimes not knowing is better, especially if it keeps you safe."

I pull away from her. "No. I'm done with that. I deserve to know."

"Emery, please—"

I cross my arms over my chest. "You know something, I know you do." I watch her eyes fill with panic. "You need to tell me the truth—for once in my life."

She sucks in a breath. "You're right." Her voice is barely above a whisper.

"Right about . . ." My voice trails off as realization hits me like a ton of bricks. My magic. I can't connect to the elements because my magic isn't elemental.

Then what the hell is it?

"Mom?" My voice shakes.

She deserves to know. Remington's voice and the memory of that night at the club echoes in my head, making my stomach roil.

"He knew," I breathe, staring at my hands in my lap as the world spins around me.

Mom grabs my shoulder. "Emery, what—"

"Who is Remington Henstridge, and how did he know about my magic before I did?"

"H-Henstridge?" she asks, pulling her hand back. "How do you know that name?"

Anger flares through me. "What? No. You don't get to ask questions. Who is he?" Based on the fact that everything I've been told over the last two weeks seems to have been a lie, I have to assume what Nova told me about Remington is as well.

"It's complicated, Emery."

I stare at her in disbelief. "Let me *un*complicate it." My voice is low, harsh. "I thought Remington was a figment of a night-mare I had. Someone who stood by and watched while I killed everyone I love with my magic. It wasn't real, though. But then I saw him, and he was very much real. He confronted me as if he knew who I was, but up until that moment, I thought he was just someone I made up."

Her jaw is tight, and her eyes are honed on me like a hawk's. "What did he say to you?"

I shrug, swallowing past the mounting panic in my chest. "Kit showed up before he could say a whole lot. He told me our families went way back and said that he always gets what he wants." It didn't make any sense, and if I'm being honest, I chalked it up to him baiting Kit, which makes sense since some-thing clearly happened between the two of them.

"Emery . . ." There are tears in her eyes, but I can't read her expression.

I lift my hand to move the hair out of my face, and the muscles in my arm tremble, making my fingers shake. "Our families knew each other," I say in a quiet voice, biting the inside of my cheek as my eyes burn. "He's not an elemental Wielder either, is he?"

She shakes her head, her eyes filled with dread.

My jaw clenches so tight that tension fills my temples, and I turn away as my pulse spikes. "Why . . . why was I kept in the dark again?" My whole body vibrates with anger, and I ball my hands into fists, getting up. "Why won't anyone tell me the freaking truth?"

Thunder cracks through the air, and I flinch, my eyes flying upward to find the sky overcast and gray where it was bright and blue only a minute ago.

Mom's eyes go to the sky before she jumps up and rushes toward me. "Emery, please listen to me." Her tone is borderline frantic.

I clutch my chest, finding it impossible to swallow. "Did I . . . Oh my god. I can't—"

She grabs my arms, pulling them away from my chest. "Breathe." Her voice is firm. She says it again and again, and finally, I'm able to pull air into my lungs.

I squeeze my eyes shut, dragging in shallow breaths as she rubs her hands up and down my arms. When I open them, the sky is back to normal. Slowly, I lift my head and meet her gaze. "You need to tell me everything."

Her bottom lip trembles, but she clenches her jaw to make it stop. "All right." She swipes at the tear that escaped and nods toward the chair. "Please sit."

I drop back into the chair and face her directly. "My magic isn't elemental, so what is it?"

Mom takes a deep breath, exhaling through her nose. "There

isn't a name for it. The Elders . . ." She shakes her head as if she can't believe she's having this conversation with me. "The type of magic you have was banned years ago. It's manipulative and dark, so the Elders deemed it too dangerous to exist."

My head feels as if it's full of cotton. "Because it was dangerous enough to kill the Wielders that could use it if they didn't learn how to control it?"

Her voice is strained when she says, "No, honey."

"But that's what happened to Dad." My stomach sinks, and I force out, "Right? Please tell me, of all the things you've lied about, the way my father died isn't one of them."

Her eyes shift between mine, glassy with unshed tears. "I'm so sorry, Emery."

I don't miss a beat. "What happened?"

She closes her eyes as tears roll down her cheeks. There's a painful moment of silence, and then she cleaves my world in two. "He was killed by the Elders."

CHAPTER NINE

I can't speak. The world dims and my ears ring. I watch my mom's mouth move, her eyes frantically searching mine, but I don't say anything.

Slowly, things start to come into focus. The trees blowing in the wind. The chime above us. The cold air seeping into my lungs as I open my mouth and choke on the dryness of my throat.

"Why?" I croak.

She frowns. "There was a time when large groups of the Wielders with dark magic turned against the Elders. Defied their laws and manipulated humans to gain positions of power. It started a war with the Elders that resulted in those Wielders— and everyone with their same magic—being rounded up and thrown into prisons around the world that blocked their abilities. Except, not being able to use their magic turned it against them. None of the prisoners survived long. It didn't take long for word to spread, and any Wielders with that kind of magic who hadn't already been detained by the Elders scattered and went into hiding."

I want to crawl out of my skin. "Did my dad go against the Elders to gain power?"

"No, but he was discovered alongside others who were thought to have done that—including Remington's parents."

Relief flutters through me for a brief moment, knowing my father wasn't one of the bad guys. But it doesn't really matter how it happened. I still lost him. "I don't know how much more I can handle," I admit in a whisper.

Mom wraps her arm around me and guides me into the warmth of the house, and I don't fight her. I don't have it in me.

Once we're in the kitchen, Kit takes one look between the two of us and says, "You told her." Panic etches into his features, and his face quickly becomes something I no longer want to look at.

My eyes burn with tears, but I don't fight them back. "This whole time . . . You've been lying to me since the day we met, Kit." I shake my head as a tear slips down my cheek, and I finally look at him again. "You knew I'd never be able to wield the magic you were trying to teach me."

He rakes his fingers through his hair, messing the blond strands that fall into his face, which has quickly filled with despair. "I'm sorry. I didn't know what to do. I wanted to help you. We thought that maybe if you spent enough time with all of us, surrounded by the elements, that you could learn our magic."

"We?" My gaze flicks toward my mom before returning to Kit.

"Nova and I. The others don't know your magic isn't elemental."

I nod, swallowing hard. "Has that ever happened before? A Wielder with dark magic learning elemental magic?"

Kit hesitates. The silence in the room is heavy, then he whispers, "Not that I know of. There isn't . . . Emery, you're one of few Wielders with dark magic left."

My jaw clenches as the bit of food in my stomach threatens to make a reappearance on the kitchen floor. "You had no right to keep this from me."

"We know," Mom says, "but it was the only thing we could think of to keep you safe. If the Elders find out . . ." She trails off as if she's run out of breath. "Please don't give up on this."

The oven timer beeps, and I tear my gaze away from her. This conversation is far from over, but I need to give my head a second to catch up.

Mom shifts past me and walks to the oven, sliding the turkey inside.

I take that opportunity to leave the room, not stopping until I'm in my bedroom with the door shut and locked. I grab my bag off the floor and dig through it, throwing my clothes on the bed until I reach the book at the bottom. I pull it out and start from the beginning, reading every single word on every single page. Granted, I probably should have done this when I found the book, but the last thing I expected was a whole different story from the one I was given on my birthday.

Mom and Kit leave me alone, and I spend the afternoon reading the rest of Dad's book. Unfortunately, I come across no insight as to why the Elders banished our magic. Just a bunch of spells that could get me killed if I use them.

I toss the book to the side and bury my face in the mountain of pillows at the head of my bed. I'm at the mercy of Kit and Mom to answer my questions, and having no way to find answers on my own makes me feel . . . well, pretty damn hopeless. How can I be sure what they tell me is the truth? What's to keep them from lying to me again?

There's a soft knock at my door, but I ignore it.

"Emery?" Mom's voice is muffled from the hallway. "Dinner is ready."

I'm not the least bit hungry, but the sooner the niceties are over, the sooner I can ask more questions.

Sitting at the kitchen table with a plate full of my favorite holiday foods should make me feel all warm and fuzzy. Instead, my stomach feels as if it's filled with gravel.

We all pick at our food, sitting in heavy silence.

Mom takes a sip of her wine, sneaking a glance at me from across the table. "I baked your favorite pie."

I poke at the pile of mashed potatoes on my plate with my fork. "Thanks."

"You've barely eaten anything," she says in a gentle tone.

"I'm not hungry." The fork feels heavy in my hand.

She sighs. "Emery, please try to understand. We only kept this from you to—"

"Keep me safe?" I cut in, throwing the napkin onto the table beside my plate. "My ignorance could have gotten me killed."

Kit's face pales. "No one is going to hurt you, Emery. We won't let them."

"Is that supposed to make this okay? Everyone has been lying their asses off to me about my life, but hey, it's fine because you were all just trying to keep me safe."

He shakes his head. "That's not what I'm saying. I just don't want you to worry. Now that you know the truth—"

"I want to learn my actual magic," I cut in, leaning back in my chair. "There's no sense in continuing to teach me magic I'll never be able to wield."

"Of course there is," Mom says. "If we can figure it out, if you can learn to wield elemental magic even though that's not what you were born with, it very well could save your life." She takes a quick look at Kit. "Your magic . . . it's rooted in manipulation. M-maybe you can learn to manipulate the elements," she stutters, clearly grasping at straws now.

I thrust my fingers through my hair, pressing them into my scalp to ease the tension forming there. "You want me to live a lie to stay alive?"

"If that's what it takes." Her eyes are wide, and her tone is desperate. "I can't lose you, Emery. I already lost your dad because of this magic. I refuse to let it take you, too."

I look to Kit. "This was your plan since I arrived at Nova's?"

He nods, but doesn't say anything; his face is filled with shame. The sight makes my stomach hurt, and I have to remind myself that it's his fault. He decided to lie to me. They all did.

Swallowing, I clear my throat before speaking again. "And Remington. He's like me, so what does that mean? What is it he wants?"

A muscle ticks along Kit's jaw. "Revenge."

I blink at him. "Revenge for what? And what does that have to do with me?"

Kit sighs as if he doesn't want to tell me. "It has to do with your magic. Because it isn't grounded in anything natural, it can be . . . transferred."

As if I need something else to make my head spin. "Transferred to what?"

"Another Wielder with the same magic."

A chill races through me, making the hair on my arms stand on end. "Wait. He wants my magic for himself?"

Kit nods tightly, his shoulders stiff with tension. "More magic equals more power. As you can imagine, Wielders like you are very hard to come by. I haven't come across another aside from the two of you in years. Remington must've done some digging through his own family history and made the connection between you and your father."

"If Remington put that together, who's to say the Elders haven't as well?" My pulse spikes at the thought of them coming after me.

"They can't track you," Kit says. "It's one of the only ways Remington and the few others left have managed to evade them. Because of the origins of your magic, they can't reach it with their own."

"Origins?" I echo.

"You remember what I told you about elementals being angelic descendants?"

I don't like where this is going. "Uh-huh."

"The dark Wielders are descended from demons."

I inhale slowly through my nose, then blow the breath out through my mouth. "That's . . . just great."

"The Elders can't track you for that reason, but Remington can. Just like you can track him. The two of you need to be relatively close, meaning you can't track each other from separate states or anything, but if you were in Helen or here, for example, and he was in Savannah or Atlanta, it would work."

I'm not sure which is more terrifying—being a descendant of demons or being connected to Remington.

I wrap my arms around myself. "So not only do I have to worry about the Elders finding out about me, but now Remington is going to try to steal my magic?"

"He can't steal it. You would have to give it to him willingly, and it's not a back-and-forth thing. If you give it up, that's it. It's gone."

"So it's a one-and-done sort of deal? No take-backs?"

Kit nods.

"Okay, but why would I do that?" The second the question leaves my lips, I can't help but think, *to save myself from the Elders and get my life back?*

It's almost as if Kit sees that thought pass over my face, because he says my name with such urgency, my eyes widen.

"Can you blame me for thinking about it?" I say.

Mom catches on and frowns. "Honey, you don't want to do that."

"No?" I challenge. "Pretty sure it would make things easier for everyone." At this point, why on earth would I want to keep it?

She looks at the table. "Your parents wouldn't want that for you."

"Would they want me to spend my life scared and hiding because of something I was born with?" I read the passages where my dad worried about what would happen when I was born. How do I know he'd want this? And what about what *I* want?

"Please just take some time. This is a lot to process," she says. "I don't want you to do something you'll end up regretting."

I look over at her. "Do you wish you had magic?" If she were in my position, would she want to give it up?

She blinks in surprise. "I . . . don't know. Sometimes, I guess."

"Even with all the bad parts?"

"You have to take the bad with the good, just like with anything, Emery." What a mom response.

Glancing between her and Kit, I sigh. "I'm kind of tired. I think I'm going to lay down for a while."

Mom frowns. "Okay, honey. I'll check in with you in a little while. Don't forget there's pie." She tries to smile, but I can see the pain in her eyes.

I get up and carry my plate to the kitchen, dumping the food into the trash under the sink. On my way past the table, Kit makes a move to stand, but I shake my head and keep going.

I need to get out of here. This place—my home—suddenly feels suffocating. The moment I'm alone in my room, I reach for my bag, fishing through it until I pull my phone out. Cringing at all the missed texts and calls from Lana and Jessa from the last two weeks, I type a message in our group chat.

I'm sorry for the silence. I'm in town for the weekend. Can we meet? I'm desperate for a reminder of what normalcy feels like. Even if that means sneaking out before pie.

Lana responds first. *Emery! Where the hell have you been? We've missed you!*

Jessa's message follows right after. *Let's meet up in an hour! Just finishing dinner.*

Sounds great, I type back.

I'll pick you up soon, Lana says, and I send a thumbs-up emoji.

I walk down the hall to the bathroom and get in the shower, cranking the dial to the hottest setting as I scrub my skin until it tingles. After I wash my hair, I turn the water off and wrap myself in a fluffy robe, tying my hair up with a towel.

Once I'm back in my room with the door shut, I shrug out of the robe and tug on my favorite pair of black leggings, pairing it with a simple tank top and maroon cardigan.

My phone chimes from the table beside my bed, and I reach over to read the new message.

Here!

Be right out, I type back and shoulder my bag, slipping my phone into the front pocket. I step into the hallway and creep down the stairs, holding my breath until I reach the front door. I quickly tug on my hiking boots, pausing when I hear soft conversation coming from the kitchen. I can't make out what they're saying without getting closer, and I don't want to risk them hearing me, so I slip out the front door and hurry down the driveway.

I drop into Lana's passenger seat and buckle myself in before looking at her. "Long time no see," I say, going for a light tone as I attempt to complement it with a smile.

She puts the car in drive and pulls away from the house. "Too freaking long, Em."

"I know, but it's . . ." I stop myself before I can lie to her face. Am I really going to sit here and do exactly what I'm angry at Kit and my mom for doing to me? The reasoning is the same —to keep her safe—so why is it so hard?

"It's what?" she asks, glancing between me and the road as we get closer to Jessa's. A perk of living in a small town—our houses are about ten minutes apart.

I press my lips together. "Complicated."

Lana shakes her head, but keeps her gaze forward. "What does that mean?"

I glance at my lap. "I want to tell you, Jessa too, but it's not —can we just talk about something else, please?"

We pull onto Jessa's street and stop in front of her townhouse. Lana taps the horn before glancing at me. "She's going to want to know why you left just as much as I do."

Jessa hurries outside, zipping up her jacket before piling into the backseat. Her dark brown hair is a windblown mess around her face, and she tries to blow it away. "Em! O-M-G, we've missed you. Please tell me you're coming back to Covington. It's so boring without you."

I turn in my seat to smile at her. "I've missed you guys, too. I would love to come back, really, but I don't think I can. At least, not right now."

Her brows furrow as she ties her hair back. "Why not?"

"Why don't we go somewhere to chat?"

Jessa looks at Lana. "What's even open? It's Thanksgiving."

We end up at the Starbucks off I-20. We're the only ones in the café, and after ordering chai lattes, we sit around one of the small round tables.

"Thank you for not giving me crap about everything," I say, glancing between the two of them as they sip on their drinks. "I know I've been a bad friend not answering texts."

"We were just worried about you, Em," Lana says. "Nothing about your leaving made sense. Two and a half months into our senior year of high school, and you switch schools out of the blue?"

"You're right. And it really wasn't up to me. I hope you know if it had been, I wouldn't have left. Especially not without talking to you both about it."

Jessa frowns. "So why did Holly make you leave?"

I bite the inside of my cheek. "She was worried about me. Some therapist at the hospital in Atlanta told her about issues that orphaned children can experience in their teen years." It sounds ridiculous to my own ears. "I didn't really understand it for a while, but I do now. I never learned how to properly cope with the loss of my parents, but with the help of my mentor at this new . . . school, I'm doing a lot better." It's half of the truth. Sort of.

Lana reaches across the table and puts her hand on top of mine. "We're your best friends, Em. If you were struggling with something, you could have told us."

Jessa nods. "We would've been there for you."

I exhale slowly. "I know, and I'm sorry. I just . . . didn't know how."

Lana squeezes my hand. "We love you."

I smile despite the ever-growing pit in my stomach. I hate lying to my best friends. I've never wanted to tell the truth so bad in my life. *What would happen if I did?* I look at my friends. *Would they believe me?*

"Does this mean you're coming back to school?" Jessa asks. "It's senior year, and we're going to start applying to colleges soon. You should be there for that."

"I'm taking online classes," I say, "probably for the rest of the school year. But we can work on college applications together." I haven't given any thought to what happens after high school—I've been a little preoccupied as of late. My future is still too much of a dark hole of unknown; the thought of applying to colleges seems pointless right now.

Jessa nods. "Think of how cool it would be to share a dorm!" She downs the rest of her latte while Lana and I just sit and stare at her. "I'm gonna get another. Anyone else?"

I peer down at my almost-full cup. "I'm good."

"Same," Lana adds with a hint of an amused smile.

"I'll get it for you," I say, standing and taking the empty cup from her hand and tossing it in the trash near the register.

"Oh, wait," she calls after me. "Can I get an Earl Grey tea

instead?"

"You got it."

The barista is talking to a customer in the drive-thru, so I scan the menu while I wait my turn.

Out of nowhere, the back of my neck starts to tingle. My chest tightens, and a flush creeps across my cheeks. I suck in a breath, but before I can turn around, his bemused voice hits me like a jolt of liquid energy, sending shivers through me.

"What the hell is a macchiato?"

My voice doesn't work, and my feet are cemented to the floor as the barista turns to face me, her eyes getting stuck on the guy lurking behind me for a long moment before focusing on me.

"What can I get you?" the barista asks with a smile.

I swallow, looking to the side to catch him in my peripheral. "Tea," I finally say. "Uh, Earl Grey."

"Sure," she says in a pleasant tone, and I pay before she walks to another counter to make the tea.

"You need to leave," I say under my breath. My heart is racing so fast it's painful in the way it thumps against my chest. As much as there's a part of me that wants to ask Remington the questions Kit either won't or can't answer, this is the worst time for it. I can practically feel Lana and Jessa's eyes on us—well, on *him*.

"But I still don't know what a macchiato is."

I grit my teeth. *Is this guy for real?* "It's espresso with foamed milk."

The barista returns with Jessa's tea before Remington can respond.

"Thanks," I mumble, finally turning around. I force myself to meet his gaze when I say, "You can't be here."

He opens his mouth to respond, but instead, he grins, turning toward the table where Lana and Jessa are sitting.

"What are you doing?" I growl at him.

His gaze focuses back on me, his eyes sparkling with amusement. "Aren't you going to introduce me to your friends?" He looks past me toward the table again, lifting his hand in a wave.

I slap it down. "No. You need to leave."

His jaw hardens as those ice-blue eyes snare me in place. "Hmm. Not yet."

"What are you doing?" I push. "They don't know anything. You can't—"

"They don't know anything because you're being smart and keeping it to yourself, or because I showed up before you could tell them?"

My eyes widen. "I wasn't going to . . ." I shake my head. "How is that any of your business, anyway?"

The corner of his mouth curls into a wicked smirk that reminds me just how dangerous his attention is. "Don't worry, little bird. I'm here to help." He brushes past me and drops into my seat, taking a drink from my latte before I can snatch it away from him.

I set Jessa's tea on the table in front of her, but she doesn't even notice.

"Who are you?" Jessa asks, her chin propped on her hand. "A new friend of Emery's?"

He smirks at her. "Something like that."

I cross my arms, standing at his side. "No," I say quickly.

"Wait," Lana adds. "Are you dating?" She looks between him and me. "Is *this* why you really left Covington?" Her tone is joking, but her words make my eyes widen.

I say, "No!" in the same moment Remington says, "Yes."

"The plot thickens," Jessa says with a little grin in my direction.

"No," I repeat, grabbing his shoulder and digging my fingers in hard. "Rem—"

"Fine, fine. No, your lovely little friend and I are not dating. She has magic in her blood, which is why she had to leave. She's learning how to use her magic and, you see, she can't do that around humans."

Lana and Jessa stare at him, blinking. They don't say anything for several seconds, then they both look at me.

"I . . ." Words have completely escaped me. I thought I had accepted that they couldn't know the truth, but now that it's out there . . .

What the hell just happened?

Lana speaks first. "He's joking, right?" Her laugh is breathy and uneven.

My gaze drops. I can't look at them as I shake my head. When Remington starts whispering under his breath, words I can't begin to understand, my head whips up, and I suck in a breath. Lana and Jessa are slumped against each other with their eyes shut. They look as if they fell asleep in conversation, not like Remington caused whatever this is.

"What are you doing?" I hiss, shaking his shoulder. "Stop it!"

Remington stops speaking, and the girls open their eyes, looking thoroughly confused. They look at each other and frown before glancing back at me.

"Sorry," Jessa says as her brows knit, "do we know you?"

My stomach plummets as both of my best friends look at me as if I'm a stranger. I stumble back. "You . . ." Shaking my head as tears blur my vision, I can't find the strength to push Remington away when he takes my elbow and walks me out of the café.

Once we're outside and the cold air hits me, I shove him away. "What did you do?" I say through my teeth.

He shrugs, adjusting his black leather jacket, and I stomp back over to him. Before I know what's happening, my palm cracks against his cheek. Pain explodes in my fingers, but I don't care. I shove him hard as a tear slips down my cheek. I swipe at it angrily and advance again, curling my hand into a fist before swinging it toward his face.

He manages to dodge it and maneuvers himself behind me, drawing my arms behind my back.

I snap into fight mode, trying to break free from his grasp, but any movement I make sends pain shooting down my arms. "What did you do?" I snarl through shallow breaths.

"Quit acting like a rabid animal, and I might feel so inclined to tell you."

Trying to break free again, I kick back in an attempt to catch him in the shin, but completely miss. He lets go of my arms only to spin me around and pin me against the side of the building. It's completely dark out, which means no one will see us—not that there's anyone around.

I shove against his chest, but he doesn't budge. "What did you do to them?" I demand, my wild curls hanging in my face and my chest heaving between us. "You need to go back in there and fix whatever dark magic crap you did to make them forget me." Tears spring in my eyes at the thought of my best friends having no recollection of the years we spent growing up together.

Remington tilts his head, watching me for a moment before he pushes the hair out of my face, tucking it behind my ear. "Dark magic," he muses aloud, his lips quirking.

I look away from him, forcing myself to focus on the line of trees across the street. Until Remington grips my chin, forcing my gaze back to his. "I know about your magic," I tell him, my jaw clenched tight.

His tongue darts out, wetting his lips. "Don't you mean *our* magic?"

I glare at him in response.

He nods, his fingers drifting from my chin to trail down my neck before his hand falls back to his side. "So then, you must know what I want. Unless Kit meant to leave you completely in the dark."

"You want my magic because it will give you more power." I

fight the urge to roll my eyes; this guy is such a cliché. "If you think you can use my friends to make me give you—"

Remington's deep laugh drowns out my words. "I'm not going to reverse the spell, Emery. I manipulated their memories and removed you completely. You want to fix it? Learn the magic and do the spell yourself."

"Are you insane?" I hiss. "I can't just—"

"Oh, but you can." He taps my nose quicker than I can smack his hand away. "You just don't want to."

"They don't deserve to have their heads messed with."

He shrugs. "What I did was a favor to you."

"Screw you," I snap. "You have no idea what I've gone through in the last two weeks."

Remington rolls his eyes. "Yes, yes—poor you. Let's just pause everything so you can have a moment to wallow in your existence."

"You are such an asshole." This time when I push against his shoulders, he backs off, and I walk toward the parking lot around the side of the building. I pull my phone out of my pocket to call a cab and find a slew of missed calls and texts from Mom and Kit. *Crap.*

Remington moves toward me. "What are you doing?"

"What does it look like? I'm going home."

He snatches my phone away with a laugh. "Don't bother. I'll take you. I think you and I have more to talk about."

Now it's my turn to laugh. "I don't need your help."

He tilts his head, watching me too closely. "You have no idea how wrong you are about that, little bird."

I stare into his eyes. "Go to hell." Grabbing my phone back, I dial the number and order a ride. When I turn back around, Remington is gone, and there's a newly hollow feeling in my chest.

CHAPTER TEN

"Where have you been?" Mom demands the second I walk in the door.

I drop my bag on the bench, kicking off my boots as Kit walks into the hallway, his eyes dark and his mouth set in a tight line. "I went for coffee with the girls. I needed to get . . . out."

Her arms are crossed over her chest, and she pins me with a stern look. "And you didn't think it was a good idea to tell us you were leaving? Kit is here to make sure you're safe, and you just—"

"I'm sorry," I snap, cutting her off. "It was stupid. I messed up and I never should have gone." My throat constricts as tears prick my eyes.

"Could I speak to Emery alone?" Kit asks my mom.

She nods, pulling me into a hug and kissing my cheek before she says, "I'm going to head to bed." She pulls back, hesitating for a long moment before walking down the hallway and up the stairs.

I walk into the living room, sniffling as I try to stop the tears from gathering.

"Talk to me," Kit says in a soft tone from behind me.

I drop onto the couch, wanting nothing more than to bury my face in my hands and sob. Kit sits down beside me, angling his body toward me. "What happened?"

I stare at my lap. "We were at the café. I made up some ridiculous story about why I left Covington. I wanted to tell them the truth, Kit, but I couldn't do it."

He nods. "That's a good thing."

"That I lied to my best friends?" I shake my head. "It doesn't even matter."

He goes to reach for me, but he must think twice about it, because he pulls his hand back. "What do you mean?"

I open my mouth, then close it when nothing comes out. And then I blurt, "Remington showed up and manipulated their memories of me." My voice cracks and my chin quivers. "They have no idea who I am." I clutch my chest, the pressure building there feeling as if it's going to explode any second now.

His eyes fill with anger, and he jumps up from the couch, but I step in front of him.

"He can't get away with this. This is exactly the type of behavior that made the Elders ban your magic."

I flinch at that. "He said that I could reverse it if I learned the magic he used to take their memories."

"That kind of magic is—"

"What I need to figure out if I'm going to fix this."

"I'm sure there's another way," he says in a tight voice. "I'll find him. You can track him, and I'll make him fix whatever he did to them."

"No," I say in a low voice, panic creeping in at the thought of Kit and Remington going head-to-head. Whatever happened between them . . . I'm too scared to ask right now, especially with the way they responded to each other at the club the night I met Remington. "Maybe this is for the best." I don't believe the words even as they leave my lips. "Now there's no chance of them finding out about my magic." I drop back onto the couch.

"That may be true, but they didn't deserve to have their memories messed with by dark magic." Kit shakes his head, sitting back down. "And you didn't deserve to watch it happen."

My eyes sting with unshed tears, and my muscles are exhausted. I just want to go to bed.

"Did he say what he was doing there?"

"No, but we both know he wants my magic, and it seems he's going to make a game of getting it."

Kit thrusts his fingers through his hair, exhaling a harsh breath. "I'm sorry. If I could change your magic, I would do it in a heartbeat."

"Thanks," I mumble. "I guess there's no sense in you being my mentor anymore."

"I'm not giving up yet," he says, brushing his thumb along his bottom lip. "Besides, all the magic stuff aside, I want to be your friend."

I arch a brow at him. "Why?"

He laughs dryly. "You really need to ask?" With a sigh, he says, "Because I like you, Emery. You're fierce and strong and about a million other things that make me admire you."

Despite the pain burrowing in my chest, I manage a weak smile. "I like you too." I lean back into the couch cushions and exhale slowly. "What am I supposed to do now?"

"Enjoy the rest of your time at home. Nothing is going to change in the next two days. We'll figure everything out when we get back to Nova's."

"Are you sure it's such a good idea for me to go back?"

He offers a dazed look. "What are you talking about?"

"If the Elders find out Nova has been harboring a dark Wielder—"

"Don't worry about that," Kit cuts in. "No one is kicking you out, Em. We will figure this out."

"I just . . . I don't want to get anyone in trouble."

He bumps me with his shoulder. "No one is getting in trouble." His voice is smooth; he sounds so sure.

"All right." A tiny bit of pressure releases from my chest as I glance around the living room. "Did my mom set you up in the guest room?"

He smiles. "Yes. She's been very welcoming."

"That's her." Getting up from the couch, I stifle a yawn. "I'm going to bed. I'll see you in the morning."

Kit nods. "Have a good night."

I climb the stairs and into bed without so much as changing my clothes. The effort involved would tip me over the edge, and having a breakdown right now isn't . . . I am so sick of crying, exhausted from being blindsided each way I turn, and the fact that there seems to be no end in sight makes it difficult to breathe without feeling as if someone has their fingers wrapped around my throat.

Kit and I get ready to head back to Nova's the next morning. The plan was to stay for a few days, but after everything that went down yesterday, I decided it was best we get back.

Mom hovers around my bedroom while I pack my bag, adding a few more of my favorite sweaters from my dresser.

"Are you sure you have to go back so soon?" she asks from the doorway.

"Yeah," I say without turning to look at her, tossing another T-shirt into my bag before zipping it shut. "I have to keep training, plus I left my computer there. I don't want to get behind with school stuff." It's the only normal thing I have going for me.

Hope shimmers in her eyes. "So you've decided to keep training with Kit?"

I pause, this time facing her. "No. I haven't decided which type of magic I'm going to focus on yet." I hold up my hand when she opens her mouth. "Before you remind me how dangerous my bloodline magic is, don't. Even if I were able to wield elemental magic, wouldn't it be smart to learn the other as well? Leaving it unchecked seems like a disaster waiting to happen."

"But—"

"This is my choice, Mom." My voice isn't unkind, but it is stern.

She opens her mouth as if she's going to argue, but then she stops herself. "Okay," she says instead, her voice filled with uncertainty.

"I'll talk to Nova when we get back. Now that my lineage is out in the open, I'm hoping he'll share some information on my real magic. He's got a million books in that study of his. There has to be something in there."

"I hope so, honey, for your sake. But please, whatever you learn, just be careful." She sniffles, her eyes glassy. "I wish there was more I could do. I've done a pretty lousy job at this mom thing lately, and I'm so sorry for that."

I frown at her, pulling the bag onto my shoulder. "Please don't, Mom. You've done the best you could. Yeah, you messed up when you kept things from me, but besides that, you've been the best mom I could ask for. You gave up your life to raise me, and I will forever be grateful for that."

Her chin wobbles as she fights back tears. "You were the best thing to happen to me, Emery. Never forget that." She pushes away from the doorway and walks to me, wrapping her arms around me tightly. "I know things are harder than they've ever been, but your parents would be so proud of you."

I swallow my own tears and hug her back, wishing now more than ever that I could stay. I miss my bedroom and this town and my school. I miss my mom.

Finally, we separate and head downstairs where Kit is waiting by the front door.

"All set?" he asks.

I nod, turning to hug my mom once more.

She kisses my cheek. "Please let me know once you've gotten back to Nova's, okay? And keep me posted on . . . everything."

I offer a watery smile. "I will."

She takes my face in her hands gently. "I love you, Emery."

"I love you," I whisper back before stepping away and walking out the door. My heart is beating too fast; my chest feels as if it's going to explode. I need to get out of here before I burst into uncontrollable sobs. Hurrying to the car, I toss my bag in the back and climb into the passenger seat.

Kit gets behind the wheel, sliding the key into the ignition. "You're sure you want to leave today?" he checks.

I nod slowly, biting my bottom lip to keep it from trembling.

He starts the car, then pulls away from the curb, waving at my mom where she stands on the front porch while I stare out the windshield.

I fall asleep on the drive back to Nova's and wake to Kit shaking my shoulder gently. When I open my eyes and see the cabin-like house, my stomach drops. As much as I know this is where I need to be, it doesn't change the fact that I would rather be pretty much anywhere else. Mom and Kit seem to be convinced that if there's any chance of me picking up elemental magic, I need to be surrounded by other elementals. I'm not sure how much of that is merely wishful thinking—probably most of it—but I decide not to contest it. I need to see Nova anyway.

I grab my bag out of the backseat and drag my feet toward the front door.

Lydia meets us on the porch, smiling wide. "I didn't think you were coming back until Saturday."

I force a smile. "Uh, yeah. I changed my mind. Figured it was best to stick to my routine here as much as possible."

Lydia glances between Kit and me. "Did something happen?"

Kit forces a laugh, and if it wasn't for the stiffness in his shoulders, it would sound more believable. "Relax, Lydia. Everything is fine."

She keeps her eyes on me. "Well, I'm glad you're back. I know you haven't been here all that long, but it was weird not having you here for a day."

I press my lips together. "Thanks."

The three of us file into the house, and Kit closes the door behind us. I walk through the entryway and down the hall, dropping my bag on the floor inside my bedroom door. I jump when I find Lydia leaning against the wall opposite my room.

"Are you going to tell me what happened?"

I frown. "You heard Kit. Nothing—"

"I don't buy it. You were so excited to go home for a few days. There's no way training and schoolwork convinced you to come back after one day."

"Yeah, you're right. But it's not something I can talk about. Not yet."

Lydia arches a brow as she walks into my room. "Uh, okay then." She drops onto the bed, smoothing her hands along my fleece blanket. "Is there anything I can do to help?"

I plug my phone into the charger on the nightstand and shake my head. "I appreciate it, though."

She exhales heavily. "Fine. You'll let me know if that changes though, right?"

This time, when I smile at her, it's genuine. "Of course. Seriously, thank you. You've been . . ." I shake my head. ". . . the nicest person since I got here. You've had no reason to be my friend, but you have. I can't tell you how much I appreciate it."

She jumps up from the bed, grinning. "You're so cute." She throws her arm around my shoulders and hugs me against her side. "We're friends for life now, Em." She winks at me before dancing out of my room, and I can't help but laugh at her exit.

I shove my clothes into my dresser and go to find Nova in his study.

"Welcome back," he says when I step inside and close the door.

"Thanks."

"I spoke to your mom." His tone is level. "I understand she told you about your lineage."

I stand near the door while Nova remains seated behind his desk. "Uh-huh."

He nods. "I imagine you have some questions for me."

Crossing my arms, I will my jaw to unclench. "Yes, I do. I don't want to talk about why you and everyone else hid important things from me. I don't care about whatever explanation you have."

Another nod. "What would you like to know?"

I glance around the room. "Do you have any resources I could use to learn about my magic?"

He gestures toward the chair across from him, but I shake my head and stay where I am. He exhales slowly. "I do, though I would be irresponsible not to warn you against looking too deep into them."

I arch a brow at him. "The night we met, you told me if I didn't work with my magic it would consume me. Does that no longer apply, or . . . ?" I leave the question open, waiting for him to respond.

Nova takes the reading glasses off the top of his head, setting them beside his laptop before standing and walking around the desk. He walks to one of the many bookshelves lining the study and trails his fingers along the spines until he stops on one, pulling it off the shelf.

I walk over and peek at the cover. It's empty of words, though there are symbols pressed into the soft leather material. "What is it?"

He holds it out to me. "A very dangerous history lesson."

I take the book and flip it over in my hands. "So there are no spells in here?"

"No. I think you should learn about this magic before you practice it."

My eyes narrow slightly, but I keep them focused on the book. "That didn't seem to apply to the elemental magic you had me training to use."

"That's different." He doesn't go into the *why* of that statement, and I don't have the energy to push it. Besides, I'm fairly certain I know the answer. It's been a broken record since I learned the truth about my bloodline.

I clutch the book to my chest as I step away from him.

"If you'd like to discuss anything once you've read that, you know where I am."

I nod and make a quick exit. Once I'm behind a closed door, I take a deep breath and flip the book open.

CHAPTER ELEVEN

Clarity is a fickle thing. When they say ignorance is bliss, *believe them*. Perhaps next time I will.

The afternoon slips away from me as I spend hours reading the leather-bound tome Nova gave me. The paper is yellowed and the words are hand-written, smudged from age.

I've learned so much about the dark Wielders. The information overload is overwhelming, to say the least, but I remind myself I asked for this. I demanded the truth, and now that I have it, it's up to me to figure out a way to handle it.

The earliest known Wielders—dark and elemental—date back over 500 years. As a species, they survived plagues and wars, but it wasn't until about 200 years ago they were discovered by a tiny sector of the government. Before then, they kept their abilities a secret from the humans. Once Wielder magic came to light in 1820, the Accords were signed between that government agency and the Elders, which protected Wielders against persecution because of their magic. Well, at least the ones who had elemental abilities. I skimmed through the pages that described the hunt for dark Wielders, holding my breath until it moved on to speak more about the Accords. Not shocking—there was fine print which stated that should the country need the use of magic, the Wielders would oblige. According to the book, that hasn't happened—yet. Nova doesn't seem concerned about the possibility, but why would he? He's not a Wielder.

I close the book and drop it onto my bed. *That's enough reading for now.*

"Yeah?" I call out when someone knocks on my door.

"It's me," Kit says, his voice muffled. "Can I come in?"

"Yeah," I say again, moving the book to my nightstand as he walks into the room, leaving the door open as he moves toward the bed. "What's up?" I ask.

His gaze flits to the book. "Doing some light afternoon reading?" His tone is teasing, but I can't even fake a laugh right now. He drops onto the end of the bed, angles his body to face me, and rakes his fingers through his hair. "You can ask me anything, and if I know the answer, I'll give it to you. But as I said, I don't know a lot about dark magic."

I nod. "So if I want to learn that, I'm pretty much on my own."

A muscle ticks along his jaw. "I'm sorry."

Pressing my lips together, I reach for him, resting my hand on his arm. "I know you wanted to help me, Kit, but—"

"Want." His eyes meet mine. "I still want to help you, Emery."

I hesitate, pulling my hand back. "How?"

"Same as before." Kit slaps his thighs and stands. "Let's run through some exercises. You can try whatever feels most natural to you." He holds his hand out toward me. "What do you say?"

I worry my bottom lip, blinking at his hand for a few extra seconds before taking it. I have to try anything at this point. My knowledge of the Elders may be limited, but my fear of them finding out about me is certainly not.

In the backyard, Kit messes around with his magic, igniting

the flames in the firepit. He lifts then drops his hand, making the flames climb and fall with the movement.

"Show-off," I mutter under my breath.

Kit turns to me, and the fire returns to a normal flickering height. "Try it," he suggests.

I shake out my arms in an attempt to release the tension in my muscles and close my eyes. Breathing deeply, I try to recall the passages from my dad's book. The words that made me feel close to him. Frustration flares to life in my chest, making it tighten as I think about how much easier this would be if my dad were here to teach me. Frustration quickly sparks into anger. My breathing quickens and my body heats. Sweat dots my brow and upper lip as I keep my eyes shut.

The sound of Kit's voice is dull and far away. What is he saying? Do I care?

My face burns, and I'm faintly aware that it's painful. Someone grabs my arm and tugs me backward. My eyes fly open, and I choke on thick smoke when I suck in a breath. Everything is heavy and fuzzy, and I can't move.

"Emery, back up!" Kit's voice comes out clearer now, and his grip tightens on my wrist, yanking me away from the massive flames.

"What the hell?" Lydia shrieks, racing toward us as she lifts her arms and conjures enough water to destroy the flames. The firepit sizzles with steam left over from the flames as she turns toward us. "Are you guys okay? What happened?" Concern is mixed with confusion on her face.

"It's okay, Lydia," Kit assures her.

She focuses on me. "I didn't think you had fire magic."

I open my mouth to respond and start coughing on the smoke still hanging in the air. I barely manage to force out, "I don't."

Lydia blinks at me, then flicks her gaze toward the remaining smoke. "What would you call that, then?"

The thought of lying to another person, someone who has

been nothing but nice to me since I got here, makes my stomach sink. Before I can stop myself, I blurt, "Dark magic."

Her eyes widen as she turns her attention to Kit. "She's kidding, right? Please tell me this is some messed up joke."

I frown, shaking my head even though she's still looking at Kit. I shouldn't have said anything, but I couldn't help it. If my magic doesn't consume me, all the secrets and lies will.

Kit's jaw is set tight. "Lydia—"

Her mouth drops open as horror fills her expression. "If the Elders find out, Kit, we're all screwed." She sucks in a breath. "That's why . . . Remington knows about her, doesn't he?"

My throat goes dry when I open my mouth to speak. "Yeah. He's . . ." I trail off, because the task of summing him up in a word seems impossible.

Lydia finally looks at me. "I don't know what to say."

"Me neither."

Her brows knit as she stares at me. "I'm really sorry, Em." She steps toward me and throws her arms around my neck, knocking Kit away.

Tears clog my throat as I hug her back. "Thanks," I mumble. "Things are kind of crazy right now," I say, pulling back so I can face her again. "I know everyone deserves to know who they're living with, but please let me be the one to break the news."

She nods. "So only Kit knows?"

"And Nova."

"Of course." She heaves out a sigh. "I wish there was something I could do to make this better for you, Em."

"You being here—being my friend—that does more for me than you will ever know."

Lydia blinks back tears. "I'm not going anywhere."

"I think that's enough for today," Kit says, and I am so not going to argue with that.

Lydia gives me another hug before going back inside, and Kit and I trail behind her.

"Do you think I could borrow your car?" I ask him.

He casts me a sideways glance, his expression still shadowed with concern. "I don't think so."

"Why not? I'm not going to take off. I chose to come back here, remember?"

He seems to consider that. "With what just happened at the firepit, I don't think it's a good idea."

I stop walking. "That was . . . It's fine as long as I don't think about it too hard." Evidently, emotional outbursts are bad for control when it comes to magic. Noted. "Please, Kit? I just want to go into town for a little while and do some homework at the café."

He stops a few paces ahead of me and looks back over his shoulder. "What if I take you?"

"Haven't you had enough of me this weekend?"

Kit chuckles. "Nah, you're not so bad to hang with."

"Gee, thanks." I bite the inside of my cheek, trying to come up with a way to tell him I want to be alone without sounding mean. "I'm going to be studying the whole time, probably with headphones in. It wouldn't be very fun for you just to come and sit there." I don't bother adding that it would look creepy. And I don't need a babysitter.

"I don't want you going by yourself," he pushes as I walk to catch up to him.

"I'll only be gone a couple hours." There's a bit of an edge to my voice. "Please," I say again. "If anything starts to feel weird, I'll come right back here. I promise."

"Do you even have a driver's license?"

I blink at his last-ditch attempt at stopping me. "Yes."

Kit presses his lips together and exhales through his nose. "All right," he finally says, fishing his keys out of his pocket and handing them to me. "But I'm going to check in with you every half hour, and you better answer me."

I nod, grabbing the keys, and smile at him as we walk inside.

"Thanks, Kit."

He shoots me a wink and disappears into the living room.

The café isn't too busy when I arrive. I order a caramel latte and find a seat near the back of the room. I stick in my headphones and pull out the second book Nova gave me this morning once I told him I read the other one. I should be catching up on homework, but this seems more important right now. My schoolwork can wait.

I quickly get lost in the series of incantations and instructions for creating spells with objects and natural elements. Anyone else looking at this could read it as fiction, but knowing the truth attached to it makes me shiver.

As I turn the page, someone drops into the seat across from me, and I glance up, freezing before I rip out my headphones.

"What are you doing here?" I demand.

Remington grins at me. "You're not very good at hellos, are you, little bird?"

"Uh, not for people who want to steal from me, no."

"So dramatic."

"I'm not giving you anything. I don't care how dangerous it is or that the Elders would kill me if they found out."

His brows rise. "Looks like you got the whole story, huh?"

"Probably not," I grumble, "but I know more than enough to know you getting what you want isn't a good thing for anyone but you."

"You don't even want your magic."

"You have no idea what I want," I snap.

Remington arches a brow. "No? Tell me I'm wrong." When I remain silent, his gaze drops to the book on the table. "Hmm. Read anything interesting?"

"Yes, actually. There's an incredibly interesting paragraph I just came across that talks about what a creepy stalker you are."

He leans across the table as his eyes flick across my face. "We keep ending up here, you and I."

"No," I say, "you keep showing up where I am. There's a difference, and it's very much illegal." My voice sounds casual, but the hammering in my chest is proof I'm way out of my element when it comes to Remington.

He chuckles, his eyes sparkling with amusement, and the sound brings heat to my cheeks. It's too comfortable. Too intimate. "Cute."

"What's your play here, Remington? You ambushing me in the middle of a café filled with—"

"Ah," he cuts me off, glancing around with a smug expression.

The café is completely empty. As in, no customers and no one behind the counter.

My mouth goes dry. "What did you do?" I force out.

"Magic." He shrugs. "You should try it," he adds.

"I'm serious. Where did they go? What did you do?" I repeat as panic closes in, making my chest tighten.

Remington rolls his eyes. "Relax, little bird. Everyone is still here. You just can't see them, and they can't see us."

"What?"

He drags his tongue along his bottom lip. "Think of it as an alternate dimension woven in reality. Except, I froze time for everyone else. It's simple manipulation of reality."

I don't have the emotional bandwidth to even begin to wrap my head around that.

"Fix it." My tone is sharp, and there's a hint of desperation there that I fight not to cringe at.

He tilts his head to the side. "You're so uptight, Emery."

"Because you're—"

"What? The big bad wolf?" His eyes narrow, but the smirk

on his lips remains. "And yet you haven't run away from me this time."

"Fix it," I say again, glancing around at the silent room. This is too freaky.

"Hmm, okay. But you have to do something for me."

My gaze snaps back to him. "The hell I do."

He purses his lips. "Ah, well. I guess those poor people will be stuck in an endless in-between dimension forever."

"Remington," I hiss. "You can't."

"Sure I can, little bird. Unless, of course, you agree—"

"Just let them go," I cut in, and my voice cracks.

He sighs as if this whole thing is a mere inconvenience for him. He blinks slowly, and the room blurs before shifting back to normal. People are chatting around us, the coffee machine behind the counter is hissing, and there's a radio station playing soft rock.

My eyes widen at how easily he managed whatever that was.

Remington leans back in his chair. "I'll pretend not to notice you looking impressed."

Smug bastard.

I scowl. "More like disturbed."

He stares at me for several seconds, clearly enjoying this.

"Are you going to tell me what you want, or are you just going to keep staring at me?"

"I don't know. I'm quite enjoying the staring."

I gape at him. "You . . . I can't deal with this right now." Shoving my things into my bag, I push my chair back and stand.

Remington follows, grabbing my wrist before I can move past him. The contact sparks with energy, and I immediately try to pull away.

"Whatever you're doing, stop it," I growl under my breath. "Someone is going to see."

His mouth is close to my ear when he says, "I'm not doing anything."

Feeling bold, I twist my wrist in his grasp and wrap my fingers around his wrist. The energy bolts through me, and my gaze flies to his. "What is that?" I breathe.

"Magic." His voice drips with amusement before his tone becomes more serious. "We feel each other's magic when we touch because it's the same."

I pull my hand away and sit back down. "Tell me why you want mine."

Remington returns to the chair across from me. "It holds power," he says, as if it's the simplest thing in the world.

"So what? You don't have enough?" I gesture around the room. "Seemed like you had plenty a few minutes ago."

His eyes flick between mine, and for a second, I catch a glimpse of pain in his gaze. It's gone when he blinks.

"The Elders are as much a threat to you as they are to me," I point out. "You think having *more* of the magic they banned will somehow help you?"

"It would help *you* to get rid of it," he says.

"Right. I'm sure you're really concerned about *me*."

A smirk touches his lips. "I think we could help each other."

"And I sometimes think coffee counts as breakfast. Doesn't mean I'm right."

He chuckles, but his expression turns serious a moment later. "What's your plan then, little bird? Are you going to keep playing house with a bunch of elementals? What are you going to do when the Elders come by to check on things, hmm?"

I cross my arms over my chest, but I can't ignore the way my pulse races. What *am* I going to do in that scenario? Nova must have a plan; otherwise, him letting me stay there wouldn't make sense. Maybe continuing to try elemental magic isn't the worst idea, but could I actually trick the Elders into believing I'm like Kit and the others? And am I willing to risk my life to find out?

"Why don't you worry about yourself instead of popping up out of nowhere and trying to scare me?"

He purses his lips. "I could help you, you know."

My arms stay crossed. "Pass." There's zero chance that offer comes without strings, and I don't think I'm prepared to pay the price.

"Oh, come on. You've got to admit, I'd be a much better mentor than your current situation."

I scowl. "Look, I have no idea what the deal is between you and Kit—"

Remington cuts in with a harsh laugh. "Of course he didn't tell you. Ever the golden boy. Wouldn't want anything to tarnish that pristine reputation of his."

"Reputation?" I shake my head. "I don't care about that. Besides, that's not the point."

"Then please enlighten me as to what is." He taps his fingers against the table. "Is it going to take long, though?" He cranes his neck to look at the menu on the chalkboard behind the counter. "Maybe I should order a coffee. Huh. Those muffins look pretty good too."

"You think this is a game," I hiss, and he turns back to me. "I'm not going to play. You want more magic? Go find another Wielder, because there's no way in hell you're getting mine."

"You think I haven't tried? Dark Wielders aren't exactly easy to find, as you can imagine."

"You seemed to find me just fine," I remark, bitterness laced in my tone.

"I got lucky," he admits with a tight jaw. "I'd been away for a while, searching the West Coast, when I decided to come home. Imagine my surprise when I felt that pull I'm sure you feel right now."

I grip the strap of my bag tighter. "What's your point? Why do you even want more power? You seem to have plenty."

"If I thought my answer would change your mind, I might just tell you. Except, that information in the wrong hands could pose a challenge."

I have no idea what that means, and I don't think I'm prepared for the answer. I school my expression into indifference despite the jackhammering pulse beneath my skin. "That sounds like a *you* problem."

When I get up this time, he doesn't try to stop me.

Back at Nova's, I leave Kit's keys on the kitchen counter and shut myself in my room, changing into sweats before crawling into bed. Staring at the ceiling for a while, I can't help how my mind spins. *How am I supposed to figure this out?* The books are helping a little, but I can't help thinking that I've barely scratched the surface on what there is to know about my magic. The thought that no one here will truly be able to help me only renews the sense of helplessness that clung to me when I first arrived.

I watch the sun fall behind the trees out my window, and once the sky goes dark, I finally close my eyes.

His voice is warmth and silk, and the desire to wrap myself in it consumes me with each word he speaks. "If you do this, there's no turning back, little bird."

"I don't care." My voice doesn't tremble. In fact, there's a lilt of excitement in it that makes me shiver.

Jessa kneels in front of me, tears streaking black mascara down her cheeks. She looks pathetic.

My hand curls into a fist, and the tighter I clench, the quicker the color drains from her face. She gasps for air, her eyes wide and pleading . . . and it only heightens the euphoria.

"Pl-please," she gasps, fresh tears wetting her face as she reaches for her throat—as if that will help.

I laugh in the same moment a scream tears through the air. I whip around and find Lana racing toward us. Remington steps out of the way and fades into the background as Lana drops to the floor in front of Jessa.

"What are you doing?" she shrieks at me. "Stop this! You're going to kill her!"

"That's the idea." With a flick of my wrist, I snap Jessa's neck without even placing a hand on her.

She crumples, knocking into Lana, and they end up in a sad little pile on the floor.

With a sigh, I lift my gaze to find Remington. He stares at me, watching my every move, his expression unreadable.

Power buzzes through me, and I close my eyes, reveling in the exhilarating pleasure of it.

My eyes snap open, and I bolt upright in bed. The sheets are soaked with sweat, and I can't stop shivering. Hot tears burn my eyes as I try to blink them away, but I eventually give up and let them fall.

CHAPTER TWELVE

I walk around the house in a daze all morning. Not even a double shot of espresso can pull me out of it. The second one makes my nerves vibrate anxiously, but I'm still exhausted. It clings to my muscles, attempting to lure me back to bed, but the renewed fear I have of my dreams keeps me away.

I need to figure out why they're happening. Maybe then I'll learn how to make them stop. Though I have an awful feeling those answers are tied to getting a grip on my magic, which seems more and more impossible every day.

Nova takes one look at me on my way back to the coffee pot and gives me the day off from my online classes.

"Do you want to talk about it?" he asks, leaning against the counter.

"I think we both know it'd be a waste of time." I pour coffee into my mug, leaving enough room for cream, and sprinkle the top with cinnamon.

"I don't know that, and neither do you." His tone is gentle—he wants to help.

Taking a sip of my coffee, I turn toward him. "I'm okay, but thanks."

He gives me a look, knowing full well I'm lying, but I hurry past him before he can say anything more, stopping in my room to grab Dad's book and the blanket off the back of the couch before slipping outside.

After walking around the grounds for a bit, I end up at the mausoleum. Setting the blanket on the cold stone floor, I sit cross-legged and open the book.

For an hour or so, I recite some of the easier incantations, practicing a cloaking spell to hide the burning candle on the ground in front of me. The heat from the flame still warms my hands, but the candle itself isn't visible. Feeling the power of my magic zipping through my veins—it's intoxicating. My eyes close of their own volition as my heart beats steadily in my chest. This feels *right*. Not strained or forced. It comes easy and . . . natural.

Though, as great as it is, it's child's play compared to what Remington can do. Compared to what *I* could do if I had the tools to advance my abilities.

I exhale a heavy breath and stand, leaning against one of the stone tombs as I thumb through the book again. One entry catches my eye, and I trace the worn paper with my finger. It's another cloaking spell, but on a larger scale. It talks about hiding your appearance, altering it so you go unrecognized. Huh. That could be interesting. Changing my appearance on a whim.

I read the passage in my head a few times before I start reciting it aloud. My skin tingles with magic, and I gasp softly. *Did it work?* I grab my phone and flip the camera on, frowning at my regular reflection. I'm not sure why I'm so disappointed. I didn't really think it would work, did I? Maybe I just don't have enough magic to make it work.

Or maybe you just need to practice it.

That tricky little voice at the back of my head is probably right.

I practice the cloaking spell every day for a week. For whatever reason, I can't let it go. Perhaps there's a part of me that believes it could be useful for the day the Elders find out about my magic and come looking for me. That fear is a constant alarm in the back of my mind, but maybe it wouldn't be so loud if I actually had a plan. But to come up with a plan, I need information. Information I can only get from—*no*. Not an option. I wouldn't ask Remington for help even if I knew the Elders were coming tomorrow.

What if you didn't ask him?

I rake my fingers through my hair as I stare at the stone wall across the room. I can't seriously be considering this . . . except I am. If I can cloak my appearance from Remington, maybe I can get into his place and find something that will help me advance my magic. Wielders seem to keep books about their magic, so maybe Remington has one.

A plan starts to form in my head before I can talk myself out of it. I recall flipping past a sleeping spell a couple of days ago, so I turn back to it and spend the next two hours memorizing it. It seems easier than the cloaking spell, but I'll need both if this plan is going to work. But will the cloaking spell hide my magic as well? Otherwise, the whole thing is pointless, because he'll sense my magic and know it's me.

I read the instructions again. It doesn't say anything about masking my magic, but at this point, it's a risk I'll have to take. Even if his magic recognizes mine, that's what the sleeping spell is for. I just have to get close enough to touch him to activate it.

Of course, the whole thing is reckless, but if I'm going to survive in this life, I have to take some risks and have faith that it'll work out. At least, that's what I tell myself as I continue to practice the spells.

Standing in the bathroom a few days later, the reflection in the mirror startles me. She is dark-haired with bangs and curvy. Her emerald eyes are wide, fanned by thick, dark lashes. Of course, she *is* me. I've been working on this spell for days now and finally feel confident enough to put it to work. That, or I'm so desperate for information I've manifested some semblance of confidence. Whatever it is, I'm going with it.

"This is so weird," Lydia says from beside me, meeting my gaze in the mirror.

I wanted to keep everyone out of this, but when she walked in on me while I was practicing the spell last week, she wouldn't let it go until I told her—and then she immediately wanted to help. Not that there's much she can do, but I think having her around is keeping me from going into full panic mode.

"Tell me about it," I mumble, fixing my bangs so they sit evenly across my forehead.

The human cloak I'm hiding under is rocking a pair of sleek black heels and a wine-red cocktail dress I would never pick for myself—which is precisely why I'm wearing it. I matched my lip color to the dress and went for a smoky-eye look.

"Remind me why you're doing this and keeping it from Kit."

I tell her what I'm looking for, and she nods. "And I don't want to tell Kit because he'll try to stop me."

"Definitely," she agrees. "I'll cover for you, but please be careful."

"I will." Remington isn't going to hurt me, especially while he thinks there's a chance he's going to get my magic.

Lydia checks to make sure the coast is clear so I can slip out of the house without being noticed. I grab Kit's keys off the hook beside the door, and I don't stop moving until I'm pulling out of the driveway. He's under the impression I'm borrowing his car to study at the café again, which makes me feel a little bad for lying. Though, compared to everything he kept from me, this feels like a drop in the bucket.

When I arrive at the club, there's already a line around the corner. My chest is tight, but I force myself to step in behind the last patron and wait. Tendrils of dread wrap around my stomach, and at one point, I'm worried I may vomit. I barely manage to swallow the panic as I make it to the door and past the bouncer. I don't miss the way he eyes me—as if he's hungry—but I try to ignore the creepy shiver it shoots up my spine as I hurry inside.

At the bar, I order a whiskey sour and sip on it as I canvass the crowd.

"You look bored."

I turn toward the friendly male voice and am met with a warm smile. This guy looks at least thirty. His hazel eyes are slightly bloodshot, and his cheeks are flushed.

"I'm actually, uh, waiting for someone—a friend." I glance away for a moment before looking back at him. As much as I need to blend in, talking to someone over a decade older than me in this setting is making my skin crawl.

He chuckles and takes a swig from his beer. "Understood. Have a good night, gorgeous." The man shoots me a wink before turning and disappearing into the crowd.

I let out a breath and take a long drink. *I hate this.*

"Was that guy bothering you?"

My back stiffens at the familiar voice. Even cloaked, my body responds to him, and I don't like it. "I'm fine," I say, turning toward him, dragging my eyes up his body. He's dressed in all black. A plain V-neck and jeans with combat boots. When our gazes collide, I can't look away; his eyes are liquid silver in this light. "Thanks, though."

Remington tilts his head, making his inky dark hair fall into his face as he watches me, and my breath catches.

Oh no. This was a bad idea.

"Can I get you a refill?" He nods toward my empty glass, pushing his hair back.

"Oh, um, sure. Thank you."

He waves the bartender over and orders me another, as well as a beer for himself. With a new drink in front of me, I decide it's now or never.

"I don't think I've seen you around before," he comments before I can say anything.

I try for a light chuckle, but it comes out a little strained. "Yeah, this isn't usually my scene." I take a drink. "I was meeting a friend, but I think she ghosted me."

"Sounds like a bad friend," he says flippantly, sliding onto the stool next to me.

"Yeah, well." I shrug. "I'm not about to go home now. It'd be a waste of this outfit."

Remington pulls his bottom lip into his mouth. "Hmm. That would be a real tragedy."

"Wouldn't it, though?" I reply in a cheeky tone.

The corner of his mouth tugs up. "You are something else," he murmurs, and I can't help the heat that floods my cheeks. "Dance with me?"

My eyes widen. We can't touch. I have no idea if that'll affect the cloak, and I'm not about to take that chance. "No. I mean, I can't. I don't dance."

He laughs, shaking his head. "Then you must be a very good friend. You got all dressed up and came out to a club, and you don't even dance."

I exhale on a laugh. "Yeah, I guess so."

His eyes flick across my face. "What's your name?"

I smile. "Doesn't matter. You'll never see me again."

Now it's his turn to look at me wide-eyed, though his expression quickly shifts into one of amusement. "No?" He leans closer, and I hold my breath. "That's a shame."

I turn my face so my mouth is close to his ear and murmur,

"Why's that?" I try to tell myself I hate this, but really, my heart is racing with excitement. Being someone else, being around *him* in this moment is . . . enjoyable. Dangerously so.

When he leans in again, I freeze, panic seizing me, and dump my drink into his lap.

He jumps up, setting his beer on the bar as he glances down at his pants.

"Crap! I'm so sorry!" My voice squeaks, more from nerves about how close he was getting, but it works in my favor.

The corner of his mouth curls upward, and he chuckles. "Don't worry about it. I live upstairs."

I grimace. "I really am sorry. I don't know what happened."

He's still smiling at me when he says, "Do you want to come up? I could make you another drink, as long as you promise not to throw it on me."

I open my mouth, then press my lips together. "Yeah, sure." I shove down the panic making my thoughts scatter and remind myself this is one step closer to getting what I came for.

He nods toward the other side of the room, and I slide off the barstool, following him through the crowd of sweaty drunk people who think sticking their butts out while their arms are waving in the air is dancing.

The music starts to get quieter as we walk down a dim hallway, past a couple groups of people waiting to use the bathroom. The faint smell of pot tickles my nose, and I hold my breath for a few seconds until it passes. At the end of the hall, Remington pulls out a key and unlocks a heavy metal door. There's a small landing and a flight of stairs, which we walk up, and he opens another door into an open-concept apartment.

The entry opens right into a spacious kitchen with shiny black countertops, stainless steel appliances, and a massive island that divides the kitchen from the rest of the loft.

"I'll be right back," Remington says before disappearing down a hallway.

My eyes dart around, taking in the cool-toned, masculine space. The ceiling is high with exposed industrial pipes, making the loft feel bigger. The far wall is exposed brick and a few windows covered by heavy gray curtains.

There's an entertainment centre against the adjacent wall with bookshelves and a large flat-screen. A black leather couch and a dark wood coffee table tie that section of the room together. I hold my breath, biting the inside of my cheek as I itch to rush over to the bookshelf and start searching. *Would he really leave a book of magic out in the open?*

"That's better," Remington says as he comes back into the room wearing a gray T-shirt and black joggers. Casual and comfortable has never looked so good. Wait, what? No. Oh god, I can't stop staring at him.

The plan, I remind myself. *I need to remember why I'm here.* Distract him enough that his guard is down, and then use the sleeping spell I've been practicing. Once he's out, I'll have about twenty minutes to search this place. Hopefully, I'll find a book of spells and be able to get out of here quickly.

The thought did cross my mind to ask him for it, but the last thing I want is to feel as if I owe Remington anything. From the little I know of him, I can tell he's the type of person to collect tenfold.

I force a smile, leaning against the end of the kitchen island. "Again, I'm sorry. I swear, I'm not usually that clumsy."

"No?" He walks closer. "Did I make you nervous?"

"Maybe," I offer, watching him close the distance between us as my heart kicks up.

He stops an arm's length away. "Drink?" His voice is lower, softer. It catches me off guard, and I stand there staring at him. "Are you okay?" he checks, looking me over.

"I'm good." Aside from the heart currently attempting to beat its way right out of my chest, I'm totally fine. I need to pull myself together and just do this. Grab him and activate the sleeping spell. I've made it this far; I have to keep going and get what I came for. I can't get lost in the way he's looking at me. It's as if I'm the only other person on the planet, and it's making my head so light I can't focus.

Remington steps in once more, stealing the remaining distance between us, his breath stirring the hair across my forehead. The faint smells of lemon and fabric softener tickle my nose, stealing my focus.

My gaze drops to his mouth, and before I can stop myself, I lean up and press my lips against his. My pulse spikes when he starts kissing me back, and I don't immediately feel the pull of his magic. *Holy crap.* The cloak blocked my magic. Relief floods through me as his hand slides up my arm and cups the side of my face, tipping my head back and deepening the kiss. I'm so happy the spell worked that I momentarily forget what I'm doing here.

He nips my lip before leaning back and looking at me with a hooded gaze. "When I saw you tonight, I didn't think you'd be interested."

I press a finger to his lips. "Perhaps you underestimate your charm."

He closes the distance between us again before I can utter the words that will knock him out, and my eyes shut, waiting for another fiery kiss. The anticipation is almost as addictive as the kiss itself, but I'm too light-headed to recognize the full extent of how dangerous that is. Remington grips my chin and kisses my cheek. His lips graze my jaw, then the shell of my ear before he whispers, "Perhaps you're right about that, little bird."

My entire body goes rigid. "Wh-what?" I blink my eyes open as he steps away.

His eyes are narrowed on me, and his cheeks are as flushed as mine certainly feel. "Care to explain what you're doing here, Emery?"

I stare at him, but my throat is too tight to respond.

His lips twitch. "Come on. I think we're close enough now."

Swallowing hard, I cross my arms. "How did you know?"

He arches a dark brow. "Emery." His voice is filled with disappointment.

My jaw clenches. "How long did you know it was me?"

Remington purses his lips in thought. "Hmm . . . Was it when we got up here, or when I saw you at the bar? Or maybe it was the moment you walked into the club."

"You knew the whole time," I breathe.

He nods, amusement glimmering in his eyes. "I'd know you anywhere."

"No," I say through my teeth. "I used a cloaking spell. I practiced all freaking week."

He snags my chin again and looks into my eyes. "Don't feel bad. Had it been anyone else you were trying to fool, I imagine it would've worked perfectly."

I pull away from his grip. "Then why didn't it?"

Remington exhales slowly. "You have so much to learn."

I shake my head, my brows tugging closer. "If you knew this whole time, then why'd you go along with it?"

He glances at the floor for a moment before looking back at me. "Maybe because I knew how much it would piss off your precious Kit." Remington holds my gaze as he says, "Or maybe I wanted to kiss you."

My heart stutters. "You—"

He sighs, cutting me off—not that I had anything intelligent to say at that moment anyway. "Why are you here?" he asks.

I lick the dryness from my lips and catch Remington's gaze dropping to my mouth. Granted, he's not very subtle about it. "I don't know," I lie. "I needed a night out." The floor vibrates against my feet from the bass of the music playing downstairs.

He laughs. "Right. And the real reason?"

Anger lashes through me, and I glare at him. "I don't know. Maybe I wanted to kiss you," I throw back at him.

His smirk is downright wicked. "Oh, yeah? Well, mission accomplished."

I deflate, muttering, "I hate you."

"You *want* to hate me," he corrects, the smirk fading from his lips.

"Why do you have to be pretty much the only other person with dark magic?" It's more of a complaint than a question—I know the answer.

"Because the world is a cruel, cruel place."

I glower at him. "Which leaves me no choice but to come to you."

His brows lift. "That's why you came? What's with the whole disguise, then?"

I press my lips together. There's no point in continuing to lie now. "I was going to use a spell to knock you out and then search this place for a book or something—*anything*—that could help me get a grip on what's going on inside of me."

He tries not to laugh. "Kit the cat just not cutting it?" He tsks. "Donovan will be so disappointed."

I roll my eyes. "You're a real ass, you know that?" I push past him to head for the door, ready to pretend tonight didn't happen.

He wraps his fingers around my wrist, stopping me. "A sleeping spell?"

I pull away and cross my arms at the amusement in his voice. "I don't need you to make fun of me. This is already bad enough."

"You think that kiss was bad?" He whistles. "Ouch."

"I . . ." My cheeks burn, but I force myself to hold his gaze. I'm not about to stand here and admit that he's the first person I've ever kissed. I want to be angry that I wasted my first kiss on Remington, but it . . . it was a good kiss. "Forget it."

"Try it," he says.

I pause, arching a brow at him as my arms fall back to my sides. "What?"

"The spell."

"Why would you—"

"I'm curious if it would've worked. You know, had I not made you from the beginning of your little undercover mission."

"No," I say through my teeth. At this point, I'm convinced it wouldn't have worked anyway; I just want to get out of here.

Again, I walk toward the door, my boots thudding against the old wood floor.

"Emery."

His deep voice makes me pause, but I keep my back to him. "Don't," I warn. If he keeps pushing, I'm going to snap, and I'd rather not find out what my magic is capable of above a room full of humans. The pressure building in my chest acts as a warning; I need to listen to it and remove myself from the situation before someone can get hurt.

"I don't understand it," he muses.

I spin around, but stay close to the door. "What?"

"You're so protective over something that's caused you nothing but grief, little bird."

My pulse ticks faster at the nickname. It's too familiar, too intimate. I hate it. *No*, I correct myself. *I hate that I don't hate it.*

I pin him with a glare. "I don't have to understand everything about my magic to know that you getting what you want is dangerous for everyone."

He folds his arms over his chest. "So you'd rather keep what's making you miserable than give it up and return to your life?"

I open my mouth to respond, but hesitate at the last second. "It doesn't work like that," I say after a beat of silence.

He grips the back of his neck, shrugging. "It could. I can give you everything you want—"

"You're wasting your breath," I cut him off. "There is no chance I'm letting you have my magic. None."

"Fine," he says in a tight voice. "When it starts to consume you, and Kit can't help you control it, you know where to find me."

I pull the door open, slamming it shut behind me and hurrying down the stairs, pushing my way through the chaos of hot, writhing bodies. My pulse doesn't return to a normal pace until I'm several blocks away.

My hand shakes as I reach for the phone tucked into my bra before stopping myself. There's no use in calling Kit. He can't do anything about Remington. This is my battle. Even though I'm still not sure what exactly I'm fighting for.

CHAPTER THIRTEEN

After the epic failure at Remington's, I spend the following morning in bed. I'm at a loss. I can read Dad's book over and over again, but it's not going to give me the answers I need to get through this.

Lydia snuck into my room last night after I got back from my "studying session" and sat on the end of my bed while I told her what went down. As much as I hadn't wanted anyone to know what I was up to, it was nice to have someone to vent to—and Kit wasn't an option. He would flip if he knew where I went instead of the café.

I roll onto my back and sigh at the ceiling. Drumming my fingers on my stomach, it growls in response. I guess I'll have to get out of bed eventually and eat something.

It takes more effort than I care to admit to haul myself out of the comfort of my blankets and shuffle into the kitchen. In the fridge, I find the fixings for an egg salad sandwich, and when I close the door, Kit is standing there. His eyes are filled with concern, which really doesn't help my overall mood, so I turn away from him without a word and start building my sandwich.

"You shut yourself in your room when you got back last

night," he says, standing on the other side of the kitchen. "You want to tell me what's going on with you?"

I stir the egg salad mixture in a bowl before spooning some onto the bread. "Not really. It doesn't matter anyway."

"I can see you're upset."

"Yeah, well, there's nothing anyone here can do about it, so I'm not sure what else there is to say." That was harsh. I set the spoon in the sink before turning to Kit. "I'm sorry. I know you're trying everything you can."

His hands are shoved into the pockets of his jeans. "Not everything."

I frown. "What are you talking about?"

He nods toward my sandwich. "Eat that, then we'll talk."

After lunch, I follow Kit out to the mausoleum.

"What are we doing in here?" I ask him, tugging the sleeves of my heavy sweater down to cover my hands. Gloves would've been a smart idea.

"Before I tell you, I need you to know that I'm only doing this because it is the very last resort. The Elders periodically check in on facilities like what Nova is running to ensure proper teaching methods are being used. They are unscheduled visits, but I caught wind from a friend of mine that they'll be stopping at our place soon, and I had to make sure you would be safe."

The color drains from my face as my pulse kicks up. "What does that mean?" My voice wavers, and I hate how weak it sounds.

Kit steps toward me and grips my shoulders, firm but not in a way that hurts. "I'm not going to let anything happen to you, Em."

I open my mouth to respond, to ask him how he plans to make sure of that, but I don't get the chance.

"Don't lie to the poor girl, Kit the cat." Remington appears in the doorway of the mausoleum and leans against the stone. The candles around the room flare to life with inky black flames, filling the space with heat and an ominous glow.

"What are you doing here?" I snap at him.

Remington rolls his eyes, and the candles return to normal. "Put the claws away," he mutters dryly before shifting his gaze to Kit. "You didn't tell her?"

"You have the worst timing," Kit mutters. Then he says, "Emery, you were right. No one at Nova's can help you with your magic. Not in the way you need."

"He's right. They won't be able to help you, little bird." Remington adds.

"I'll take my chances," I shoot back. It's not what I want, but I'll be damned if I let him have the satisfaction of hearing me say that I . . . need him.

He arches a brow. "You really don't want to make it out of this alive, do you?"

I cross my arms. "What are you doing here, Remington?"

His lips twist into a smirk. "Hmm," he hums, "I love the sound of my name on your lips."

"Enough," Kit says in a sharp tone, then focuses on me. "I asked him to come. Clearly, it was a mistake."

My eyes widen. "Uh, you think?"

"Hurtful," Remington cuts in with a mock pout.

"Are you going to take this seriously?" Kit grumbles, his face tingeing with red as he glares at Remington.

"Uh, probably not. Where's the fun in that?"

Kit closes his eyes as if he's attempting to calm himself. "I'm sorry, Em. I should've known this was a bad idea." He shakes his head. "Let's just go. We'll figure something else out."

Remington laughs. "Good luck with that. She needs me, and you *hate* that she needs me." His voice is smug, and his eyes glimmer with arrogance. He's asking to get punched in the face.

I open my mouth to shut that down, but Kit beats me to it.

"The hell she does," he growls. "I was wrong to ask you here. You are the absolute *last* thing she needs."

He smirks. "That's not true, Kit the cat, and you know it."

"Okay," I rush to say, stepping between in an attempt to diffuse the tension. Facing Kit, I meet his gaze, my eyes pleading with him. "You were right. As much as we both hate it, he's the only one who knows how my magic works." I lower my voice. "I don't know what you had to offer to get him here, but I'm thankful you care for me so much that you did." Does that mean I'm happy about Remington being here? Hell no. After last night, the last thing I want is to be left alone with him.

Worried you'll kiss him again?

I shove that thought away. I want to learn my magic. If working with Remington is the compromise I have to make in order for that to happen, I'll just have to endure it.

Kit's brows furrow. "Emery—"

"I'll meet you back at the house in an hour." He doesn't need to be here for this, and I have a feeling it would be a lot harder to focus with him watching like a hawk.

His jaw clenches, but he keeps his eyes on me. "No. There is no way I'm leaving you alone with him."

I press my lips together, praying to any god who will listen that Remington doesn't bring up last night. "Kit."

He opens his mouth as if he's going to argue, but at the last minute, he snaps it shut and glares at Remington. "You hurt her in any way, and you won't have to worry about the Elders. I'll kill you myself."

I frown at his back as he walks away.

"Do you think he ever gets tired of being so high and mighty?"

I jump at the sound of Remington's voice way too close to my ear, whirling around to face him. Big mistake. We're practically nose-to-nose. His breath tickles my cheek and smells faintly of oranges.

I take a healthy step back. "Do you ever get tired of being so annoying?"

The corner of his mouth kicks up. "Nope. Especially considering how much I know you secretly enjoy it."

I cross my arms, pinning him with a glare. "Oh, good. So you're annoying *and* delusional."

Remington drags a hand through his hair, chuckling silently. "We only have an hour. I'm more than happy to continue bantering with you, though I imagine you'd like to learn something in our time together."

When it's clear he's waiting for me to answer, I nod. "Can I ask you something, and can you promise to answer honestly?"

He purses his lips, considering. "Hmm, yes and no."

Annoyance flickers through me. "God, do you have to be so infuriating?"

Remington tips his head to the side. "That's your question?"

"No." Dropping my hands to my sides, I breathe out a sigh. "Why are you helping me? Is it because you think I'll give up my magic still, and you want it to be more useful when I do?"

He looks at me, his amused expression smoothing into one that could almost be mistaken as thoughtful. He steps toward me again, and this time, I don't move away. "Does it really matter? We both have reasons for doing this."

I arch a brow. "That's a non-answer if I ever heard one."

Remington grins. "You've already made up your mind about me, little bird. With Kit's help, I'm sure, but all the same. I'm not here to change that."

"I haven't—" I start to disagree, but stop myself. Maybe he's right. Maybe I did write him off as the bad guy because of Kit. Well, that, and because of what he did to my friends, and the fact that he wants to steal my magic to make himself more powerful. You know, typical villain stuff. "Fine. Maybe I have . . . or *had*. I don't know. You are very confusing."

"Why? Because I keep you guessing? Because you never know what I'm going to do next?"

"Uh, yeah. Pretty much."

His grin remains. "Come on. Let's practice some evil and corrupt magic before I send you back to Saint Kit." Bitterness weaves its way through his voice, and I wonder if I'll ever work up the nerve to ask one of them why they have such a burning hatred for one another. Certainly, it must have to do with more than just different magic.

"Tell me what you've learned on your own so I have an idea of where to start."

I tap my hands against my thighs, a little unsure how to handle his sudden change in tone. I'm not used to the serious, non-arrogant version of Remington.

"Well, I've been reading my father's book," I tell him, and he nods. "A lot of it is just ramblings about spells, but not the actual spells themselves. There were some, though, but I'm not sure I want to delve into a lot of them."

His chin dips slightly, and his eyes hold a curious light. "Do you have the book with you? I'd be interested to read what he had to say."

"No." I'm glad it's hidden in the dresser in my room at Nova's, because the idea of putting it into Remington's hands makes my chest tighten.

"Hmm, that's too bad."

I nod, wetting my lips before giving him the rundown on what I've read. "After struggling to learn the elemental stuff with no success, the feeling of my magic actually working . . . it made me feel more powerful than I ever thought possible."

"Be careful, little bird. Working with dark magic—it can be very addicting."

I push my fingers through my unruly curls to move them out of my face. "I don't understand. Are you trying to talk me out of this?"

His smile is faint. "I'm just trying to make sure you have all of the information before making a choice." He touches my forearm, and the crackle of energy warms my skin. It doesn't shock me as much anymore. In fact, it's oddly pleasant. Something else I need to be careful of. "It's your choice, Emery."

My breath catches, and I meet his gaze. It's soft and focused solely on me. "I want to learn."

"Then congratulations. You just upgraded mentors."

I roll my eyes. "You are such an asshole to Kit."

The amusement in his eyes fades. "Yeah. I'm awful. This isn't news, Emery."

Crossing my arms over my chest, I shoot him a dry look. "Right, but you're not always." My voice lowers, almost as if I'm afraid to say what comes out next. "Not with me."

Remington cocks his head to the side, studying me. "Don't read into it. Whatever I do serves my own purposes. Get that twisted, and you'll be sorry."

I blink at him, my lips parted slightly. "You don't scare me, Remington."

He moves closer, and his breath stirs the hair at my temple. Lifting his hand to my face, he grips my chin between his fingers. "No?" His eyes search mine. "Why do you think that is?"

I chew my lip. "I don't know. Probably a little stupidity on my part. Though, you haven't hurt me yet. Sure, it's because you want something from me, but I figure so long as that's true, I'm safe."

His eyes darken as they drop to my mouth. "That's a mistake." His voice is low and gravelly.

"Oh well," I murmur, shrugging.

He just stares at me for a few beats. "You are—"

I shift away from him. "Are you going to teach me something or what? I don't have all day."

Remington chuckles. "What do you want to learn?"

I purse my lips, thinking about it for a moment. "What's the coolest thing you can do?"

He arches a brow at me. "Define 'cool.' Because I have a feeling your definition is very different from mine."

I almost pout. "What is that supposed to mean?"

"Nothing. This magic is unlike anything you've dealt with before. Those parlor tricks you've been taught are worthless."

"I know that," I snap. "But I did something one time . . . with fire. When I thought I had earth magic. I tried to extinguish the flames with dirt. I thought it was working, but when I opened my eyes, the flames were black."

Remington doesn't look surprised. Curious, maybe, but that's about it. "Your magic can manifest in different ways. That was likely less of anything you did and more of the magic trying to exist outside of you."

"You make it sound like a monster."

"It can be, which is why if you don't know how to deal with it, it does have the power to hurt you—or worse."

I nod. "Is this the part where you tell me how much easier things would be if I just gave you my magic so I wouldn't have to worry about it anymore?"

He smirks. "Sure, little bird. It's true, but I won't repeat something you already know. I'd like to save my breath for something more important."

My eyes widen. "Are you . . . coming on to me?"

Remington laughs. "Not in the slightest." He leans in until his lips are level with my ear. "There would be no question in your mind if I was. Trust me."

A flush spreads across my chest, and I fight the urge to back away. My pulse is thrumming beneath my skin, and my stomach is a mess of nerves.

He leans back and looks into my eyes. "Would you like that?"

My mouth dries right up, and I swallow hard. "I . . . Are you joking?"

"Sure."

I can't get a read on him, and it's threatening to drive me insane.

"Whatever game you're playing, I don't want to be a part of it. I don't trust you, and—"

"You don't trust me, or you don't trust yourself around me?" He regards me with a thoughtful expression, a dark strand of hair falling into his face.

"What's it matter?" I ask without thinking.

Remington shrugs. "I suppose it doesn't. I was just curious."

"Well, quit it. And start helping me, or you may as well leave."

"And then where would you be?"

"I'm not doing this with you." I keep my voice level, refusing to bait him anymore.

He holds his hands up in defeat. "All right, all right. What should we start with?" he muses aloud, tapping his finger against his lips.

"Something I won't screw up?" I offer.

"Perhaps we should start with a cloaking spell," he suggests with a devilish grin.

"Funny," I deadpan as I lean against one of the massive cement boxes.

He tries to hide his grin by pressing his lips together. "Okay, only seriousness from now on."

I arch a brow, not believing that for a second. "Fine. I want to learn what you did at the café the other day. With the alternate reality or whatever."

"That isn't really an easy spell to start with. It was actually a combination of a few different ones."

"I'm a quick study," I argue. "At least show me how to change what I'm seeing."

He opens his mouth, but rethinks that choice and closes it. He nods again. "Let's give it a shot." Remington walks around the small space, shrugging off his leather jacket to reveal a long-sleeved, tight-fitting shirt. My shoulders tense when I realize I'm staring at his chest.

He catches me, his eyes noting my posture as he walks closer. "You need to relax if you want this to work."

"That's not exactly easy to do around you."

Remington touches my shoulder. "I'm not going to hurt you, Emery. I need you to trust me right now. We want the same thing, which is for you to gain control of your magic and advance your abilities."

I exhale, closing my eyes in an attempt to concentrate.

"That's it," he murmurs, pulling his hand away. "Now, picture what you want to see. It helps if it's somewhere you're familiar with."

I keep my eyes shut, cringing as I ask, "I'm not going to, like, teleport there or something by accident, am I?"

He chuckles. "No."

"Well, I don't know!"

"Just try it," he suggests, and I'm surprised not to hear any arrogance or amusement in his voice. He's actually taking this seriously.

I clench my hands into fists for a moment before opening them, trying to release the tension through my upper body, then take a deep breath to center myself. The first place that comes to mind is the living room at home. Not Nova's, but the house I grew up in—my home. I concentrate on what I recall most about the space—the warmth and comfort I feel when I'm there. It's a safe space. I picture holidays spent in this room, opening gifts on Christmas morning with my mom, and weekend movie nights eating pizza and way too much junk food with Lana and Jessa. The smell of Mom's cinnamon apple candle tickles my nose, and

I suck in a breath, keeping my eyes closed. I'm too scared to open them.

"Don't be afraid." Remington's voice is soft. "Open your eyes, Emery."

After a moment of hesitation, I blow out a breath and slowly open them, blinking a few times as the room focuses. "Oh my god," I whisper, turning to face him. We're standing in the wide archway into the living room. My gaze bounces around the room, recognizing each detail until it comes back to Remington. He's watching me.

"I'm doing this?" I ask in a low voice, worried he's going to reveal that he's actually the one making the room appear around us.

He tilts his head to the side, searching my face. "I'm not doing anything, little bird," he assures me.

"Holy crap." I breathe out a laugh. "This is incredible. It feels so real." I shake my head, still wrapping my head around the fact that *I* did this.

"You're manipulating the space we're in," he explains. "But you're also manipulating what you and I are seeing. It would become more difficult if there were more people, but like anything, the more you practice, the easier it will come to you."

"You're saying that I'm manipulating your mind?"

He nods. "I'm allowing it, but yes."

I arch a brow at him, and the scene around us blurs a little. "What do you mean, *allowing it*?"

"Exactly that. I've been at this longer than you. I could interrupt your magic at any time with my own."

"Nice brag," I say without thinking.

His lips twitch. "For most people, though, they wouldn't even notice it. They wouldn't know how to guard their mind against your magic because they don't know it exists."

"That seems unfair," I comment.

"That's life. It's also one of the many reasons our magic is not approved by the Elders."

"I mean, I can sort of understand that. Kit and the others can control the elements, but we can control—"

"Everything." He shrugs, glancing around the room. "I'm assuming this is your home."

I follow his gaze. "Yeah."

"Cute."

I roll my eyes. "Is there more?"

Remington's gaze shifts back to me. "Like what?"

"I don't know. Can we interact with the objects around us?"

Shaking his head, he says, "What you're managing now is surface-level magic. The things you see aren't really here." He nods toward the staircase. "If you tried to go upstairs, you'd likely walk into a stone wall. We're still in the mausoleum."

"It just looks so real."

He inhales slowly, then blinks, and the room vanishes, leaving us standing back in the candle-lit stone room. His eyes dance across my face, and when our gazes lock, he says, "Appearances can be deceiving."

"How poetic of you," I mutter, glancing at one of the candles. The wax has melted significantly; I didn't realize how much time had actually passed. "I'm almost afraid to ask, but how did I do?"

The corner of his mouth curves into a slow grin. "Huh. Not bad for a rookie, I guess."

My eyes narrow, and I immediately regret asking. "Why do you have to be so—"

"Handsome?" he offers, tilting his head to the side. "Charming?" He leans in close, and I hold my breath. "Downright—"

"Infuriating," I cut in, pushing my fist against his stomach in an attempt to put space between us. I'm met with hard resistance, and my eyes fly to his, but he's staring at my mouth.

"I can't stop thinking about what your lips would taste like if I kissed you right now."

"Peppermint," I blurt. Yep. Pretty sure my brain has short-circuited.

His brow quirks as he flicks his tongue over his bottom lip. "Is that so?"

"It's lip balm," I mumble. *Oh god. I need to stop talking.*

His eyes sparkle with amusement. "Yeah?" He holds my gaze as if he's waiting for me to say something, but I've got nothing. "Come on," he says. "You should head home before Kit comes looking for you."

I open my mouth to . . . what, *thank him*? It feels like an odd thing to do, considering he likely only did it for his own gain. He must truly believe I'll hand over my magic one of these days.

"It's okay," he says, "you don't have to say it. You don't trust me, and that's fine." He dips his face closer to mine, lowering his voice as if he's all of a sudden concerned about being overheard —in a mausoleum. "For what it's worth, I'm proud of what you accomplished today, and you should be too."

I stare at him despite the growing urge to look away. His gaze makes my skin tingle in ways that have me questioning why on earth I'm drawn to him. Can I chalk it up to a side effect of having the same magic? Probably not, but it'd be easier to have something that's out of my control to blame for my ridiculous attraction to Remington.

He pulls away, and I drag air into my lungs while he grabs his jacket and shrugs it on as we walk out of the mausoleum together.

I get back to Nova's just in time to sit down for dinner. Lydia made a roast that smells amazing and has my stomach growling before I can get my jacket off. Everyone is already at the table when I walk in, and my eyes go to Kit. He's looking at me with one brow raised. I offer a faint smile and nod at him.

"Hey," Lydia says as I sit in what has become my normal place at the table. "Where have you been?"

Nerves unfurl in my stomach. "Oh, um, I was just doing some training."

Realization flickers across her face as she pauses in the mashed potatoes mid-scoop.

"But Kit was here," Zoe says.

"Right." My eyes flick toward where Nova is sitting at the head of the table, his eyes on me. He nods once, and I take that as permission to tell the others about my magic. "Kit is no longer my mentor."

"Why not?" Zoe asks, and I ignore the excitement in her eyes. She *really* wants Kit to herself.

Without preamble, I say, "Because I'm not an elemental Wielder."

Lydia sinks into her chair, staring at the plate in front of her without saying a word. She's known about my magic for a few days, but it seems as though she's shocked I just put it out in the open.

"What the hell, Nova?" Zoe snaps, turning a glare on him. "You've been harboring a dark Wielder? How long have you known about this and put us all at risk?" she demands.

Nova's expression remains impassive as he regards her. "I knew about her magic when I brought her here."

She drops her fork onto her plate, vibrating with anger. "You have got to be kidding me."

"Easy, Zoe," Mason says with a strained expression, shifting in his seat and looking to Nova as if he wants to trust his decision, but this is too much.

"I didn't know about my magic—my real magic—until I went home for Thanksgiving. I had a feeling something was off, but it wasn't until that trip that it was confirmed. Since then, I've been trying to learn it."

"Are you crazy?" Zoe chimes in, her eyes wide. "The Elders will punish all of us if they find her here."

My jaw clenches as bile rises in my throat. The thought of putting anyone here at risk because Nova is protecting his dead best friend's daughter . . . I can't carry the weight of that. "I should leave," I say in a low voice.

"What?" Lydia's voice is filled with a mix of sadness and confusion.

"Zoe's right. If that's a possibility, then it's not fair for me to stay. My magic shouldn't pose a risk to any of you."

"You're not leaving," Nova's tone is final. "I made a promise, and I intend to keep it."

"What?" Zoe snaps. "Are—" Nova holds up a hand, and she stops talking. Scowling at me, she shoves away from the table and storms out of the room. A few seconds later, her bedroom door slams shut.

"Nova—" I start.

"We will discuss this after dinner," he tells me before scanning the rest of the Wielders at the table. "If anyone has anything they would like to say, you may do so once we've eaten."

The rest of the meal is silent.

I push food around my plate, my appetite having vanished since telling the truth. Once Kit, Nova, and I are the only ones at the table, I set my fork aside. "I can't stay. It's not safe—for anyone." Now that I'm working on my magic, getting a better handle on it, I should go home. If leaving Nova's means the rest of Wielders under his roof are safe from the Elders' judgment, it seems like the best option at this point—the *only* option, really.

"I promised your father I would protect you no matter the cost. It's not something I would do for anyone else, but you are an exception."

I swallow past the dryness in my throat. "Why?"

He almost smiles. "When you were born, he and your mother asked me to be your guardian—after Holly, of course. We may not be related by blood, but the day your parents asked me to take care of you, you became family."

My eyes burn. "So you should understand why I need to go."

"We can find another way," Kit says.

"No." My tone is firm. "I appreciate what you both have done for me, even if it took me a while to get on board with the whole magic thing, but this needs to be my decision." I stand, glancing between them. "The Elders have taken enough from me. I won't let them have the satisfaction of finding me here." I take my plate to the kitchen and give them one last look. "I'm leaving in the morning."

CHAPTER FOURTEEN

The world shakes violently, pulling me from a dreamless sleep. I gasp as Kit's face comes into focus. His complexion is white as a sheet, and his eyes are dark and tired.

"What the hell?" I grumble. "What are you doing?"

"Get up."

"What time is it?"

"*Emery*." His tone shoots ice through my veins.

I sit up, swinging my legs over the side of the bed as Kit steps back. "What's going on?"

"Samuel called to warn me," Kit says, storming over to my dresser. He starts throwing clothes over his shoulder at me. "They're on their way."

"Who?" I rub my eyes, grabbing the clothes out of the air before they hit me in the face.

"Sam's one of the Elders. They were planning to check in here in a few days, but someone tipped them off."

Tipped them off? Realization slams into me, stealing the breath from my lungs.

"What do we do?" My voice shakes. Kit keeps his back to

me while I change. "How did this happen?" I grab my phone off the table beside the bed as Kit turns back around.

"We have to go."

"We?" I shake my head. "No. You can't get caught with me, Kit."

"Take my car." My heart lurches as my gaze snaps to the door where Nova is standing. "Drive to Covington," he continues. "Holly is expecting you. The two of you will need to get out of the state."

"And go where? For how long?" I vaguely notice Kit tossing my belongings into my duffle bag.

He walks into the room and takes my hand, dropping the keys into my palm. "Your parents had friends in New Orleans."

I gape at him as he steps back. "Dark Wielder friends?"

He shakes his head. "But they knew about your father's magic. I'll call them when you leave and let them know you're coming."

Kit zips up my bag and shoulders it. "I'll walk you out."

My stomach drops. We all should've been more prepared for this to happen, but for me at least, there was a naïve part of me that didn't think the Elders would come. Not like this.

Lydia is standing near the door with Mason beside her. They're both in pajamas, and Lydia's expression is a heartbreaking mix of exhaustion and concern. She pulls me into a hug, holding me to her so tight it hurts, but I don't pull away.

Mason's jaw is clenched, and his lips are downturned.

"Be careful," Lydia says as Mason pulls her back.

I nod, sniffling as I struggle to fight back tears.

Nova and Kit walk me to the SUV. Kit puts my bag in the backseat and, without hesitation, wraps his arms around me.

I close my eyes, my cheek pressed against his chest. My bottom lip trembles, and I bite it to keep from crying.

"We'll figure this out."

I pull back and look him in the eyes. "How?"

"I'm going to do my best to reason with them," Nova says. "You just worry about getting home. We'll keep you posted here." His eyes shift to Kit for a brief moment before returning to me. "Go."

With tears in my eyes, I get behind the wheel and start the car. I roll the window down, and Kit steps up to the door. Nova stands back a little, his expression grim.

"Be careful," he says.

"You too. I—"

The passenger door opens, and my heart slams against my ribcage as my head whips around to find Remington dropping into the seat next to me. "What are you doing?" My voice is high and uneven.

"Road trip," he says with a grin.

I turn back to Kit to question this, but he looks as surprised as I am.

Nova steps up and puts a hand on Kit's shoulder. Maybe he recognizes that I'm probably safer with Remington if the Elders find me. "Drive," he tells me. "Don't stop until you get to Covington."

With a shaking hand, I type the address into the built-in GPS, shaking my head at the digital clock next to it. It's two-thirty in the morning. I put the car in drive and grip the wheel until my knuckles turn white. A sob builds in my throat as we move down the gravel driveway, and I hold my breath in an attempt to push it down.

The cold air prompts me to roll up the window, drowning the car in silence, save for the pounding of my heart in my own ears.

"Take a breath," Remington says.

I gasp for air, my chest rising and falling fast. "What the hell is happening right now?" I turn onto the dark back road and press the gas harder. "How did you . . . ? Why are you here?"

"You woke me up."

I turn toward him to find his jaw set tight. "Huh?"

"There was a ripple of magic. It quite literally shocked me awake."

"That's crazy," I say, my eyes back on the road.

"You're scared, and your emotions are heightened," he explains in a much more level voice than mine. "Your magic responds to that."

"Great. I'll add that to the ever-growing list of things that are going wrong."

"There's nothing wrong about it, little bird." He sighs. "Why don't you pull over and let me drive?"

I hit the gas harder in response. "You've evaded the Elders this long. How does this work?"

"We keep moving."

My pulse surges at his use of *we*. "Why did you come?"

"I wouldn't be a very good mentor if I abandoned you this soon out of the gate. We just started working together." There's a tinge of amusement in his tone. *How is he making jokes right now?*

"So it has nothing to do with wanting to make sure you don't lose your chance at more power?"

He reaches in front of him and messes with the dashboard. A few seconds later, warm air tickles my cheeks. "You said it, not me."

I shake my head. "Nova thinks he can talk them out of this witch hunt."

Remington shifts his seat back a bit, stretching his legs out. "You sound doubtful."

"I've never seen these centuries-old Wielders, but the fact that they're coming after me in the middle of the night doesn't make me feel very confident they'll just be cool letting me exist with this magic." Before he can say anything, I add, "Don't bother reminding me that you could fix that." I peek over just in time to see the smirk on his lips.

"I wasn't going to say it."

We drive in silence for a while. I follow the GPS while Remington shuffles through the music library on his phone. I'm not sure why it surprises me that I like the songs he plays, but I keep that to myself.

"What's your plan here?" I ask. "Are you going to follow me and my mom to New Orleans?"

"Hmm. New Orleans?"

"Nova said my parents had friends there, so we're going to lay low for a while, I guess."

"Seems like a good idea," he says.

"Seems like the *only* idea," I point out.

"Maybe for now."

I press my lips together, not sure what to make of the ominous tone of his voice, but I decide not to ask. I need to focus on getting home so Mom and I can keep moving.

We're halfway to Covington when I ask the question that's been nagging me whenever I see Remington and Kit together.

"I don't think you want to know, little bird."

There's a sharp edge to my voice when I say, "I asked the question."

"I lost someone close to me," he says, "and Kit could have stopped it from happening."

My mouth goes dry. "I . . . I don't know what to say." I have at least half a dozen follow up questions, but they all feel selfish to ask after he shared that. *Who did he lose? How long ago was it? What happened?*

"You don't need to say anything." He changes the song and turns the volume up a bit.

"I'm sorry, Rem," I finally say, and my pulse jumps. *Rem? Where did that come from?*

He turns his body toward me. "Finally giving me a nickname?"

"I don't know," I mumble, my cheeks heating. I catch his faint grin before staring out the windshield.

"I like it."

All right then.

The closer we get to Covington, the harder I find focusing on the road. My nerves are making my stomach upset, and there's a dull ache in my temples, like when the weather changes quickly and messes with the air pressure.

I pull onto the gravel road, driving for a few minutes before turning into the driveway and frowning at the house. All of the lights are off, including the porch lights she always leaves on at night. Her car is in the driveway, and I slow to a stop next to it, shifting the SUV into park.

"It doesn't look like anyone's awake," Remington says.

My breath catches in my throat. "I don't . . ." I'm unbuckling my belt and reaching for the door before I can finish my sentence. I rush up the steps and grab the doorknob, shocked to find it unlocked.

The passenger door shuts behind me, but I'm already halfway down the hall, shouting for my mom before Remington catches up to me, flicking on the light in the foyer.

"What—"

"She's not here," I gasp out, my chest heaving as I struggle to breathe. I fumble my phone out of my pocket, and my hands shake as I find Nova's name and call him.

The line rings once. "Emery." His tone cracks a hole in my chest.

I squeeze my eyes shut. "No." My voice cracks. "Please don't . . ."

"They have her."

"Why?" I press my hand against my forehead, willing my head to stop spinning. "I don't understand."

"The Elders want you to turn yourself over." Nova's voice is strained. "A couple of them just left. Kit and Lydia are coming to get you and—"

The phone slips out of my hand, clattering against the wood

floor as my knees buckle. I manage to grab the banister at the stairs to keep upright, but Remington rushes forward, his eyes wide with . . . panic?

"Emery, what—"

"My mom," I croak. "They took my mom."

His expression darkens. "What did Kit say?" he asks in a low voice, bending to retrieve my phone and holding it out to me.

I shake my head, taking it from him. The call disconnected, and honestly, I need a second to process what just happened, so I slip it back into my pocket. "That was Nova. He said Kit's coming here."

"We shouldn't wait for him. Let's—"

"I'm not going to let her get hurt because of me," I cut him off. "She gave up her whole life to take care of me when my parents died. I can't let anything happen to her, Rem."

He nods. "Then we'll get her back."

I swallow past the fear clogging my throat. "The only way I see that happening is if I give them what they want."

His jaw tightens as his eyes flick between mine. "You do that, and you're dead."

"Maybe not. They didn't start out intending to kill the dark Wielders—"

"They didn't stop imprisoning them as soon as they found out what was happening either."

I throw my hands up and snap, "What else am I supposed to do?"

"You won't like my answer."

"Tell me."

"Accept the fact that you won't see your mom again."

I slap him across the face so hard that sharp pain shoots up my arm and tears fill my eyes.

He rubs his jaw, his eyes narrowed. "You asked."

"You want me to let my mom die because you want my magic. You're a selfish asshole, and I want you gone. Now."

Remington doesn't say anything, doesn't try to change my mind. He turns and walks out of my house, closing the door behind him.

I sink to the floor and let out the sob I've been holding back since leaving Nova's.

CHAPTER FIFTEEN

I pace the house for over an hour, trying to think of a scenario where I save my mom's life without losing my own. Nothing seems plausible when the Elders are using an innocent person to get to me.

What are they doing to the dark Wielders they find, now that they know the cells they were putting them in blocked their magic to the point of killing them?

I probably should have asked that question a long time ago.

I'm dozing in and out on the couch in the living room when headlights flash in the front window as Kit's car pulls into the driveway. My muscles are heavy as I get up and walk to the front door, meeting them on the porch.

Lydia throws her arms around me until I can't breathe. When she pulls back, her face is filled with concern.

Kit walks up the steps behind her, his mouth set in a tight line. "Where's Remington?"

I glance at him. "I sort of slapped him across the face and kicked him out."

His brows rise. "Sort of?"

"Okay, I did. But he deserved it."

Neither Kit nor Lydia comment on that as we walk inside, and I close the door, flipping the lock over. In the living room, we sit around the coffee table, and I can't stop my knee from bouncing.

"What did the Elders say?" I ask Kit.

He takes a deep breath. "Nova was prepared to lie to them. You were gone, so he was going to tell them that you'd been with us a month ago for a day or so before leaving. He was going to send them looking for you in Washington."

"Do you think that would've worked?" I'm not sure why I ask. It doesn't matter now.

"It would've been a temporary fix."

I chew my bottom lip, tearing at the skin until I taste blood. "How did they find my mom?"

Kit drops his gaze to his lap, and I look toward Lydia, who looks as if she's about to burst into tears at any moment.

"Kit?" I push.

"Zoe told the Elders there was a dark Wielder in Covington. She thought doing that wouldn't bring attention to Nova's, and they would put it together that you were Simon Leclerc's daughter."

"It didn't go as planned, though," Lydia adds. "Considering Nova's is the only facility for Wielders in the area, the Elders figured you'd been staying there."

My nostrils flare. "Why would Zoe do this?"

"She was jealous of you from the moment you arrived at Nova's," Lydia says. "She's had feelings for Kit since she met him."

I freeze, turning my attention to Kit. "My mom's life is in danger because Zoe has a crush on you?"

His face pales. "There's more to it than that. Her parents were associated with some of the dark Wielders at one point, so she has resentment toward them."

"How is that my fault?" I clench my hands into fists.

"It's not," Lydia rushes to say.

"She admitted what she did after Samuel and Myra left, and Nova asked her to leave."

"What's that matter? The damage has already been done." I shake my head. "Where are they keeping my mom?"

"Their main facility in Roswell. It's a little ways outside Atlanta."

I nod, gripping my thighs. "And they want me to go there?"

"They would arrange for you to be picked up at Nova's, but Emery, that's not going to happen."

"I can't let them hurt my mom," I whisper. "Maybe if I turn myself over to them, they'll see I'm not a threat." It's a terribly naïve idea, but it's the only option I have that protects the people I care about. "Is Nova in trouble?"

Kit presses his lips together and won't meet my gaze, so I turn to Lydia.

She frowns. "They, uh . . . they shut down his facility."

That punches the air out of my chest. "Wh-what?"

"They wanted to detain him along with your mom, but Samuel managed to talk them out of it," Kit says.

"Yeah, because he's pretty much the only sane one," Lydia grumbles.

"What do you mean?"

Her brows knit. "The Elders are so old. I mean, Sam's one of the younger ones, but the others . . . they're so set in the old-time ways of magic."

"The old-time ways," I echo. "Like dark magic being so much more dangerous than elemental?"

"Yeah," she says. "Which in some cases, sure, but even elemental magic in the wrong hands can be dangerous."

I rake my fingers through my hair, my eyes burning from lack of sleep—and from crying. "There has to be a way to convince them I'm not the enemy."

Kit sighs audibly. "Maybe, but I don't think we're going to

come up with that tonight. We all need to get some rest. We'll head back to Nova's tomorrow."

As much as I want to go back tonight, to figure this out right now and make sure my mom is returned safely, exhaustion clings to me like soaking wet clothes.

"I'll sleep in my mom's room. Lydia, you can take mine, and Kit—"

"I'm fine on the couch."

Lydia and I walk upstairs together, and she grabs my hand before I turn toward Mom's room. "I know things are really bad right now, and you're going out of your mind with worry and fear, but I . . . I have hope." She squeezes my hand.

"Thanks," I say in a quiet voice. I'm glad she does, because I can't seem to find a shred of it inside myself.

***

The following morning, Lydia drives Kit's car back while he and I take Nova's SUV. Traffic is light, and we pull into the driveway at Nova's a couple hours later as he steps onto the porch. The grass is covered in frost, and my breath fogs the cold air, making me shiver the moment I open the passenger door.

"I'm so sorry," I tell him, throwing my arms around his neck.

His arms come around me. "You don't need to apologize, Emery."

I pull back enough to look at his face. "I don't know how this got so messed up," I whisper.

"I know," he says. "It's not your fault."

"Isn't it?" I ask as he ushers me into the warmth of the house.

"No." His voice is soft but firm.

Kit and Lydia follow us inside, and I gasp when my eyes land on a stranger sitting on the couch in the living room.

"Nova . . ."

"It's okay," Kit says. "That's Samuel."

The 'sane' Elder. Great. He's still an Elder, and I'm still considered a criminal to them just for existing.

"What is he doing here?" I don't want to say the words on my tongue, but they tumble out anyway. "Did you tell him I was coming back today?" I'm looking at Nova as my eyes burn.

"Of course not. He got here only a few minutes before you did."

Kit walks into the living room, and Samuel stands as the rest of us join them. I hang back near the entryway, my nerves crackling with energy and my feet ready to bolt at a moment's notice.

When I meet Samuel's pale green gaze, I square my shoulders, feeling as if I need to appear calm and collected even as my pulse is racing and my heartbeat is in my throat. He has curly black hair and is dressed far more casually than I was expecting. The guy is wearing a black pullover sweater and faded blue jeans. His expression is curious as he looks me over; he can't be much older than Kit. Late twenties, *maybe* thirty.

"Emery Leclerc," he says in greeting.

"Hi." That's all I've got.

He offers a faint smile. "You look just like your father."

His words are a slap to the face, and I suck in a breath, my jaw clenching. "Don't talk about my father," I say in a low voice.

He nods. "Of course. I'm sorry."

I blink at that. He's . . . *sorry*? "What have you done with my mom?" I demand. "I want to see her."

"She's okay," he assures me. "The others would like you to come to our facility, and they will allow her to return home."

"The others? Are you not including yourself in that statement?"

Samuel shifts his gaze to Nova. "I don't necessarily agree with some of the things they do, or how they choose to uphold the laws put in place centuries ago. I would like to see a change. A few of us would, actually."

There's a tiny spark in my chest. I want to believe that's what hope feels like, but I'm wary of it. I don't trust this guy, but it would appear that Kit and Nova do—at least to some extent, or he wouldn't be here.

"What kind of change?" Lydia chimes in, leaning against the wall beside the front window. Mason slips into the room at some point and joins her.

"I'm not denying that dark magic poses a risk. We've seen it used for evil in many ways, but that was a generation ago. Perhaps it's time to . . . re-evaluate our stance on the matter."

I hold my breath, too scared to speak. If what he's saying is true, if the dark Wielders no longer had to worry about being caught by the Elders, I could get my life back. I could learn my magic and finish high school and travel the world and do, well, anything I want.

"You know how the others feel," Kit says to Samuel. "You know their views haven't changed, and I'm not sure what could possibly make them consider it."

"You're right," Samuel replies. "There's no denying the risk involved." He turns his attention to me. "You would need to come with me to Roswell. Once you're there, they'll let your mom go, and we can work on convincing the others the assumed threat we've been chasing for years deserves another chance."

"No," Lydia says, and my gaze turns toward her as she looks toward Nova. "Do you really think it's worth risking Emery's life?"

I swallow a sigh. We're going to continue going in circles with this argument. "I want to go."

Everyone turns their attention to me, but I don't cower away from it. I look at Samuel and repeat myself.

He nods. "Good. We should leave soon."

"I'm going with you," Kit says, his shoulders stiff.

"You know you can't," Samuel tells him.

A muscle feathers along his jaw, and he opens his mouth to speak, but Samuel stops him with a hand on his shoulder.

"I know you want to make sure she's safe. You'll have to trust that I will do my best to ensure that, Kit."

He narrows his eyes at Samuel. "You'd really stop me from going to protect her?"

"It'll be more effective if Emery goes alone, proving she cares more about keeping her family safe than about herself or the magic inside of her."

"It's my choice," I point out, "and I've made up my mind."

Kit falls silent, and the rest of the room follows suit.

For someone who didn't leave her tiny hometown for the first eighteen years of her life, I've done a lot of travelling in the last month. Granted, I haven't left the state, but still.

My stomach is a ball of nerves as I sit next to a stranger—an Elder at that. I have to remind myself that people I trust in turn trust him, but it doesn't make what I'm doing any easier.

"Have you considered this before?" I ask. "Offering the dark Wielders the chance to live the same way the elementals do?"

Samuel taps his finger against the steering wheel. "Myself and a couple of the others have discussed it. Never anything concrete, for fear of being overheard by the rest of the council."

"What do you think would stop all of you from considering it?"

He purses his lips. "Fear, probably. Many of them have been around a long time, Emery. They've seen the evil your magic can bring."

"Couldn't the same be said for elemental magic?"

"In some respects. But with elemental magic, it's rooted in nature and requires balance. That's the biggest difference. Your magic isn't tied to anything like that, which makes it very easy to spiral into immeasurable power. In the wrong hands, that is deadly."

"Anything in the wrong hands can be deadly," I offer.

Samuel nods. "You don't need to convince me."

I stare out the window for a while, jumping when an incoming call chimes through the car speakers.

Samuel answers in a low voice. "Be there in about twenty minutes, Myra."

"We have a problem." Her voice sounds unnaturally deep.

"What is it?"

"Stephen was pressing the human for information. He thought she might know of other dark Wielders from hiding Emery all these years, but he couldn't get anything from her. She was adamant that she wouldn't be used to hurt her daughter."

My eyes go wide, my posture going ramrod straight in my seat. "She doesn't know anything!"

"Samuel," she says in a stern voice; she didn't know I'm in the car with him.

"What happened?" I demand, gripping the door handle because I need *something* to hang onto.

The line is silent. Then she says, "You should turn around and take her back to Nova's."

Samuel grips the wheel tighter. "Myra, what happened?"

"She made sure we couldn't use her to force Emery's hand. Cyden found her in one of the guest suites this morning. She was already gone."

A scream tears through my throat as I fight against my seatbelt with nowhere to go.

Samuel pulls over, jerking the car into park as he curses under his breath.

My shoulders shake, and my chest explodes with pain. I sob so hard my vision dances with black dots. I can't breathe. *This wasn't supposed to happen.* When I start slamming my fists into the dashboard in front of me, Samuel doesn't try to stop me.

Dizziness floods in as I continue to cry, and I have to make an effort to force air into my lungs in between sobs. I cover my face, my skin hot to the touch, and pull my knees up to my chest.

I barely recognize the movement of Samuel turning the car around. Everything in me hurts as I swallow past the bile rising in my throat and sag against the seat.

CHAPTER SIXTEEN

When we get close to Helen, I wipe the wetness from my cheeks. My eyes feel hot and puffy and my throat hurts. I have to clear it twice before my voice works.

"I don't want to go to Nova's."

Samuel looks over at me, his lips set in a frown. His eyes fill with pity. "I don't know where else to take you."

I close my eyes for a few seconds, then let out a shallow breath and give him an address.

His car slows to a stop at the curb fifteen minutes later, and he turns to me. "Are you sure?"

I nod blankly.

"Emery, I'm—"

"Please just . . . don't."

I get out of the car on shaky legs and suck in a long breath of cold air before walking toward the building. It's too early for people to start lining up outside, but the door is unlocked.

I step inside the empty club, blinking at the space in daylight. It's . . . smaller than it looks at night. My boots echo on the worn laminate floor as I cross the room, heading toward the hallway that leads—

You're making a terrible mistake. Turn around, Emery. Don't go through with this. You're angry and scared and acting based on those emotions. You'll regret this.

The words slow me, but still I end up at his door, eyes burning with more tears. My hand shakes as I lift it, but the door opens before I can knock.

Remington's eyes are so light blue they're almost gray. They flick across my face, filling with shock before he steps aside to let me in.

I hesitate, my feet like anchors to the floor outside his loft. Finally, I push past the fear and walk inside before Remington closes the door behind me. I wrap my arms around myself to combat the chill in my bones.

"It's a little early for a booty call, little bird, and I honestly didn't expect to see you around here after our last interaction." He smirks. "What's up?"

A million thoughts go through my head, but the loudest one is screaming at me to get rid of my magic.

"You can have it." My jaw clenches, and I swipe away the tear that rolls down my cheek. When he doesn't say anything, I glance at him, and his expression isn't what I expected. "Thank you," I croak, turning my gaze to the basketball game on the TV until Remington steps into my view.

He frowns, shaking his head in confusion.

"For having the decency to at least pretend to look surprised."

He nods and licks his lips as if he's preparing to speak, but he doesn't. He just looks at me.

I adopt his confusion, fully expecting him to gloat.

"Drink?" he asks.

"No. Let's just get this over with."

He cocks his head, watching me. "This?"

I exhale a sharp breath, my throat thick with fresh tears. "Are you really going to make me say it again?" My voice trembles, but I stand as tall as I can. "You're getting what you want, Remington. Do you have to be like this?"

He laughs. The bastard actually *laughs* at me.

I take a swing at his face, but he catches my wrist before my palm can collide with his cheek. His fingers wrap around tightly, and he tugs me forward, so close our chests brush.

"You asshole," I say through my teeth, hot tears burning my eyes. There's no point in trying to hide them from him, and I don't have the strength to fight them back.

His jaw is sharp enough to cut stone, and heat radiates from him as he stares at me. His eyes are hard, unforgiving, but there's something else in them too. Something I can't decipher for the life of me.

Remington dips his face so we're nose-to-nose, a breath away, and murmurs, "I've changed my mind."

My stomach plummets, and I shove away from him. "What is that supposed to mean?" I shake my head. "All you've wanted since we met is my magic. Now I'm here, handing it to you on a silver platter, and you've *changed your mind*?"

"That's what I said."

"No. No, I don't accept that."

His lips twist into a cruel grin. "No? Why not, little bird?" He steps closer, and I immediately retreat. He follows until my back hits the wall, and then he cages me in with his arms. "Hmm? Is your power not everything you dreamed it would be?"

I swallow past the lump in my throat. "Why are you doing this?"

Remington exhales slowly, his breath stirring the hair at my temple. "You made me the villain, Emery." He leans in, brushing his lips along the shell of my ear. "I'm just playing my part."

My entire body shivers, and I close my eyes at the sensation. "So take it," I force out.

Remington shifts back just enough to narrow his icy gaze on me. "Why *now*?"

Anger bubbles in my chest, and I snap. I grab the front of his shirt and push hard, moving us away from the wall. "Why do you care? You've waited all this time for me to hand over my magic, and now I am. Quit dragging this out and just do it!"

He glances down to where I'm white-knuckling his shirt, then back up at my face, his lips pressed together. "He didn't tell you, did he?"

"What?" is all I say. I don't have the energy to play his games.

He shrugs. "Kit or Donovan. I was sure one of them would as soon as they found out."

My hand falls to my side, but Remington's shirt remains wrinkled. "What are you talking about?" My voice is lower now, uneven.

Remington steps in and grips my chin, holding my gaze. "I don't need you to *give* me your magic, Emery." He laughs, but it's dry and humorless. "I could have taken it from you, and there would have been nothing you or Kit or anyone else could have done to stop me."

I slap his hand away and stumble back, my pulse racing beneath my flushed skin as I sniffle. "You're lying."

"And yet, you look afraid of me all of a sudden," he muses, his eyes flicking between mine.

"Then why didn't you?" I challenge. "Since you found out, why didn't you take my magic?"

He wets his lips, and I loathe that my stomach flutters at the sight. "Because," he says simply, "I wanted you to surrender to me."

My breath gets stuck in my throat. I blink at him, but he doesn't say anything, doesn't move. "Fine," I finally say, forcing an even tone. "Take it. You were right, I don't even want it. It's caused me so much pain—you'll be doing me a favor."

Remington lifts his hand to my face, and I freeze as he takes a strand of my hair between his fingers before tucking it behind my ear. "I've thought about it, little bird." His eyes meet mine. "A lot. But I meant what I said. I don't want it anymore."

Defeat weighs heavy on my chest, but I manage to get out, "You haven't told me why."

"Why," he echoes, pursing his lips. "Because I'd like to offer you a compromise."

"You—you're giving me a choice?"

The corner of his mouth twitches. "A novel concept to you these days, I'm sure."

I look away, mostly because I can't deny that. My choices have pretty much all been taken away from me as of late. And the one time I did make a choice, I was too late . . .

"Emery." Remington's voice catches my attention, and I turn back to him. "You have the potential to be so much more than you are. So much more than you *were* while you were stuck with Donovan's clan of misfit Wielders. Listen to me very carefully, little bird. Our abilities recognize each other because our magic is the same. Kit can say what he wants about it being dark and dangerous, but the two of us together are more powerful than he could ever dream of being."

"I don't care about power," I say firmly.

Remington looks at me as if I have three heads. "You are something else, aren't you?"

I meet his gaze and hold it. "I don't want to be a part of this anymore."

"I know you're worried about your mom, but your magic can help get her away from the Elders."

I shake my head, struggling to keep the tears at bay. If I have to say the words . . .

He closes the space between us as he stares into my eyes. "Emery—"

"My mom is dead, Rem," I say, and his face blurs as more tears gather. They fall down my cheeks as I blink.

He starts to reach for me, but stops himself, crossing his arms over his chest. "What happened?"

"She wouldn't let them use her to get to me. So she . . . I don't know what she did, b-but she's . . . she's gone." I can't bring myself to tell him the full truth. *My mom killed herself so the Elders couldn't use her to leverage me into turning myself over to them.*

"I . . . I'm sorry."

I nod. "Now you know. So, please." My bottom lip quivers. "I don't want to live with this for another second. It has cost me too much." I sniffle and correct myself. "It has cost me everything."

Remington's jaw is hard, and there's anger in his eyes. "They can't get away with this," he says, his arms falling back to his sides. There's sadness in his voice that surprises me. So much so that I don't know what to do with it.

"What are you saying, Rem?"

He lifts his hand and brushes his thumb along my cheek. "I want you to help me destroy the Elders."

My pulse jumps, and my throat goes dry as he pulls his hand back. "What?"

"They've killed so many of us. Your family . . . and mine."

There it is.

His jaw clenches, and he clears his throat before saying, "Both of my parents." I knew his parents had died like my father did, but I'm not prepared for him to take a shallow breath and say, "And my sister, Aurelia."

"Your sister . . ."

I lost someone close to me, and Kit could have stopped it from happening.

Remington must see me put it together, because he says,

"They dated for a while." His jaw hardens. "And he was with her when the Elders found her."

I'm afraid to ask, but the words fall out of my mouth anyway. "Did he . . . ?"

Pain crackles across his face. "He says he didn't tip them off, but it doesn't really matter. He let them take her."

My lips part in a soft gasp. "I . . ." I don't have time to think about what I'm doing. I close the little distance that remains between us and wrap my arms around his neck, holding him tightly. "I'm so sorry," I murmur, because even as pain flows through my veins, I can't help but want to comfort his loss too.

Remington stiffens, but slowly he relaxes and slides his arms around my waist, dropping his forehead to my shoulder.

I may feel utterly lost in this moment, but I decide one thing for sure. I'm going to help Remington avenge his family—I'm going to avenge *mine*.

CHAPTER SEVENTEEN

One week later, we lay my mom to rest with a small group of her friends at the cemetery in Covington. They believe she passed suddenly from a brain aneurysm, but her death—and the truth of how it happened—continues to weigh heavy on my chest.

Between Nova, Kit, and Samuel, they were able to convince the rest of the Elders to allow me the chance to bury the last member of my family in peace. On the condition that Samuel would return to Roswell with me shortly thereafter.

I didn't tell anyone what happened that night after Samuel brought me back to Helen. When I returned from Remington's, Kit was sitting on the porch. He didn't ask questions when I sat beside him, and I didn't speak either. After learning the part he played in Remington's sister's death, I didn't really know *what* to say. So we sat in silence, watching the darkest parts of the sky fade into morning.

A hand touching mine pulls me back to the present, where Margaret, a woman from my mom's church, is looking at me. Birds chirp in the distance, and the cold air makes me shiver and hold my coat tighter.

Kit leans down and whispers to me, "Do you want to say anything?"

All eyes are on me. I should say something. I have to; my mom gave up everything for me.

With a deep breath, I smooth my hands down the front of my knee-length black dress and walk around the closed black casket, my boots leaving footprints in the small dusting of snow on the ground. Tiny flakes fall from the sky as I turn to face the small crowd.

My lips part in surprise when I see Jessa and Lana huddled together near the back, their eyes glassy and their noses red, either from the cold or from crying, I'm not sure which. *Of course they're here. They didn't forget my mom.* My head spins with the logistics behind the spell Remington did, but I can't focus on that right now.

"Go ahead, honey," Margaret says to me.

I nod without looking at her and start speaking to the crowd. "After my parents died, Holly gave up her life to take me in and raise me." Swallowing the lump in my throat, I continue. "She was there for every major event in my life, and knowing that she won't be anymore . . ." I trail off. I'll end up crying too hard to speak if I go down that road. "She was the most selfless person I've ever met. Everyone in the community loved her, and she adored all of you," I say, looking out across the familiar faces. Nova stands in the second row with Lydia and Mason, and my gaze holds his for a moment. "Living in a small town gives us the unique opportunity to know everyone around us, and I think I can speak for everyone here when I say that we were all exceptionally lucky to have known my mom." My eyes burn as I fight back tears. "Bad things happen. Things that *shouldn't* happen, they just do sometimes. But Holly wouldn't want us to be sad forever. When I think of living the rest of my life—or even just today—without her, it makes me not want to do it, but I know in my heart that it would hurt her if I didn't. I hope you'll join me in remembering the good times, even when it might be easier to cling to the sadness we're all feeling now." My eyes drop to the closed casket as a tear rolls down my cheek. "I'm going to make this right," I whisper, squeezing my eyes shut for a moment until my bottom lip stops trembling.

I walk back to stand next to Kit while the casket is lowered into the ground. Margaret begins a prayer, but I barely hear her. Kit has his arm around me as if he's worried I'm going to collapse. I don't mind it . . . I don't really feel it, actually. It's as if I'm living outside my body. Watching everything from a different perspective. I desperately want to get out of here. Being around my mom's friends while they talk about her and cry over coffee and sandwiches isn't something I can handle.

The minute the service is over, I head for the car. Kit is a few paces behind me, but makes no attempt to catch up. He's giving me space, and I appreciate that more than he probably knows.

"Emery," a familiar voice calls out, and I stop, turning my head to see Lana and Jessa walking toward me. Their eyes are rimmed in red and a little puffy from crying, but they both smile at me.

"Um, hey. Thanks for coming," I say hesitantly, because I figure that's customary.

"Of course," Lana says before throwing her arms around me, hugging me so tight it's hard to breathe, but I don't care. When she pulls back, Jessa replaces her.

"Is there anything we can do?" she asks, rubbing my arms as if she's trying to keep me warm.

You can tell me what's going on. They aren't supposed to remember me. Remington blocked their memories of me. Unless . . .

"My dad made a casserole," Lana says, cutting into my thought spiral. "I was going to drop it off this afternoon."

I force a smile, glancing to where Kit is chatting with

Margaret before looking back at the girls. "That's really nice, thanks."

"It's nothing," she tells me. "I can't imagine what you're going through right now. I'm so sorry we haven't kept in touch." Her brows knit as her gaze flits between Jessa and me. "I don't really know what happened."

I give her shoulder a squeeze. "Please don't worry about it. I'm just so glad you're both here."

The girls wrap me in a group hug, and I close my eyes. I'm not going to speculate on what made Remington decide to lift the spell, but I needed this.

After everything is said and done, Kit takes me back to the house.

"Thanks for being there today," I tell him, taking off my boots and hanging my coat in the front hall closet.

"Of course." His voice is tight. "I'm not sure what happens now, Em. Samuel isn't coming today, but we need to figure out how this is going to work when he does."

I nod. "Can we figure it out tomorrow?"

His expression softens. "Of course." He starts to take his coat off, but I shake my head.

"You should head back to Nova's." I wrap my arms around myself. "I need some time."

"I . . . Are you sure?"

"Yes." I don't meet his gaze. "I'll, uh, call you tomorrow."

Kit hesitates at the door before opening it. "Get some rest."

I stand in the doorway while he walks down the steps and gets into his car. Once he's gone, I shut and lock the door, shuffling into the living room as exhaustion clings to my muscles.

Collapsing on the couch, I stare at the picture frames above the fireplace. The realization that I am truly an orphan now slams into me with the weight of a transport truck. My stomach knots, and a dull, pounding behind my eyes threatens to turn into a migraine at any moment.

I get off the couch and walk aimlessly around the house, stopping in front of my mom's bedroom. I pull the door shut before I can think about stepping inside. Nothing good could come from that right now. I lean against the closed door and slide down until I'm sitting on the floor. This feeling of emptiness is painfully familiar. I don't remember all of the details after my birth mom died, but this hollowness . . . I'll never forget it.

Tipping my head back against the wood, I let out a shaky breath. "I'm not sure how to do this without you," I say, tears gathering in my eyes for what feels like the hundredth time today. "There's still so much I don't know." I sniffle. "I don't know what to do, Mom." Tears wet my cheeks, but I don't bother wiping them away. Instead, I pull my knees up to my chest and drop my forehead onto them, crying harder. I cry until I can't breathe, until I'm choking on tears and gasping for breath.

The sounds fade as exhaustion siphons the energy from me. I lift my head and dry my cheeks before getting off the floor. I walk to my room and grab my duffle bag off the floor, dropping it onto the end of my bed before unzipping it and pulling out Dad's book. Before I can stop myself, I walk back to Mom's room and open the door. I close my eyes for a moment, overwhelmed by the smell of her floral perfume, and then I force myself to refocus.

Mom has always kept an insane amount of candles around the house, so I gather them on her dresser and light them. I open the book, sitting on her bed as I flip the pages. I've been reading it for weeks and still don't have a full grasp of its contents, but I don't have the luxury of time anymore.

I land on one of the pages I dog-eared and read it a few times as I walk around the bedroom, picking up a few of her things. Her favorite book, a hairbrush, and the necklace my birth parents gave her for being the maid of honor at their wedding. I set everything out on the bed and rub my hands together to warm them.

I close my eyes and breathe deeply as I try to focus. I center myself and think about my mom. Everything she's done for me. It's always been from a place of caring and love. All she ever wanted was to keep me safe and make sure I had the best life possible. And in the end, she paid the ultimate price for it—one she shouldn't have had to pay.

I have to fix it.

I open my eyes and scan the worn, handwritten pages of the book. Searching for something that can help me undo it. For anything that will bring her back.

The hair at the back of my neck stands straight as my skin starts to tingle. I hold my breath, closing my eyes with a sigh as I set the book down. "What are you doing here, Rem?" Maybe I should be shocked that he came to Covington, or that he let himself into my house somehow, but I can't find the will to care at this point.

He ignores the question. "You want to tell me what you're doing?"

Blinking my eyes open again, I look over at where he's leaning against the doorframe with his arms crossed over his chest. His dark hair is pushed back, and he's wearing all black— a leather jacket over a V-neck that's so tight it's practically a second skin, and washed-out jeans with combat boots.

"I'm going to fix this," I say, my voice wavering near the end.

Remington frowns at me. "Fix it?"

I finally meet his gaze. "I'm going to bring her back."

His jaw tightens. "The woman you watched being buried just hours ago." He shakes his head. "Emery, you're talking about necromancy. You can't bring someone back from the dead." His voice is gentle, which for some reason fuels the fire in me.

"Why not?" I snap. "She didn't deserve to die!"

He steps into the room, leaving a good amount of space

between us. "Nature has to have a balance. You can't do this without setting that off."

I shake my head. "Our magic isn't based on nature, remember? That's why we're so dangerous." My tone is laced with bitterness.

Remington sighs, letting his arms fall to his sides. "I don't mean it like that. Even if you're somehow able to pull this off, you can't be sure it'll work the way you think it will. I'm so sorry, I am, but your mom is gone. If you bring her back, there's no telling how it will affect her. She won't be the person you knew."

"I don't care," I say through a fresh batch of tears. *I need my mom.*

"And what of you?" he asks, coming closer again. "A spell like this isn't for baby Wielders. It could very well kill you in the process, and then what? What was it for?"

My jaw clenches. "I have to try!"

He pins me with a narrowed gaze. "If you try to go through with this, you could die."

"I can't . . ." My bottom lip trembles. "I don't have anything left to lose, Rem."

His gaze is laser-focused on me as he closes the rest of the distance between us and takes my face in his hands. "That's not true. You have so much ahead of you, and you're going to figure everything out, but not tonight and not like this."

I blink, and tears roll down my cheeks. "I have to try," I choke on my words.

Remington thumbs my tears away. "I'm asking you, please, do not do this."

My eyes flick between his. "You could help me. Maybe if we did the spell together, it would have a better chance of working." Hope blossoms in my chest. I have to believe that with Remington's help we could bring my mom back. I watch his jaw work, and my stomach drops. "But you won't."

"I'm not going to argue with you. This isn't happening. I'm sorry. You need to sleep and to grieve."

More tears spill down my cheeks, and I swallow hard. "Rem, please. She didn't deserve this."

He pulls me against his chest and holds me there while I cry. "I know," he murmurs into my hair.

"Help me," I cry against his shirt. "Please. I'll do anything. Just please, help me bring her back."

He smooths his hand down my hair but says nothing, and I don't have the energy to pull away from him. I grip the front of his shirt and hang on with every ounce of strength I have left.

"Come on," he says softly, pulling away before he guides me out of my mom's room, closing the door behind us. We walk down the hall in silence until we reach my room.

Having the guy from my nightmares standing in my bedroom is an odd thing. Definitely not the weirdest thing to happen since I found out the truth about myself, but still pretty jarring.

I sink onto the end of the bed and run my fingers along the fuzzy blanket under me. "I don't know what to do without her, and I . . . I just thought . . ." I stop talking, shaking my head. "I'm sorry."

Remington walks in and kneels in front of me, placing his hands on my knees and warming my skin. "You never have to apologize to me. Ever."

I blink at him. "You are very confusing." Pushing my fingers through my hair with a sigh, I add, "Can I ask you something?" When he nods, I say, "Jessa and Lana were at the funeral today. They remember me."

"That's not a question, little bird." His tone isn't mocking, and his expression remains impassive.

I glance down to where my hands are sitting in my lap. "Thank you." I probably shouldn't thank him, given he was the one who blocked their memories, but he made the choice to undo it so they could be there for me today.

He nods and captures my chin in his hand, tilting my head back to look him in the eyes. "Get some rest." Remington steps away and turns toward the door.

"Where are you going?" I don't know why my voice is tinged with panic, but it stops him from leaving.

He faces me again. "I should go."

I chew my bottom lip. "What if I want you to stay?"

"Well, I'm not going to curl up in a ball on the floor like a dog." His tone is teasing, but I can't find the will to smile.

"That's not what I meant." I scoot back until I reach the headboard and pull the blankets back on the other side of the bed.

Remington hesitates for a few seconds before walking around the bed. Instead of sliding under the sheets, he pulls them up and sits on the edge of the bed. He removes his shoes before lying on top of the blankets and leans against the headboard, glancing over at me.

"I dreamed of you before we met," I murmur, sliding down until my head rests on the pillow. I'm not sure what makes me tell him, but it's out there now.

Remington stills next to me. "Are you sure?"

I almost laugh, though the situation is as far from funny as it could be. "You think I'd mistake you for someone else?" I shake my head. "That night, when I saw you at the club, I thought I was going crazy. Hallucinating the hauntingly handsome guy from my own personal hellscape."

He just stares at me. "I really don't know what to say to that. What happened in the dream?"

I don't bother telling him that it happened more than once. Glancing past him to the window, I say, "In a nutshell, I kill everyone I care about with dark magic while you stand by and watch."

Remington frowns. "That's—"

"Disturbing? Yeah, I know." I run my fingers through the

blanket between us. "Look, I . . . I'm sorry I painted you as the villain," I say.

"I was," he says. "At least in your story."

"You wanted to get back at the people who stole from you. I understand that now more than ever."

He crosses one leg over the other, letting out a breath. "And I was willing to sacrifice you to get it."

My breath catches. "What made you change your mind?"

A ghost of a smile touches his lips. "You."

A flush creeps across my cheeks. "I guess I should take that as a compliment."

His responding chuckle is soft. "You took me by surprise, that's for sure, little bird."

I roll onto my side, resting my cheek on the pillow as I face him. Something in my chest flutters, and I press my lips together. "And now we're a team. Who would've thought?"

"I don't think your elemental friends are going to be very agreeable to that," he comments.

"I don't care." This is about my family, and I need to make things right. That's all I care about right now.

"Okay," he murmurs, reaching over and brushing his knuckles across my cheek.

I close my eyes at his touch, finding myself wanting to lean in, to lose myself in it. Instead, I open my mouth and ruin the moment. "How are we going to stop the Elders from hurting anyone else?"

His hand stills against my skin before he pulls it away. "We don't need to talk about that right now."

I open my eyes. "They gave me today, but they'll be waiting for me to arrive at their facility. I've still agreed to go to them, but it could be a good thing. Samuel and some of the others want to see change in the way things are handled."

Remington's body stiffens. "And you believe him?"

"The night my mom . . . We were heading toward Roswell

when I found out. Samuel turned the car around and brought me back to Helen. He brought me to you," I add, adjusting the pillow under my head.

"What are you saying?" he asks in a low voice.

I pause, considering it. "I have a way inside, Rem. We can use that to our advantage."

His lips twitch. "Yeah? You gonna go all vigilante on me and try to take them out all by yourself?"

"No," I grumble. "I don't know."

"You should sleep now. Tomorrow is another day." He rests his hands behind his head, closing his eyes as his chest rises and falls with a deep breath.

I lay there watching his face. My eyes fall to his lips, and I press mine together, reminded of the way his kiss sparked something inside of me.

"Emery." His voice slices through the silence. "Not that I mind you staring at me, but there will be plenty of time for that once you've gotten some rest."

My cheeks flush as I roll away and close my eyes. I listen to the sound of our combined breathing and let it lull me into the darkness.

CHAPTER EIGHTEEN

I notice his presence is missing the moment I wake.

I push the blankets off and get out of bed, frowning at the funeral attire I fell asleep in. I strip out of the black dress and get in the shower. I grab an old T-shirt and pair of yoga pants and get dressed before going to the kitchen for coffee. Despite the sadness that clings to me like cobwebs, I smile when I find a fresh pot of coffee already made. Next to the machine is a sticky note with a phone number with the letter 'R' scrawled below it.

I pull out my phone and type, *Thank you.*

You're welcome. A few seconds later, another message comes through. *Did you know you snore?*

My eyes widen. *I do not!*

You definitely do. It's cute.

I narrow my eyes at the screen. *I'm blocking this number.*

If you think that will keep me away, you've learned nothing.

I try to ignore the way that makes my chest flush and type back, *You're such a pain.*

Ha ha. I'll be back later. Taking care of a few things.

The smile slips from my lips. *What things? Should I be worried?*

No need to worry. Enjoy your coffee, little bird.

I bite my lip and consider dialling his number. I can't help but think something isn't right, but I have a feeling he won't tell me over the phone either, so I set my phone down and pour myself a cup of coffee.

After a few bites of cold sympathy casserole, I take my coffee and go upstairs to crawl back into bed. My life feels as if it's at a standstill at this point, and shutting out the world seems like a far easier option than, well, anything else.

I doze in and out of restless sleep for the duration of the morning after checking in with Kit and Nova with a quick text.

My eyes flutter open to the sound of knocking at my front door shortly after noon. I roll over, groaning as I reach for my phone as it rings again. Lana's number lights the screen, so I answer it.

"Hey, Em," she says. "Can we come in?"

"I wasn't planning to see people today," I say around a yawn. "Don't you guys have school?"

"We brought snacks," Jessa says in the background.

I manage a small laugh. "Do you still have a key?" I really don't want to get out of bed.

"Of course. See you in a sec."

The door opens downstairs, and a minute later, Lana and Jessa are walking into my room. Their hands are full of take-out bags and candy.

"Are you trying to comfort me or put me in a sugar coma?"

Jessa smiles, setting her arm full of candy on the end of my bed before kicking off her shoes and crawling in next to me. Lana joins us a minute later with a giant brown bag. She sits cross-legged and digs into the bag, pulling out several containers of fries, handing one to each of us before unwrapping a cheeseburger for herself.

We sit in silence for a few minutes, stuffing our faces with the greasy goodness.

"Thank you for coming," I tell them. "If I'm being honest, I'm pretty lost right now."

Lana sets her half-eaten burger on the foil wrapper. "That makes total sense."

Jessa nods. "We're here for you, whatever you need. We're not going anywhere."

For the afternoon, I allow myself to be distracted by junk food and high school gossip.

I take my mom's car and drive back to Nova's late in the afternoon after texting Remington that I was leaving Covington.

I pull into the driveway a couple hours later, and the front door opens when I beep the lock on the car. Kit steps onto the porch as I approach the steps, slinging my bag over my shoulder.

"I didn't know you were coming back today," he says with an odd edge to his voice.

"I thought . . ." I trail off. "Sorry, I meant to text you."

"No worries. Why don't we go for a walk? Lydia and Mason are out, but I'm sure they'll be happy to see you later."

"It's freezing out here. I just want to get inside. Plus, I need to talk to Nova." I climb the steps, but Kit doesn't move away from the doorway. "What's going on?" I ask.

His jaw works. "Zoe is getting her things. If we knew you were coming back today, Nova never would have allowed it."

I freeze, flexing my fingers to keep from clenching them into fists. "She's here?"

"Emery—"

I shove past him, dropping my bag in the process. My boots thud against the floor as I storm through the house, anger burning in my veins. When I reach her room, I throw the door open without warning.

Zoe sold me out, and now I have nothing.

My focus narrows on where she's throwing clothes into a suitcase, and I snap. Launching myself at her, magic overcomes me in a haze of rage. I feel my control snap in a reverberation of energy, and Zoe whirls around, her eyes wide and blank as if she can't see. Vindication fills me at an alarming rate when she starts screaming, and my fist flies toward her face. I hear a crunch when it smashes into her nose, and blood gushes down her face, covering her mouth and chin, dripping through her fingers as they cradle her face.

I advance again, but someone grabs me around my waist, hauling me away as Zoe falls to her knees, crying in pain.

"Let me go," I shout, clawing at the arm around me as I try to cling to the euphoric energy zipping through me as I somehow continue to manipulate Zoe's vision. I don't want to stop. It feels too good.

"Snap out of it, Emery." Kit's voice is harsh in my ear as he shakes my shoulder with his other hand, and my breath hitches when I whip around and find Nova standing behind us.

Zoe whimpers, looking up at us as recognition flares to life in her red-rimmed eyes. Looks like her sight is back.

Kit pulls me the rest of the way out of the room before I shove away from him. The three of us walk down the front hall and around to Nova's study.

"She deserved that," I say through my teeth. *I would've done a lot worse if Kit hadn't stopped me.* I shiver at the thought, my jaw clenched so tight my temples start to throb.

His brows tug closer as we stop outside the door to the study, and he shakes his head. "This isn't you."

"My mom is dead," I whisper, sniffling as tears blur my vision. "I have no idea who I am."

"Emery," Nova says, and the sadness in his voice makes my chest tighten.

"The Elders won't get away with this without consequence," I vow, following him into the study with Kit walking behind me. "We're going to punish them for what they've done."

Nova frowns before looking at Kit. "I think you should go make sure Zoe finds her way out sooner rather than later."

Kit nods tightly and leaves the room, closing the door behind him.

"Talk to me," Nova says in a gentle tone.

I chew my lip for a few seconds, going back and forth between wanting to trust Nova and being worried this whole thing could backfire if he doesn't see things my way. "I've agreed to help Remington take down the Elders."

Nova pinches the bridge of his nose, his brows knitting. "You know I'll do anything to help protect you, so I need to warn you against that decision."

"Something needs to change. We can try to convince the Elders that dark Wielders don't have to be a threat, but if that doesn't work? Then what?"

"I'm not sure," he says, and I see the pain in his eyes from that admission.

"I don't want a fight, Nova, but if it comes down to it . . ."

A door slams shut, and I jump, glancing toward the window behind Nova's desk in time to see Zoe hurrying down the driveway and getting into a van. It disappears down the drive, and I exhale a slow breath.

Kit returns a minute later, glancing between us. "We need to talk. Sam called me earlier." His gaze focuses on me. "You're not going to the facility."

"What?" I shake my head. "Kit, I agreed to go."

"You're not going there," he repeats, "because they're coming here."

My eyes widen, and my voice rises in pitch. "When? And is that worse or better?"

"Four days from now. They're finishing their facility tours in the Midwest. And I wish I knew what it means. Samuel and Myra and maybe one of the others are open-minded, but the rest, I don't know. He couldn't tell me why they've decided to come, but I think we need to prepare for the worst."

I need to tell Remington.

Turning to Nova, I say, "I'm not going to just sit around and wait for them to come for me." I back toward the door, shaking my head. "I can't." I walk out of his study, ignoring the two of them as they call after me.

I run into Lydia and Mason as I'm leaving through the front door. Lydia wraps me in a hug that I slip out of quickly, promising to talk to her later over my shoulder as I head to my car.

I knock on the door to Remington's loft, and it opens a moment later, revealing him bare-chested. The black sweatpants he has on are sitting dangerously low on his hips, and I have to force my gaze away, because that shouldn't be as attractive as my body seems to think it is. His hair is wet and his cheeks are flushed, as if he just got out of the shower. He tilts his head, his eyes traveling the length of me before focusing on my face.

"Hi," I finally say.

Remington leans against the doorframe, pressing his lips together against a smirk. "Hi." He rubs his jaw, glancing past me into the hallway. "You want to come in?"

I nod. "We need to talk."

He steps aside so I can cross the threshold. My skin sings at the warmth of his loft, and I remove my boots, leaving them near the door.

"Are you hungry?"

"That depends on what you can cook."

His laugh is deep. "I don't cook. I'm excellent at ordering take-out, though."

I turn and look up at him. "Seriously?" My eyes flick to his kitchen, and I'm immediately reminded of the fiery kiss we shared there. "You have an amazing kitchen, and you don't even cook?"

"Sorry to disappoint, little bird."

I shake my head, walking around him and into the kitchen. After searching the fridge and cupboards and coming up empty-handed, I laugh. "Wow," I mumble under my breath. Checking one last cupboard, I find a container of popcorn kernels. It's not exactly a meal, but I'm never one to pass up a salty snack.

I search until I find a pan and set it on the stove, pouring the kernels in before setting a lid on top.

Remington doesn't say a word through the whole thing. He just watches me with a faint smile. He disappears for a few minutes and finds a shirt before he comes into the kitchen and retrieves two glass bottles of Coke from the fridge. He carries them into the living room, and a minute later, the space fills with soft music.

Once the kernels are popped and poured into a giant bowl, I sprinkle them with salt and carry the bowl into the living room. Dropping onto the couch, I cross my legs and set the bowl in my lap.

"I have no idea what I'm supposed to do now," I mumble, shoving a fistful of popcorn into my mouth. *How do I tell him the Elders are coming here?* We haven't had a chance to discuss what we're going to do about them, and with Samuel and a couple of the others potentially leaning toward our side, I'm not sure how to broach the topic.

"You do whatever it takes to survive."

I stop mid-chew and turn to face him. "Is that what you're doing?" I swallow before setting the bowl on the coffee table.

He holds my gaze. "Some days." The corner of his mouth kicks up. "Today, however, is going significantly better than I was expecting."

I roll my eyes. "Shut up. I'm being serious. My future has literally been shot to hell. Our magic comes with a death sentence, and I—"

Remington lifts his hand to my face, grasping my chin. "You have so much to learn." He licks his lips, leaning closer as his gaze drops to my mouth. "And I fully intend to teach you everything."

My breath hitches. "Why do I get the feeling you're not entirely talking about magic?"

He chuckles. "A beautiful girl once told me I underestimate my charm, so I've been working really hard to lean into it. Seems to be working in my favor."

"You're really asking for me to dump that bowl of popcorn on your head," I remark dryly, knocking away his grip.

"Go for it," he challenges.

"Nah," I say after a beat of silence. "I like popcorn too much."

"Right." He rests his arm along the back of the couch, and his fingers brush my shoulder. "What'd you want to talk about?"

I scratch at my arm. "We need to figure out how to pull off this thing with the Elders."

"This thing," he echoes.

"Samuel told Kit they're coming here in four days." When his jaw clenches, I reach for the hand resting against his knee. "I want to make them suffer for what they did to us, Rem, but I . . . If there's a way to avoid a fight, we need to consider it." I still need to learn more about my magic, but I'd rather do that without the assumption that I'll be using it to potentially kill someone.

His gaze narrows on my hand on top of his. "You are a much better person than I am."

"What are you talking about?" I ask, pulling my hand back.

He shakes his head. "I've lived with this hate in my chest for so long."

"Do you think killing them all will let it out?"

His eyes meet mine, and I struggle to read the emotion in them. Sadness, maybe? "I don't know," he says.

I lean forward, brushing my fingers along his cheek as my pulse races. I have no idea what I'm doing, but I want to be closer to him. To taste his lips again.

"What are you up to, little bird?" he murmurs.

I bite my bottom lip and drop my hand into my lap. "I've never kissed anyone but you," I whisper.

It takes him a second, but recognition flares to life in his gaze. "Was that . . . ? No. That wasn't your first kiss."

"Yeah," I say quietly.

His thumb brushes along my bottom lip, his eyes so focused on my face I'm still struggling to find my breath. Remington leans in until I can feel his breath against my lips. "I didn't deserve to be your first, but hell do I want to do it again."

"Kiss me." The words fall from my mouth and my pulse spikes.

He cups the side of my face and rests his forehead against mine as if he's holding himself back.

I tire of waiting for him and fill the space between us. I brush my lips against his slowly, tentatively. He curls his hand around my neck and pulls me across the cushion until I'm flush against him, swallowing my moan of surprise as he deepens the kiss. My eyes close, and I press my hands against his chest, gripping his shirt between my fingers as I lean into him. His thumb brushes along my jaw, and my world narrows on the warmth spreading through me. I never want it to end.

"We should stop," I say against his lips. My voice is thick, and the fact I'm still kissing him gives my words very little impact on both of us.

"Mmm." He drags his tongue along my lower lip before nipping it. "So stop then."

I grip his shirt in my fist, trying to will myself to pull away from him. I groan. "I don't want to."

He kisses me harder for a brief, incredible moment, and then he pulls back, resting his forehead on mine. "You're right."

"Huh?" I ask, breathless, finally blinking my eyes open to look at him.

He chuckles deeply. "We need to put a pin in this for now, little bird."

Subdued annoyance flickers through me. *Since when is Remington the voice of reason?*

"Don't give me that look. I'm being good."

I roll my eyes. "I know."

"Good." He leans back into the cushions, pulling me with him so we're . . . cuddling?

"This is weird," I say after a few minutes.

His laugh vibrates against my back. "Only because you're making it weird."

I turn my head so I can look at his face. "If we're going to hang out, maybe we should talk about—"

"Nope," he cuts in. "Not tonight."

"Okay." I drag out the word. "We're just going to—"

"You need to take a beat. Just relax, okay?" He brushes my hair back. "All of our problems will still exist tomorrow. Don't worry about them now."

"I—" I stop myself and exhale slowly. "All right," I finally say.

The last thing I expected to be doing tonight was cuddling on Remington's couch and watching old sitcoms, but here we are.

I doze off at some point, my eyes too heavy to keep open. When they flicker open, I'm faintly aware of being held in

Remington's arms. He carries me down the hall into a bedroom and lays me on the bed, pulling blankets over me before walking out, closing the door behind him.

As I fall back to sleep, a flicker of fear settles over me when it dawns on me that I've grown to care for someone I never expected—someone I have the potential to lose if things go wrong with the Elders.

CHAPTER NINETEEN

I shouldn't feel cheap for sneaking out of Remington's loft if we didn't do anything, right? That would be silly. But when I wake in his bedroom with the sun just starting to rise outside his window, I panic.

Tiptoeing into the main living space, my breath catches when my eyes land on Remington asleep on the couch. He looks so peaceful, I can't help but stare.

I shake my head, hurrying toward the door. The idea of having to face him in this moment makes my pulse race.

Shoving my feet into my boots, I grab my coat and slip out the door before pulling it on. I don't stop moving until I get behind the wheel of my car. Last night was a nice distraction, but now I have to return to the real world, which means I need to practice the hell out of my magic until the last possible moment. I'll come back and work with Remington later, but I want to practice alone for a while.

I drive in the direction of Nova's, but instead of pulling into his driveway, I keep going until I reach the end of the road and park my car at the dead end. I get out, zipping up my coat before grabbing my bag from the back seat.

The wind chills me to the bone as I walk through the snow-covered brush and into the clearing, heading for the mausoleum. I'm not sure why I came here. Maybe my magic remembers this place. Regardless, I walk down the stone steps and push the door open, pulling Dad's book out before dropping my bag on the floor.

I flip through some of the pages I've read dozens of times already and land on a page of intricate spells, picking one that allows the Wielder to manipulate physical objects. I flatten the pages and rub my hands together, taking a deep breath before skimming the pages in an attempt to memorize the words.

I close my eyes, reciting the words in my head a few times before speaking them aloud as I focus on moving the stone tomb in front of me. The first couple of tries, nothing happens. Frustration builds in my chest, but I force it down, pulling in a steadying breath. I shake my arms, trying to force the tension out of my muscles so I can try again.

After another few failed attempts, I try another method. Closing the book, I set it on one of the tombs and step forward to place my palms against the stone. I drag in a slow breath and repeat the words under my breath, focusing on the rough surface under my hands. The cold stone heats against my palms, and I repeat the spell, finally feeling as if it could be working. I continue the spell, and my chest tightens with a mix of nerves and excitement . . . until the ground starts rumbling beneath my feet.

I grit my teeth, keeping my eyes shut against the panic slithering through me. I knew this wouldn't be easy, but I can't give up now. I know I can do it; I just have to keep going.

Stones chip off the walls, falling to the floor of the crypt, and the air gets heavier with dust.

Come on, Emery. You can do this. Focus. Breathe.

A sharp sound like nails on a chalkboard fills the space, and I clamp my hands over my ears, squeezing my eyes shut, but I don't stop the spell.

"Emery!" a deep voice shouts over the horrific sound.

My eyes fly open to find Remington standing in front of me, gripping my shoulders.

"What are you doing?" His eyes are blazing with emotion. I'm not given the opportunity to consider what it is. "We have to get out of here!"

I shake my head in confusion as the ear-pitching sound quiets to a dull groan.

"The mausoleum is going to collapse," he says, pulling on my arm. "We have to get out *now*." He doesn't wait for me to respond before hauling me up the stairs.

"What are you doing?" I shriek. "My dad's book is still down there! I have to go—"

The rumbling in the ground intensifies, and in a matter of seconds, the stone building collapses in on itself, leaving a thick cloud of dust in its wake.

I try to cover my face, but my lungs are still heaving, and I cough until the dust begins to settle. "No," I croak. "What did I do?"

Remington has his arm around me, holding me to his side. "What were you thinking?"

I pull out of his grasp and glare at him. "I was trying to turn the stone into marble. I didn't think . . . How did this happen?"

"Oh my god, Emery!" Lydia appears at the tree line and sprints toward us, Kit on her heels. "What happened?" she asks frantically, pulling back and glancing between Remington and me—and the destroyed stone structure.

"Uh, just a little spell mishap," I offer. "I'm fine."

Kit's eyes are narrowed on Remington. "Is this the kind of magic you're teaching her? To destroy things simply because you have the power to do so?"

"Kit," I cut in before Remington can say anything. "He saved my life." The words taste foreign on my tongue. "I was practicing on my own."

"I felt a surge in her magic," Remington explains, staying close to my side.

"He got here and pulled me out just before the building went down." I glance toward the rubble, still surrounded by dust. "I would be under all of that if he hadn't been here."

Lydia gasps. "I'm just glad you're okay."

I nod. "What are you guys doing out here?"

"We were training in the yard and heard the collapse." Her gaze sweeps between the guys before she says to Kit, "We should go tell Nova what happened."

He's looking at me. "You sure you're okay?"

"I lost my dad's book," I say, frowning. "I'm alive, though, so I guess."

His frown mirrors mine. "We'll try to get it back. It'll take some time, but I'll do my best. I know what that book means to you."

A lump forms in my throat. "Thank you."

He nods. "Nova was worried about you yesterday after you left. He wants you to come back, but understands that may not be easy for you now."

I bite the inside of my cheek. "I'll talk to him."

"Are you going to tell me what's going on?" he asks, looking toward Remington for a beat before turning back to me. "It would help if everyone was on the same page." He pushes his fingers through his hair before sliding his hands into the pockets of his jacket. "We'll go let Nova what happened." With that, he and Lydia head back to the house.

My gaze swings to Remington. "Um, thanks for . . . you know."

The corner of his mouth quirks into what I can only describe as a half-smirk. "For saving your life? You're welcome."

"Right," I mumble. *Great.* I have a feeling I'm not going to hear the end of this for a while.

I get a text from Lana while we're walking back to my car and frown.

"What's that for?" Remington asks.

I glance up, spotting what I figure is his car parked twenty feet away. "It's Jessa's birthday." I pull my keys out of my pocket and unlock the car. "I completely forgot. Lana wants to take her out tonight."

"You should go," he says.

"Really? Even with—"

"If things go south, you're going to wish you'd spent this time with your friends."

"What about practicing my magic?"

He opens his mouth, then pauses. "The reality is that your magic isn't going to grow in the next two days. You can practice certain spells so they're more familiar to you, but your abilities aren't going to grow to great heights in the time we have."

"What you're saying is, either way I'm screwed, so I might as well go eat some cake?"

His lips twitch. "Luckily for you, I've been practicing and using my magic for almost five years, and we're stronger together. We'll practice before the Elders come."

I hesitate, but ultimately, he's right. These are the important moments.

In Covington later that afternoon, I walk to the town square and move from store to store looking for a birthday gift.

I'm coming out of the flower shop my mom used to bring me to when a girl who looks to be around my age bumps into me, and I almost drop the bundle of calla lilies I'd picked up for Jessa.

"Sorry, I—" she starts, stopping when I reach out with my free hand to steady her, jerking back when a shock runs through me. "It's you," she whispers in disbelief, her hazel eyes wide. The blond-haired guy next to her pulls her away from me, and I frown.

I blink at them in surprise. Covington isn't exactly a large city. Everyone pretty much knows everyone. Even still, I say, "Do I know you?"

"You're like us," the guy says, and my gaze snaps toward him.

"What did you just say?"

His eyes are the color of wet sand, and they're currently narrowed at me. "We were passing through Georgia on our way to Houston and this morning, we felt a surge of magic."

Panic whips through me, and I take an instinctive step away from them. "I'm not sure what you're talking about."

"Whatever magic you did, it left an impression," the girl says, glancing around. "Perhaps there's somewhere more private we could talk?"

"Hold on." I shake my head. "You're telling me that you're both—"

"Wielders. Just like you. Yes."

I stare at them, stunned. It takes me a few seconds to pull myself together before I say, "How do I know what you're saying is true?"

The girl tilts her head, watching me. "You didn't feel my magic when we touched?" She holds out her arm. "Touch me again."

Hesitantly, I reach out, and the moment our skin touches, a familiar zing of energy ripples through me. The guy offers his arm next, and I experience the same feeling.

I pull my hand back as my head spins. "Okay then. Uh . . ." I shove my hand into my bag and pull out a pen and an old receipt. I scribble down my address and hand it to the girl. I'm not exactly living there right now, so I figure it's a safe enough place to meet. And I don't plan on meeting them alone anyway. "Come by in a few hours, and we can talk."

They exchange a glance before nodding. "We'll see you then."

As we go our separate ways, my heart in my throat, I fumble getting my phone out of my back pocket. I speed walk toward home as the line rings through to Remington's voicemail. Crap.

"Call me back. Now." My voice shakes, and I end the call. I send a quick text letting Lana know I probably won't be able to make it tonight before tossing my phone into my bag along with the flowers. I try to take a deep breath, but my chest is rising and falling too fast.

More Wielders like Remington and me. We knew there were some out there, but I wasn't prepared to come face-to-face with them today.

I'm climbing the porch steps when my ringtone chimes, and I snatch my phone out of my bag. "Rem," I breathe. "I may have just made a terrible mistake."

"Slow down, little bird. Take a breath and tell me what happened."

I hold the phone to my ear with my shoulder as I dig my keys out to unlock the front door and step inside, closing it behind me. "How fast can you get to Covington?"

"Emery?" The concern in his voice makes my chest tighten.

I exhale heavily, still trying to catch my breath. "How fast, Rem?"

I hear the sound of keys jingling and then a door slamming.

"I'm on my way."

CHAPTER TWENTY

I'm pacing the living room when Remington arrives, walking into the house as if he lives here. He closes the distance between us, his eyes dark.

"Tell me again what happened," he demands. "Every detail."

I rake my fingers through my hair, not surprised to find the curls tangled. "I was in the town square when this girl bumped into me. She was with a guy and they . . . they said they were like me—like us."

His jaw hardens. "Emery—"

I cringe. "They'll be here in half an hour."

"Are you insane?" His gaze slices through me, icy and intense. So much so that I want to look away.

"What else was I supposed to do? We couldn't exactly stand around in the town square and talk about magic, now could we?"

"So your first thought was to invite them to your home? Complete strangers."

"Can you quit being an asshole for a minute, please? They knew about that spell I did. The one that destroyed the mausoleum."

His brows knit. "That doesn't mean they're like us."

"I felt their magic, Rem. I believe them."

He opens his mouth to respond, but there's a knock at the door accompanied by the familiar tingle of magic—they're early.

I bite my lip. "Well, it looks like we're about to find out if they're on our side."

Remington's eyes narrow. "You drive me crazy, you know that? Always getting into trouble."

"Says the guy who has caused most of it," I shoot back before heading toward the door.

Remington catches my wrist and pulls me back. "Nope. You stay in here. I'll assess the situation and figure out what we're dealing with."

"Who do you think you are? This is *my* house."

He shakes his head. "I'm not going to argue with you, little bird." Pointing toward the couch, he says, "Go sit. And stay."

My face contorts into a scowl, but before I can speak, Remington scoops me up and walks over to the couch, dumping me onto the cushions. He's gone before I can grab him, and I'm left seething. *You'll pay for that one.*

Remington opens the door and steps outside, pulling it shut behind him.

I scramble off the couch and rush to the window, hiding in the curtains as I try to hear what they're saying. I can pull apart three distinct voices, but the actual words are muffled. Damn it.

I close my eyes and focus on the sounds in an attempt to manipulate their voices so they're loud enough for me to hear, but the moment it starts to work, there's a break in the conversation. The front door opens.

I try to move away from the window, but my foot gets caught in the curtains and my ass ends up on the floor just as the three of them walk into the living room.

Remington is wearing the most annoying grin I've ever seen, while the others are smiling politely. It's definitely forced, but I have to appreciate the fact they aren't laughing at me.

"What did I say?" Remington directs at me.

I pull myself out of the curtains and stand, pinning him with a glare. "Oh, we'll talk about that later. Don't you worry." I turn my attention to the girl. "Thank you for coming." I extend my hand as I step toward. "I'm Emery. Sorry, I probably should have introduced myself earlier. I'm sure you can understand how unprepared I was to meet you guys."

She shakes my hand. "Of course. It's no problem. My name is Adeline. It's totally crazy but really cool to meet you."

I crack a smile. "Likewise."

The guy offers me his hand next, and I shake it. "Matthew," he says in greeting.

I finally look at Remington. "You satisfied they aren't here to kill us?"

He inclines his head ever so slightly, his gaze locked on me.

"Great." Looking back toward the newcomers, I ask, "Can I get you both something to drink? I was going to put on a pot of coffee." It's pretty close to dinnertime, but I could use the boost of caffeine for this conversation.

"Sure," Matthew says, smiling. "Ads doesn't drink caffeine, but I drink enough for both of us."

"You don't? Wow, I think you're the first person my age I've met who doesn't."

She smiles shyly. "It, um, affects my abilities. The caffeine triggers my anxiety, and that mixed with the type of magic we possess—it doesn't bode well for going undetected."

"Of course. I understand. If you guys want to take a seat in the living room, I'll get that coffee started." I touch her arm. "I have some herbal tea, if you want?"

"That'd be great, thanks."

I nod before walking into the kitchen. Once I've put on the kettle and started the coffee machine, I pull down four mugs and set them on the counter.

My body tenses when Remington steps into the room, ever

aware of his presence. I keep my back to him, still pissed about the stunt he pulled when Adeline and Matthew arrived.

Remington walks closer, so close his body heat warms my back. "You're mad."

I close my eyes, clenching my jaw. "Yeah."

"Turn around and look at me." His lips are level with my ear, making me shiver.

"No," I force out. If I look at him, I'm either going to slap that smirk I know he's wearing clear off his face or kiss him. And I'm not going to risk the latter when I'm still this annoyed with him.

His hand lands on my hip, and my breathing hitches. "Inviting them here was reckless."

I spin around before I can stop myself, glowering at him. "Are you kidding?" I hiss. "What does it even matter now? We know they're not a threat. They're in as much danger as we are."

He grips the counter on either side of me, caging me in. "You got lucky it turned out this way."

My eyes narrow at his condescending tone. "Oh yeah? What would you have done if they were a threat?"

"I would have killed them." He doesn't hesitate. His voice doesn't waver.

"You—"

Remington tilts his head, his eyes searching mine. "What is it, little bird? You seem surprised."

"You speak so easily of killing," I whisper.

"I will protect what matters to me."

My gaze snaps back to his, my cheeks and chest flushed and my heart hammering beneath my breast. "Oh."

His lips curl into a grin. "You're cute."

I open my mouth to tell him off, but the whistle of the kettle stops me. Remington pushes off the counter, pouring two cups of coffee and carrying them into the other room, leaving me to catch my breath.

With Adeline's tea steeped and my coffee poured, I wait for my complexion to feel somewhat normal before walking back into the living room. I sit in the chair that puts me as far away from Remington as possible. I need a clear head right now, and he's been making that rather difficult as of late.

"So," I say, starting the conversation we're all here for, "you found me because of a spell I screwed up."

Adeline takes a sip of her tea before setting the mug on the old wood coffee table separating us. "Whatever you did, it sent out a shockwave of power."

I frown. "I destroyed a mausoleum."

Matthew's eyes widen. "No way." He sounds . . . impressed?

"Emery isn't familiar with her own strength when it comes to magic," Remington comments.

I ignore that and instead ask, "If you felt it, who's to say others didn't, too?"

Adeline arches a brow. "Are you aware of other dark Wielders in the area?"

"No," Remington says, his eyes on the mug in his hands.

She nods. "You're the first we've come across in a long time." She looks at me. "How long have you two known each other?"

"Oh, uh, not too long. It's kind of a complicated story."

Remington smirks from behind his mug, but says nothing.

"Perhaps one for another time," she suggests, offering me a little grin.

I nod. "Listen, I wanted you both to come because things around here have sort of come to a head with the Elders. At least, they're about to."

Matthew's eyes narrow, and he shifts closer to Adeline. "What does that mean?"

I tell them what went down with the Elders, losing my mom, and about Samuel leaning toward change.

"The Elders signed the Accords to protect both Wielders and

humans. What if we can prove to them we're only as dangerous as the others? If they can see we just want to live our lives, maybe they'll amend the Accords and deem our existence, you know, not illegal."

Matthew crosses his arms over his chest. "I don't see that happening."

"I realize how outlandish it sounds, but not all of the Elders agree with the way things are done now."

"That doesn't mean they'll suddenly be cool with us," Adeline says, glancing at Matthew. "I don't know about this."

I tap my thumb against the side of my mug. "It's risky, I know. But—"

"It's not a good idea," Remington says, his voice firm.

"Do you have a better one?" I challenge.

"You know I do."

"No," I say, "your idea to destroy the Elders is suicidal."

"Sounds about the same as yours."

"Destroy them?" Adeline asks, her voice cracking. "How?"

"They aren't immortal," Remington points out.

I rake my fingers through my hair, my chest tightening with frustration. "If we want change, I don't think we should go into this on the offense. Be prepared to defend ourselves if necessary, yes, but if we walk into it expecting a fight, that's exactly what's going to happen."

"I don't want to fight," Adeline says in a quiet voice. "What about Samuel? Is he willing to stand up for us?"

I want to say yes, but I really don't know. When it comes right down to it, will Samuel turn his back on the others to pursue the change he believes in? I'd like to think so, but we can't hitch our lives on that.

"The Elders are coming here in a few days, so I suppose we'll find out soon enough," Remington says, his jaw set tight.

I fight the urge to roll my eyes; he's really not helping. "You don't have to stay or take part in this. I understand it's not a small thing."

Matthew and Adeline exchange a glance before Matthew says, "We want to help, but there's just so much on the line. Can we think about it?"

"Of course." I school my expression, trying not to let them see the disappointment weighing heavy on my chest.

Adeline pulls out her phone, holding it out to me. "I realize we didn't have a chance to do this earlier. If you want to give me your number, we can keep in touch. Matt and I have a room at one of the bed and breakfasts in town."

I save myself as a contact and hand it back. The two of them stand and head for the door, Remington and I following.

Once they're gone, Remington exhales through his nose, snaring me in his gaze. "What am I going to do with you?"

"With me?" I jab a finger into the middle of his chest. "What am *I* going to do with *you*?"

He grins, sliding his hand up my forearm, and he pulls me in. "I have a few ideas."

Parts of me like the sound of that *way* too much.

"Maybe once we survive the end of the world?" I offer in a cheeky tone.

The grin slips off his lips as he sighs, dropping his forehead to mine and closing his eyes. "I'm sorry you were dragged into this life, little bird. You deserve so much better."

"Hey," I say, pulling back so I can look at him, "we're going to figure this out. I refuse to run and hide for the rest of my life. I'm eighteen years old. I want to graduate high school and go to college. Build a life for myself."

He nods. "You're very optimistic."

A smile touches my lips, and I press my palm against his chest, over his heart. "This is going to work because I refuse to accept any other outcome."

"You are incredible," he says softly.

"And you . . . aren't as terrible as I initially thought," I offer with a faint grin.

He pouts. "Mean."

I reach up and push my fingers through his hair, cupping the back of his neck as I lean into him. "You're growing on me," I admit in a whisper before pressing my lips against his.

Whatever comes next, at least we have this moment of shared peace before the chaos.

CHAPTER TWENTY-ONE

We drive back to Helen mid-morning the next day. I was a ball of nerves when we left Covington, so we took Remington's car, and he drove.

I text back and forth with Adeline during the trip, but she still isn't sure what they're going to do. I decide we can't count on them to show up, but send them Nova's address anyway—just in case.

Later that afternoon, Remington paces the living room of his loft as we wait for Kit to show up.

"I know this isn't what you wanted. But the whole revenge thing—it wouldn't have ended well, Rem. It wouldn't have brought your sister back. Not to mention the fact that you would have been killed, and everyone like us would still be forced to live in secret, fearing for their lives."

He stares ahead and continues pacing. "Yep."

I deliberately step into his path, making him stop so he doesn't plow me down. "Can you please say something else?" I snap, my voice cracking.

His jaw works as he drops his steeled gaze to meet mine. "What would you like me to say, little bird?"

My brows knit as I stare at him. "I don't know." I take a step closer, sliding my hands up the length of his chest and draping them over his shoulders. "I want this to work. And I want to know that *you* want this to work. But I think we both know there's a strong chance it won't, and then we'll have to run and keep running until we can come up with another plan."

He frowns. "What we both know is that I'm no good for you."

I freeze. "Where did that come from?"

"I thought about it the entire drive here. You'd have a better chance convincing the Elders to change their minds about dark Wielders without me. I've built a less-than-desirable reputation over the years, not to mention the prejudice they have against me because of the crimes my parents committed. The thought of that jeopardizing your chance at freedom . . ."

I grip the hair at the back of his neck as I lean up on my tiptoes. "Stop it. I don't care about any of that, okay? I'm not going anywhere." I lower my voice. "I'm not going to leave you behind, Rem."

He exhales through his nose. "You're going to ruin me," he whispers in a heavy tone, then shakes his head. "No, *I'm* going to ruin *you*." Dropping his gaze to mine again, the raw darkness there threatens to steal the air from my lungs. Gripping my chin in his hand, he tilts my face toward him. "And the worst part? I'm going to enjoy every depraved minute of it."

I swipe my tongue over my bottom lip, afraid and unable to look away from him. "Rem," I breathe, my voice trembling.

His hand is shaking against my skin. "Tell me to go, Emery. Tell me to walk away from you right now."

This is his loft, but he's right. That's what I should do. Based on what he's said, my best chance at survival is to walk away.

Then why haven't I said it? Why haven't I run in the other direction every time he's come around?

His eyes fall to where I'm biting my lip. "You can't."

I shake my head.

"Well," he says, tipping my head back and leaning toward me, "let's watch the world burn to ash at our feet."

Before I can utter a word, his mouth is on mine, and everything is set ablaze.

Our hands are everywhere. His mouth jumps between my neck and my mouth, trailing along my jaw and nipping at my bottom lip. He snakes an arm around my waist and hauls me against him as I push my fingers through his hair, tipping my head back to deepen the kiss.

There's an abrupt knock at the door that breaks us apart, our chests heaving. "To be continued," I mumble, and Remington smirks at me as he walks to the door. I lift my fingers to touch my tingling lips and cringe when the door opens to reveal Kit. One look at me and he'll know what we were up to before he arrived.

"Kit the cat," Remington drawls, opening the door wider. "I'd say welcome to my humble abode, but I really don't like that you're here, so then I'd be lying and that wouldn't be nice."

Kit narrows his eyes at Remington, but doesn't say anything as he walks past him into the loft, his eyes landing on me.

"Hey," I say, sliding my hands into my pockets. "Have you heard any more from Samuel? Does he think they'll at least consider an amendment to the Accords?"

"He isn't very confident, but it's the only chance we have."

"And if it doesn't work," Remington says in a low tone, "Emery and I will be on the first flight away from here, and you will never see us again."

"Rem," I say, shaking my head. "Please."

"He's right," Kit says.

"Yeah, fine, but we still have to try."

His jaw works as he glances between me and Remington. "You should probably stay here until this is over. It would appear to be the safest place for you. Remington has somehow managed to evade the Elders for some time."

"Because I'm awesome. That, and because the Elders aren't as smart as they want everyone to believe. A simple cloaking spell, and I'm able to manipulate how people see this place." His gaze settles on me, and suddenly it feels as if Kit isn't even here. "You're welcome to stay here, though I think you already knew that."

My pulse ticks faster as I nod at him. "I'll have to grab a few things from Nova's."

"I'll drop them off tomorrow," Kit says. "I'll let you know if I hear anything else from Sam." He turns his attention to Remington. "You understand this means you will have to follow the rules and live by the Accords, or you'll end up an enemy of the Elders once again, and you'll drag Emery down with you."

"Watch your tone, Harris," Remington growls. "I know full well the magnitude of this situation. I don't need your high and mighty attitude."

Kit averts his gaze, and his tone softens. "I'm just saying—"

"Don't bother," Remington cuts him off. "You have some nerve acting like you're better than us, especially after—" He stops mid-sentence, shaking his head. "Forget it," he grumbles under his breath before walking away. A few seconds later, the door to his bedroom slams shut.

I let out a heavy sigh and look at Kit.

"He's always going to hate me, Em," he says with a grimace. "I'll never be able to make up for what happened to Aurelia."

My forehead creases. "Is that why you've always tried so hard with me? You're trying to make up for what happened to Remington's sister?"

A muscle works in his jaw as he shoves his hands in his jacket pockets. "I don't know. Maybe on some level?" He stares at his shoes for a moment before looking back up at me. "Where does this leave us? Are we . . . I mean, can we still be friends?"

"Of course." It's something I'm still conflicted with, but Kit helped me through one of the hardest parts of my life. And while he caused one of the hardest parts of Remington's life, he's always been there for me. I don't care for Kit in the same way I do Remington—I know that now—but there will always be a space in my heart for Kit simply because of that.

"I'm sorry things didn't end up differently between us," he says.

I don't return the sentiment, but I do say, "I know, but it's okay. Really."

He offers a small smile. "I should go. I'll see you soon, okay?" When I nod, he adds, "Please take care of yourself."

"You too," I tell him as we walk to the door. I close it behind him, flipping the lock over, and am surprised to find tears gathering in my eyes.

Standing outside Remington's bedroom door, I hesitate to knock. Maybe I should leave him alone. This whole thing must be dragging up a lot of unwanted emotions and difficult memories of his sister. Though maybe he needs the comfort of knowing someone is here for him, that he's not experiencing these feelings alone. I bite my lip, battling the uncertainty.

"Are you going to continue to stand at my door?" Remington's voice is muffled through the wood. "I can see the shadow of your feet."

I open the door a crack, sticking my head inside. "I wasn't sure if you would want me to come in, but I needed to make sure you were okay." I step into the room, closing the door behind me.

Remington is sitting on the end of his bed. His hair is a wild mess of darkness, almost as if he was in here gripping it between his fingers, though I suppose some of the mess could've been made by me earlier.

"Come here," he murmurs, his eyes locked on me.

I couldn't disobey if I wanted to, not under that stare. I close the distance between us, standing before him, and he leans in until his forehead touches my stomach. "Rem?" I ask, my voice filled with worry. "Talk to me."

"Little bird . . ." he whispers. "You are too good for me."

I crouch, taking his face in my hands. "Don't say that. We've both done things we aren't proud of."

"I wanted to kill him," he says. "Standing in my living room while he was here, I thought about it. About how good it would feel to watch the life drain from his eyes." His dark brows tug closer, and the exhaustion in his eyes rips into my chest. "You are light and warmth, and if you stay here, I'll destroy it. I will destroy you."

My heart is hammering against my ribcage as I stand and then lower myself onto his lap, still holding his face between my hands. My thumbs brush along the stubble at his jaw. "Do you think so low of me that you believe you could destroy whatever it is you see in me?"

Pain contorts his face, and he grips my hips. "That isn't it at all."

"Then what?"

He shakes his head in my grasp. "I would give you the world. Anything you could imagine, I would die to make it yours, but . . ." He drops his chin. "I can't love you the way you deserve. I lost that part of me when my sister was taken from me, and I am sorry for that."

My throat goes dry as my eyes burn with fresh tears. "I'm not going anywhere, Rem. You're not going to lose me."

"Where have you been?" His words are a gentle whisper as he lowers his face to mine and kisses me until my head spins.

Everything happens so quickly and yet almost in slow

motion as we undress, exploring each other with soft touches and kisses.

Remington leans back enough to look me in the eyes. "Are you sure?"

I hold his gaze, nodding. "Yes." My fingers brush along his cheeks as my heart beats so fast it could break free of my chest at any moment. "I'm not really sure about anything else right now, but you . . . I'm sure about you."

Remington drops a gentle kiss to my forehead.

My heart pounds against my ribcage, both from nerves and excitement. "I've never done this before," I whisper.

He freezes above me, his hair hanging in his face. "Should I stop?" His gaze holds mine. "I don't want to rush this. You need to be sure."

I swallow. "I am," I assure him, pulling him to me. "Just . . . go slow."

He nods, kissing me again. "I'm glad I'm your first," he murmurs against my lips.

"First and only," I say, kissing him back, and the realization that I never want to be with anyone else steals my breath anew.

I lay in Remington's arms after being overcome with the most intense sensations I've ever experienced.

"Whatever happens with the Elders and whatever time I have left on this earth, I will spend it trying to be all that you deserve and more."

My lips part in a silent gasp, and I lean up to press my lips against his in a whisper of a kiss. "It's going to work," I say. "And if it doesn't . . ." I shake my head. "I will do everything in my power to take them down. Whatever it takes."

Remington smirks. "Easy, little bird. You talk so easily of treason, I'm a little worried I'm rubbing off on you."

I roll my eyes at his sarcastic tone. "I'm serious."

He presses his forehead to mine. "I have no doubt." He shifts beside me, wrapping his arm around my waist and pulling me against him.

I snuggle in, resting my cheek on his bare chest to listen to the steady beat of his heart. "We could just stay here forever," I suggest, yawning.

"I would give up just about everything to make that possible if I could." He smooths his hand down my hair, and I close my eyes. "You can sleep," he says, amusement making his tone soft and light.

I swallow another yawn. "I'm not tired." I don't want to sleep. Not when my reality is this.

"Uh-huh," he murmurs, pressing his lips against the side of my head.

As much as I try to fight sleep, eventually my body gives in, fading away while Remington holds me in his arms.

***

The only thing better than falling asleep in Remington's arms is waking up in them. And if you had told me a month ago I'd feel this way, I would have cackled in your face.

Remington is sleeping soundly when I open my eyes. We're facing each other with his arm draped over my waist.

I watch his chest rise and fall evenly for a few breaths before my eyes lift to his face. He looks so calm. Dark lashes fan his olive-toned cheeks, and his hair sweeps across his forehead in a mess of obsidian waves. We're only a few years apart in age, but he looks younger than he is when he's asleep. My fingers itch to reach out and touch his cheek, but I don't want to wake him. Something tells me we're not going to get much rest in the coming days. Nothing about what we're about to get ourselves into is going to be easy. Remington said we're prepared to run, but the idea of fleeing and leaving my friends behind yet again makes me want to cry.

Remington stirs, stretching slowly, and his arm tightens around me as if he needs to make sure I'm still here. When his eyes open, my breath catches at the heat in his gaze.

"Good morning," I murmur.

He drags his tongue over his bottom lip before grinning at me. "It certainly is."

I shake my head, my cheeks flushing as he pulls me against him and kisses my forehead. "You sleep okay?" I mumble.

"Never better, little bird. You?"

I nod in response.

"Are you hungry?" he asks, his fingers tracing along my bare stomach.

"I . . ." My eyes drop to the movement, and my throat goes dry. "Sure," I force out.

"Prepare to have your mind blown."

"What?" I squeak.

"The food," he says, his eyes sparkling with amusement.

"I thought you didn't cook," I point out.

He shrugs. "Breakfast is the exception. It's the superior type of food, after all."

I can't argue with that.

He untangles himself from me and gets out of the bed, walking toward the door. "You just take your time. I'll be in the kitchen." His tone is teasing, because I am very clearly staring at him. I grab a pillow from behind me and chuck it at him.

He ducks and slips out the door, chuckling as he walks down the hall.

I stay in the warmth of his bed for a few minutes more before dragging myself into the bathroom. After I've taken the quickest shower of my life, I steal one of Remington's black T-shirts, tugging it over my head and peering down to where it ends just above my knees.

Walking down the hall toward the kitchen, I comb my fingers through my damp hair. Remington has his back to me, frying bacon in a pan on the stove. The savory smell permeates the air, and my stomach growls.

"You shouldn't cook without a shirt," I say, walking into the kitchen and leaning against the counter. "You could get burned."

He turns to face me, and his eyes narrow. "Says the girl wearing my shirt."

I bite my lip, glancing down at it. "It was either this or nothing at all, so . . ."

Remington gestures to me with the spatula in his hand. "And you thought this would be my choice?"

I roll my eyes, but I can't ignore the way his words make my heart race. "Didn't get a long enough look last night?"

He doesn't miss a beat. "Never."

Shaking my head, I press my lips together against a smile and walk toward him as he turns to flip the bacon. I wrap my arms around his bare waist and rest my cheek against his back. "It smells amazing."

"There's coffee in the pot and orange juice in the fridge."

I peel myself away from him and head for the coffee maker. Because coffee. I pour us each a mug and open the fridge to find the milk, lightening my cup and adding some sugar. I watch Remington cook while I drink my coffee and attempt to enjoy this moment.

"Kit dropped off some of your things while you were in the shower. They're on the couch."

I nod, but the idea of the two of them interacting without a buffer makes me anxious. "Did he say anything about Samuel?"

"Nothing. But he mentioned that Nova's been in contact with other Wielder homes around the country. How do you like your eggs?" he throws in as if it's part of the conversation.

Once breakfast is ready, we sit together on stools at the counter and eat in silence. When we're done, I kick him out of the kitchen to shower, and I wash the dishes.

"You know," he says, coming down the hall with damp hair, "I could get used to having you here."

I press my lips together and glance at him over my shoulder. "I think we should probably get through this thing with the Elders before talking about, um, that."

Before he can answer, my phone starts ringing on the counter. I quickly dry my hands and answer it. "Kit," I say. "Have you heard anything?"

"Nova's been in contact with some of the other Wielder houses and managed to convince half a dozen of them to help convince the Elders to change the Accords. Many of them are wary, but they're putting their trust in Nova based on relationships he's created over the years."

I bite the inside of my cheek as my nerves unsettle the food in my stomach. "Everyone deserves a chance, Kit." *We should be able to live without fear of being hunted for being different.*

"I agree. Lydia and Mason are prepared to stand with us as well."

"Has Samuel spoken with the other Elders?" I ask while Remington lingers, leaning against the counter as he watches me.

Kit sighs. "Yes. They'd like to meet you."

"You say that like it's not what we wanted."

"I've trusted these people my entire life, Em, but I'm struggling with that right now. I don't know how this is going to go down, and that terrifies me."

"We'll make it work," I say, because what else is there? The only alternative would be the Elders killing me and Remington. *Or us killing them.*

"I hope that's true," he says in a low voice. "They want to meet in the clearing near the mausoleum."

The pit in my stomach feels heavier. "At the scene of my destruction. Great."

"Is Remington near you?"

"Uh-huh . . ."

"Can you give him the phone?"

I frown. "Kit?"

"Just do it. Please, Emery."

I hesitate before pulling the phone away from my ear and holding it toward Remington. "He wants to talk to you."

Remington stares at the phone with a strained expression, his jaw working before he takes it and walks away. I want to know what they're talking about, but I force myself to give him space and instead go into the living room to see what Kit dropped off earlier.

Ten minutes later, I've changed into some navy leggings and put on a bra but kept Remington's shirt on and am sitting on the couch. He comes back into the room and sets my phone on the coffee table.

"What was that about?"

"He wants me to teach you some magic in case we need to use it."

"Wasn't that our plan anyway?"

He nods, holding his hand out to me, and pulls me off the couch. "We should get started."

"Can't you just give me your magic?" I remark dryly.

Remington chuckles, squeezing my hand. "Oh, that's funny."

"Actually, I think that's what they call irony."

He rolls his eyes and finally lets go, much to my dismay. "Are you going to correct me this entire lesson, or . . . ?"

"That depends on you, my mentor." I can't help the grin on my lips.

It takes me a few minutes to get into the headspace where I can focus on the magic instead of Remington's presence so close —especially after last night.

"Take a deep breath," he says softly, and I do. "Are you ready?"

What a loaded question. Am I ready to face the Elders and potentially have to fight for my life, or run away and keep running with no end in sight? No freaking way. I want to go back to Covington and finish high school with my best friends. I want to stress over which college programs to apply to and obsess over my applications. I want to figure out what the heck I feel for the guy standing in front of me waiting for an answer.

One step at a time, I remind myself and take another deep breath. "I'm ready."

CHAPTER TWENTY-TWO

We walk downstairs to the empty club so there's more space to move around. There are also fewer things for me to break if I screw up, so really, it's a win-win.

"We're going to go over three different forms of manipulation," Remington explains, leaning against the bar. "I think we better start with cloaking." The faint twist of his lips makes me glare at him.

"I'm never going to live that down," I mutter.

He doesn't bother trying to hide his grin. "Probably not, no."

"Awesome. What else?"

"I want you to get this one down before we move on. The idea of this cloak isn't to make someone think you're another person. In this case, it will make you disappear altogether."

My stomach swirls with excitement. I can't help it—it's pretty cool. Maybe not under these circumstances, but otherwise. "So an invisibility spell?"

"Sure, if that's how you want to think of it. But you won't really be invisible, you'll just be manipulating the minds of those around you to believe you're not there."

"Like what you did that day at the café."

Remington nods. "It's easy enough when you're working with one person, but it can get tricky when there are multiple people."

"So how do I do this?"

"It's a test of willpower. You need to visualize yourself in the person's body. Visualize what they're seeing. And then you're going to alter it."

"That sounds fine in theory, but won't the Elders be able to sense a mental attack like that?"

"That's the beauty of our magic, little bird. Because it's not rooted in the elements, they can't touch it. Which means there's not a thing they can do to stop it."

My eyes widen. It's starting to make a little more sense why they wanted to get rid of the dark Wielders—they were scared. They couldn't control them. "Show me," I whisper.

Without preamble, Remington closes his eyes. Silence stretches between us, and from one moment to the next, I feel an odd tingling sensation at the back of my head. Before I can open my mouth to question him, Remington is gone. Except, I know he's not. I can sense him—his magic—but I can't see him.

A few seconds later, the sensation is gone, and Remington is standing in front of me again.

"Your turn," he offers. "When you go to latch on to someone's mind, you'll sense them like a ball of light. You'll see it in your mind and connect with it. It's different between the two of us because of our shared magic, but that's how you'll do it to someone else."

I nod and close my eyes, imagining myself through Remington's eyes. Unruly copper curls, warm brown eyes, boring old leggings, and his T-shirt. I focus on how the club appears behind me and then I visualize what it looks like without me. Instead, I picture myself back in Remington's loft, lounging on his couch as he stands in the kitchen making pancakes.

This magic is a breath of fresh air. It sends electricity through me and makes me feel as if I can do anything. Energy crackles through me; I want to feel this way forever.

Remington claps, and I open my eyes to find his shining with pride.

"Good," he murmurs, and giddiness fills my chest. "I have no idea what you did, but I didn't even feel you in my head."

I bite my lip, trying not to smile. "Guess I'm just awesome." I toss my curls over my shoulder dramatically.

"You know how to do it with one person, and while we can't practice with multiple people being the only ones here, it's the same method." He slides onto one of the barstools. "You'll see each individual mind as its own ball of light."

I nod. "What's next?"

"I want you to do that cloak again. And again. And again. Until you don't have to put effort into doing it. That's when you'll know you have a handle on it."

And so, we spend the next hour with me repeating the same cloak. He's right, though. It becomes muscle memory by the time he says we can move on.

Remington slides off the barstool, walking closer to me. "I showed you how to cloak yourself invisible in the case you need to get away. It's a defensive move."

"Okay . . ."

"What I'm about to teach you isn't like anything you've ever practiced, Emery. It's dangerous, and exactly what the Elders are afraid of."

My throat is too dry to speak, so I just nod.

"You're going to learn how to make someone think and feel as if they can't breathe. The magic won't affect them physically —as real as it feels—it will simply make them believe it."

I ponder that for a moment before asking, "Could someone with air magic actually make that happen?"

He laughs, but the sound holds no amusement. "I would

imagine so. I haven't pissed off someone with air magic enough to test that theory, though."

"Right," I finally say. "So our magic is only able to make someone *think* something is happening to them?"

He tilts his head to the side. "No. The final thing I'm going to teach you is something you should only use as a last resort. If this meeting goes nuclear—meaning, it's us or them—I want to know you have an effective offensive spell in your back pocket should you need to use it."

"You're scaring me," I admit, my brows knitting. I understand the severity of the situation, but hearing the words aloud makes it feel too real.

Remington frowns, closing the distance between us in a few strides, cupping my cheeks in his hands. "I'm sorry, but I need you to make it out of this. I will do whatever is necessary to make that happen."

I swallow the lump in my throat, wrapping my fingers around his wrists. "We're both going to make it out of this just fine."

His gaze searches mine. "I wish I shared your optimism, little bird."

I choke on a laugh. "Optimism," I echo, shaking my head. "It's not optimism, Rem—it's desperation. I can't think of any alternative or I'll lose it, and that's not going to help anyone."

His thumb brushes along my cheek as he leans in to kiss me. It's soft and quick, but my stomach is fluttering in an instant.

"You can't do that," I murmur, "if you want me to concentrate on learning this stuff."

Remington smirks. "Oh? Am I distracting you?"

My eyes narrow, but I can't find the will to be annoyed because I can't stop thinking about kissing him again. I pull his hands away from my face. "We need to focus."

"I am very focused, I assure you."

"Great. So teach me this breathing thing."

He chuckles. "All right, all right. This one is trickier because I can't show it to you like I did with the cloak, and the way I go about it may differ from what feels natural to you."

"Making someone believe they can't breathe doesn't feel natural to me at all," I point out.

"Don't worry about that right now."

"Why? Because what you're going to teach after this is even worse?"

He purses his lips for a moment before answering. "Yes."

My stomach drops. "Rem—"

"One thing at a time," he reminds me, and I nod reluctantly. "The way I learned this . . . trick, for lack of a better word, is to work with my own breathing. Each time I inhale, I pull air out of someone else, depleting their lungs' oxygen supply. With each exhale, I'm discarding it into the air. To them, they're struggling to get a breath in, but I'm not actually affecting their lungs. Just tricking their mind into believing it."

I wrap my head around his method—it seems simple enough, which makes me frown. Something so detrimental to another person shouldn't feel easy.

"Any questions?" he asks.

"I don't think so."

"Good. Now try it."

"Try what?" Realization hits me, and I immediately feel dumb. "I'm not doing that to you," I say in a voice several octaves higher than normal.

"Yes, you are. I need to know you can." He shoots me a grin. "Don't worry, little bird. I trust you."

A shiver races through me. "You . . . are you sure?"

"Come on. Give it a shot."

I curse under my breath, my palms growing damp. I wipe them on my thighs and focus my gaze on his chest, watching it rise and fall a few times as I sync my breaths with his. I inhale deeply, pulling the air away from him. I exhale a shallow breath and inhale again. My pulse spikes when Remington gasps for breath, his cheeks going pink. I want to stop, but I don't. *He wants me to do this*, I remind myself, pulling another breath from his lungs. His eyes go wide, his hand reaching up to grab his throat.

I take another breath. And another.

Finally, he lifts his hand, signalling me to stop, and I sever the connection, sucking in a sharp breath.

"That . . . was . . . good," he says in between breaths as his complexion returns to normal.

"I feel weird saying thank you," I admit.

"How are you feeling about all of this?"

"Overwhelmed, but I connected to this magic, so it's not as jarring, if that makes sense."

"If it makes sense to you, it makes sense," he tells me.

I nod. "You've been at this a lot longer than me. I'm not going to be as strong as you with all this mental stuff."

Remington's expression is thoughtful. "I've thought about that, which is why this last exercise isn't a mental one." He reaches into his pocket and pulls out a slip of paper. "This is a spell from my parents' book. I can't tell you why they had it. I've never used it, but I memorized the words years ago." He hands me the paper, and I open it, my eyes scanning the lines of hand-written text.

"What does it say?"

"Honestly, I have no idea. It's an ancient dead language that I couldn't find a record of anywhere. The rest of their book is mostly in English, which is why I know what this spell does."

I look up at him. "Which is what?"

"It allows the Wielder casting it to raise another's body temperature so high it can—"

"No," I cut him off, folding the paper over. "I'm not doing this."

"Emery, if it comes down to—"

"I said no, Rem." I hold the paper out to him, and he takes it from me.

"You'd rather die than learn a spell that could help you?"

"Help me at the cost of someone else."

A muscle ticks in his jaw. "Someone who wants you dead! The Elders are our enemies, or have you forgotten? They don't want peace with us—they don't want us to exist!"

"I know you're scared, Rem. I am too. But this—violence isn't the answer. We need to show them we aren't a threat. What you've shown me already is enough, okay? It has to be, because that . . . I can't do that."

His expression softens. "Okay," he finally says. "You don't have to learn the spell, but just know I will not hesitate to use it if I think for one second you're in danger."

My chest swells with . . . I'm not even sure what.

Remington may not think he's capable of love, but he is profoundly wrong about that.

I grab the front of his shirt and pull him close enough to wrap my arms around his neck. His arms come around my waist, and he holds me against him, resting his chin on the top of my head.

I'm not sure how long we stand there before my phone chimes.

I lean back just enough to pull it out and frown at the text from Kit. "It's time to go."

My entire body is shaking, and it isn't entirely from the cold wind whipping around us. Being forced to have faith in the same people who are the reason your family is dead . . . it isn't easy.

"You remember what I taught you?" Remington checks as we walk down the dirt road, getting closer to the clearing. His fingers are woven through mine and his thumb is tracing slow circles against the top of my hand.

I nod. "You're very thorough."

He cracks a grin. "This is true."

I stop moving and shake my head, panic gripping me so hard I can barely breathe.

Remington's eyes fill with concern. "Are you okay?"

I exhale a laugh. "Are *you* okay?" I step closer to him, wanting to shift the attention off of me. "These people killed your family. How are you not freaking out right now?"

There's a heartbeat of silence between us before Remington says, "I'm not *not* freaking out. I'm terrified with what's about to go down, but I stop myself from thinking about it. Because if I don't, I'm going to do something stupid to ruin the plan, like kidnapping your ass and getting far away from here."

I frown. "We're here to make a difference for everyone like us. We can't give up before we even start."

"You're right, and I told myself that, which is why we're still here and not on a plane to some remote island."

My responding laugh is uneven. "That sounds pretty good right about now," I admit.

He pulls me against his side and drops a kiss to the top of my head. "Come on, little bird. Let's get this over with."

We walk the rest of the way hand-in-hand, and the moment we step into the clearing, I swear the temperature drops.

I look around the wide-open space, pausing on the pile of rubble that used to be the mausoleum, and my pulse spikes like a jackhammer beneath my skin. It doesn't settle even when I spot Nova talking to a small group of people around his age. They must be the other house leaders Kit told me were coming. When I don't see Kit or the others with him, the knots in my stomach give a painful twist.

"Kit's not here," I say, low enough that Remington is the only one to hear it.

"It's fine, Emery. Just keep breathing."

I swallow the lump in my throat and struggle to blink back

tears. I suck in a breath when my eyes land on the Elders, standing in the middle of the clearing. Four men—including Samuel—and three women, all wearing heavy coats to block out the cold, and all staring at us.

My gaze goes down the line of them, each varying in age from mid-thirties to the oldest woman who appears to be at least sixty.

Nova turns around and spots us, leaving the group to walk over to one of the younger Elders. They exchange a few words before Nova approaches us.

"Emery, they'd like to speak to you without Remington." His voice is calm and steady, but his jaw is set tight, and I don't know how to take that.

Remington's grip tightens on my hand. "Not going to happen."

Nova shifts his gaze to Remington. "We're trying to avoid a fight. If this is going to work, you need to follow their directions."

"It's okay," I say in a soft tone, pulling my hand out of Remington's grasp. "Everything is going to be fine."

Seems I'm better at trying to convince others of that than making myself believe it.

I take a step away, but Remington grabs my wrist, pulling me back. His lips are at my ear, and he whispers an incantation I've never heard before. Energy zips through me, and my eyes go wide.

"What—"

"Shh," he murmurs, pressing his lips just below my ear. "Remember what I taught you. Use it if you have to. Do not hesitate."

He . . . gave me magic.

Not *all* of his magic—he wouldn't leave himself without any —but a jolt of it. It courses through me and gives me the confidence to square my shoulders.

"I understand," I whisper.

He drops a kiss against my cheek before letting go. When I steal a glance at him, his posture is rigid, and his eyes are ablaze with cerulean fire.

I swallow past the fear clogging my throat and follow Nova, keeping my chin up and my gaze trained on the Elders. The last time I saw my mom alive runs through my head, along with the reminder that these people took her from me.

Samuel steps away from the others and starts toward us.

My heart races. "Nova . . ."

"He's on our side," he reminds me, but that doesn't stop nausea from rolling through me like a tidal wave. Panic grips every part of me, like ice in my veins, but somehow my feet keep moving.

"Where the hell is Kit?"

"He's coming," Nova assures me, and I don't have time to press him.

Samuel meets us halfway across the clearing. He nods at Nova before turning his attention to me.

I stare at him, probably looking like a deer in headlights. As much as I want to be strong, I've never had a good poker face.

"A few of us tried to sway the others your way," Samuel says in a low voice.

"What does that mean?"

"This could work."

A spark of hope ignites in my chest as we walk toward the rest of the Elders. One steps forward—another man. This one appears much older than Samuel, with thinning gray hair and wrinkles around his mouth and dull green eyes.

"Emery Leclerc," he says, "Kit speaks very highly of you. Unfortunately, the same can't be said for your companion."

"What's your point?" I blurt without thinking, and Nova stiffens in my peripheral.

Off to a great start.

The Elder chooses to ignore that and instead says, "As I recall, you're quite new to your magic."

"Yes." I don't elaborate. It may not be to my benefit, but I can't bring myself to offer any more than that.

"And you've been practicing dark magic since you discovered your origins." He's not asking.

Nova clears his throat. "Cyden, Emery made a great deal of effort to learn elemental magic, as I'm sure Kit shared with you."

The Elder—Cyden—nods without taking his eyes off me. "Unfortunately, Emery, the magic you wield is not safe."

My pulse ticks faster, and my eyes jump toward the small crowd of house leaders. They're within earshot, and all of their expressions are grim. "You're wrong."

One of the female Elders gasps, and I fight the urge to roll my eyes at the theatrics.

Cyden tilts his head, his expression curious. "Oh?"

I lick the dryness from my lips. "It can be, of course. In the wrong hands. But the same could be said for elemental magic."

"Your magic is not born from the earth. It is not safe and cannot be allowed to exist. The balance—"

"You want to talk about balance?" I cut in. "Where was your concern for balance when you used my human mother to get to me?" My voice is rising with each word, and Remington comes over and stands on the other side of me.

Samuel shakes his head as Cyden narrows his eyes at Remington. He doesn't move.

"She broke our laws by keeping you hidden and for trying to pass you off as an elemental Wielder," the gasping female Elder from before says.

"Your laws," I echo bitterly, "should never have applied to her. She wasn't a Wielder and had no reason to live by your laws. All she was trying to do was take care of her family, and you punished her. There's no balance in that."

The rest of the Elders join the small group we've formed in the middle of the clearing.

My heart is racing and fear is clawing at my chest, but I refuse to cower to these people who took so much from me and from Remington.

And there's a good chance we're about to lose everything we have left.

CHAPTER TWENTY-THREE

Remember why we're here, I remind myself.

We're not here to fight. We're here to find common ground and come to an agreement on how to coexist.

I pull in a shallow breath, trying to calm my racing heart. "I don't expect you to trust me right now. What I'm asking is that you allow me—and Wielders like me—a chance. Being born shouldn't be a death sentence, and we shouldn't be punished for the mistakes of those who came before us." I look down the line of them, pressing my hands against my sides so they can't see the way they shake. "To take my life before I've even had a chance to prove myself . . . You're tipping the scale in the opposite direction of good."

"You may not have broken any of our laws yet, but Mr. Henstridge certainly has," Cyden says in response.

"What laws?" I push. "Is the punishment for breaking them death?"

A woman with sharp blue eyes, cropped black hair, and a permanent scowl steps forward. "Mr. Henstridge is irresponsible with his magic. He has used it freely around humans with no regard for the consequences of being discovered. Forget the fact he has used his power *against* not only humans, but members of this council." *If I had to bet, it was probably against her.*

My posture goes rigid. "Maybe he wouldn't have had to do that if—"

"Emery, don't." Remington's voice is a sharp whisper in my ear.

The woman shoots daggers at Remington. "The Henstridge line is—"

"Standing right here," I say, cutting her off, "wanting to come to a mutually beneficial agreement."

"How can you be sure?" another Elder asks.

"Because I trust him." I say the words without a single thought. "But you don't trust us because you're stuck in the past. We are a new generation of Wielders who want to live our lives without fear of being hunted by you, the figures meant to be leaders."

"Are there other dark Wielders in the area?" Samuel asks, glancing between Remington and me.

My breath catches, thinking of Adeline and Matthew. They're probably halfway to Houston by now. I shouldn't have figured they would show up and risk their lives, but there's a tinge of sadness in my chest at their absence. *Maybe it's for the best.* "No."

A couple of the Elders exchange glances—a middle-aged female with white-blond hair and dark eyes, and a bald man who appears slightly older than her with dark skin and light eyes that could be blue or green from where I'm standing. *Is that woman Myra?* I wish there was a way for me to know who here might be on our side . . . Though it's very clear who *isn't.*

Cyden steps forward, his eyes locked on Remington.

My jaw clenches as I watch Cyden move, and my muscles

tense. "What will it take?" I blurt as pressure builds in my chest. "What will it take for you to amend the Accords to include dark Wielders and give us the same chance any elemental Wielder would get?" My fingers tingle, and I'm not sure it's from the cold. "I've put everything on the table. You're either going to kill us anyway or—"

"With his magic and his past offenses, he is too dangerous to let go," Cyden says without taking his eyes off Remington.

"Emery," Remington says in a low voice, evidently sensing the magic stirring in me.

I barely register that Nova is touching my arm from the other side of me—a warning to keep it together.

"No," I say through my teeth. "You killed his entire family. I'm not going to let you—"

"Take it," Remington interrupts.

I whirl around, flooded with confusion. "What are you talking about?"

Remington steps around me, and when I try to stop him, Nova pulls me back. Remington meets Cyden's gaze, and I hold my breath.

"You're concerned about me having the ability to wield magic you can't control. You don't trust me because of my past, the things I've done, whatever. Fine." He glances at me, snaring my gaze and holding it. "I'll give it to her. All of it. Let her show you just how wrong you are about our magic."

That knocks the air out of my lungs faster than anything. My chest hollows out as my head whips around to see the group of Wielders Nova brought all staring at Remington with wide eyes.

Another Elder, this one with long brown hair tied back at the nape of his neck, steps forward, his boots crunching in the snow. "You'd give up your magic for—"

"I'd give up *everything* for her."

Out of all the ways I came up with for how this could go, this was nowhere near a possibility.

The guy who wanted to steal my magic when we met is willing to give up his own forever to ensure we make it out of this alive. And I'm pretty sure I've fallen in love with him.

What an awful moment to come to that realization.

Silence fills the clearing; I'm not the only one surprised by Remington's suggestion.

Cyden glances at Nova before turning his gaze toward me. "You appear shocked by this," he comments.

I try to speak, but nothing comes out. Finally, I manage to say, "It's the first I'm hearing of it." Pulling away from Nova, I turn to Remington and say, "We're not doing this. I can't . . . This isn't . . . *Why?*"

Remington moves to stand in front of me and grips my shoulders, steadying me. "Breathe," he murmurs. "If this is the only way to come to an agreement, so be it." There's a ghost of a smile on his lips when he says, "I need you to trust me now."

I press my lips together, too overwhelmed and taken off guard by this turn of events to offer a response. When I turn to look at Nova, my gaze halts on movement in the tree line. Relief floods through me as Kit walks toward us. With him is Lydia and Mason, as well as Adeline and Matthew.

They came.

As the group gets closer, the house leaders Nova was speaking to earlier move in as well.

"What is this?" the black-haired Elder asks, her scowl still firmly in place. "I thought you said there weren't any other dark Wielders in the area."

Matthew speaks up. "We were passing through when we met Emery, and she told us she wanted to work with you."

Adeline slides her fingers through Matthew's and says, "We've never hurt anyone. Never used our magic around humans. We just want to live a normal life without fearing . . . you."

Kit scans the clearing before addressing everyone. "We are

here to express our dedication to the law, Bellamy." *So Scowl Face has a name.* "To ensure we are protected and trained to wield our abilities in accordance with those laws. All of us."

Cyden regards him with a curious expression. "Mr. Harris, I must say, I was not expecting this from you."

Kit nods. "It's important to me, sir. To all of us. We need to work together, protect each other—at the very least, learn to coexist."

Nova walks closer to Kit, standing next to him. "Myself and several others have agreed to house non-elementals as long as they abide by the same rules as everyone else. We'll have mentors learn ways to help them with their unique abilities."

"Sounds like you've got this all figured out," Bellamy says.

"No," Kit says, "but it's a start. We still need your help."

"You need our *permission*," she corrects.

Kit frowns. "We would like to amend the Accords to—"

"We've heard it already, Mr. Harris."

"That's what happens when you show up late to the party," Remington says, smirking.

I shoot him a look. *Really? Now?*

Kit looks to Nova. "What's going on, then?"

Nova sighs. "Remington has offered to give his magic to Emery as a show of goodwill. To prove our intention here is that of peace."

Kit's eyes go wide, but he doesn't have a chance to respond before Bellamy says, "I don't buy it." The rest of the Elders turn to look at her. "This magic is evil and wrong and needs to be eliminated. The danger it poses could destroy everything we've built."

"Our magic can be just as destructive," Lydia shouts before snapping her mouth shut, her eyes wide and cheeks flushed— though that could be from the below-freezing temperature.

"She's right," Mason chimes in with a level voice, his fingers flexing at his sides. A moment later, the wind picks up, blowing snow off the trees surrounding us and turning the clearing into a snow globe. "We have the power to do much more than what we're taught is acceptable, but we choose not to. The dark Wielders should be given that same choice."

I shiver against the cold as snow gets stuck in my curls, and my pulse continues to race as the wind dies down. I sneak a glance at Adeline and Matthew, who stand behind Lydia and Mason. They're both pale and stiff and look as if they're about five seconds away from bolting. Understandable.

"The decision is yours," Kit says to the Elders.

Cyden takes his time, looking at each one of us before clasping his hands in front of him. "No."

My stomach drops, and the air leaves my lungs in a silent gasp. *What? They're not even going to vote on it? What the hell is the point of having a whole council of Elders if this one guy is going to call all the shots?* My control is slipping. Energy crackles through me like a live wire, and I can't stand still.

"Emery." Remington's voice is low, strained, which does nothing to calm the war of fear and anger tearing through me.

"Wait," Kit says, "please."

"Mr. Harris—"

"I've trusted and followed you my entire life. From the moment I found out magic was real, that I was a Wielder who could use the elements, I looked up to the leadership you provided. The guidance to people like Nova who have dedicated their lives to helping new Wielders, protecting them from the human world that has no idea magic exists. But now . . . You'd rather remove what you view as a potential problem than try to solve it." He shakes his head. "That isn't the leadership I grew to admire, and I hope you'll reconsider. I won't follow a group of people who refuse to give a chance to people who have done nothing wrong. I stood by once and let that happen." His gaze flicks toward Remington, and I hold my breath. "Never again."

"Kit," Samuel starts.

"This isn't right, and you know it!" The temperature in the clearing rises, and all of us watch as the snow melts from the trees and the ground in a matter of seconds. The ground dries up so fast the grass beneath our feet turns stiff and yellow.

The chill in my bones is replaced by tingling, and I watch with wide eyes as a line of fire ignites across the ground, separating us from the Elders with tall flames.

"What are you doing?" I shout at Kit, but he doesn't hear me.

The flames rise, burning so hot I turn my face away.

"Enough!" Cyden bellows, and Kit extinguishes the fire. "You have done nothing today but prove you are not to be trusted with your abilities either, Mr. Harris." He looks to the other Elders and waves to the one with his hair tied back. "Stephen, show Mr. Harris to the facility. We'll deal with him once we're done here."

Panic washes through me like ice water, and my eyes feel as if they're going to bulge right out of my face. "No!" My gaze whips to Samuel. "Don't let this happen. Please!"

Samuel's lips are set in a tight line, his eyes dark. "I believe we should give them a chance," he speaks up. "This isn't who we are, punishing Wielders who have done nothing wrong. *That* is what disrupts the balance."

"Traitor," Bellamy seethes. "You should be stripped of your title for even suggesting that we—"

"Samuel is right," the woman with white-blond hair says. That must be Myra.

Bellamy gapes at her before turning to Cyden. "We cannot allow this."

"I agree with Bellamy," Stephen adds. "We can't ignore years of history and risk giving these dark Wielders a chance." He shakes his head. "We must stay the course."

To eliminate us.

I reach for Remington's hand, fear clogging my throat to the point that I can't speak. He laces his fingers through mine, gripping my hand tight.

Cyden purses his lips, looking from us to the line of Elders behind him. He stops at the woman on the end with frizzy red hair. "Selene, you haven't spoken."

Her red-painted lips flatten. "I fear you will not like what I have to say."

My head snaps up. *Is she on our side?*

"I see," Cyden says. "And you, David?" He turns his attention to the man next to Myra.

"We do not punish innocent Wielders," he says, echoing Samuel's sentiment.

"No one here is innocent," Bellamy snaps, and when she pulls a long blade from the inside of her coat, the blood drains from my face.

"We didn't come here to fight," Nova says, holding his hands in front of him. "No one needs to get hurt."

In the time it takes me to blink, the blade slices through the air, heading straight for—

"No!" I scream as Nova's knees hit the ground, his eyes wide with confusion. The hilt of the blade sticks out of his abdomen, and his fingers hover around it. Lydia and Mason rush over, dropping to the ground on either side of him, and the other house leaders that stood with Nova at the start flee the clearing.

Pure rage consumes me, narrowing my vision on Bellamy. I don't hesitate. My magic is sharp and vicious, stealing the air from her lungs. Her eyes bulge, and she claws at her throat. I may only be making her *think* she can't breathe, but when her knees buckle and she falls to the ground, my very real knee connects with her face, knocking her out cold.

Everything happens so quickly. Stephen comes at me from the right, but I duck under his arm, and he flies toward Remington. I watch as his lips move, and I feel the crackle of magic before Stephen clutches his chest, screaming in pain. Remington shoves him to the side, and the man falls to the ground, thrashing and whimpering until his movements become jerky and he finally goes motionless.

He killed him.

My heart pounds in my chest as our eyes meet, and I bite down on my bottom lip to stop it from quivering. *This wasn't supposed to happen.* I look to where Nova is still on the ground. His eyes are open, but his face is too pale.

"Get him out of here," I yell at Lydia and Mason, and they haul him up, dragging him toward the tree line.

I step toward where Cyden is facing off with Kit, and snarl, "If Nova dies, I will end you."

"He . . . deserved it." a cracked voice says from behind me. I whirl around just in time to see Bellamy get to her feet.

Myra steps in between us. "Bell, please listen. We need to remember our purpose. We need to—"

My brows knit when she stops talking. Bellamy steps in, wrapping her arm around Myra as she falls against her.

When Bellamy steps back, I let out a shuddering breath at the blood coating her fingers and stare in horror as Myra collapses on the ground, her chest unmoving.

Adeline and Matthew rush into the madness, attacking Bellamy together. She blinks rapidly, staring straight ahead with wide eyes. They're altering her vision so she can't see.

Bellamy screams, her high-pitched voice filling the clearing to the point I want to cover my ears against the shrill sound of it.

Selene shakes her head and walks closer to the woman. A second later, her scream cuts off and her face turns red.

I made her think she couldn't breathe, but Selene is actually stopping the air in her lungs. This time when Bellamy falls to the ground, I know she won't be getting back up.

"You've . . . corrupted this . . . leadership," Cyden directs at

Samuel, wiping the blood from his mouth where I assume Kit punched him.

"No," Samuel says, closing in on him. "This leadership was corrupt from the start. I stood by too long and allowed things that never should have been done to happen. We all did. We allowed our fear of something we couldn't control drive us to hurt and kill people." He looks around the clearing, to the bodies on the ground. "Even each other."

Kit steps aside as Samuel moves closer to Cyden, and Remington pulls me against his side as he steps back too.

Cyden's voice is gravelly as he says, "We must uphold the Accords." He spits blood onto the ground.

"No," Samuel says, "We must change them. If you can't see that—"

"I will not sign these Accords." Cyden's dull green eyes narrow on Remington and me.

"You won't live to see them," Remington snarls, and my chest tightens.

"Rem—"

He pulls away before I can stop him, launching himself at Cyden. He knocks Samuel away, tackling Cyden to the ground before his fist slams into the man's jaw. It's not a fair fight by any means, considering Cyden's age.

Remington pulls his arm back to hit him again, but instead is pushed back by an invisible force. He hits the ground hard, grunting, but then he starts to laugh. "Air magic? Nice one, old guy." He gets to his feet as Cyden struggles to stand.

"You're just like your father," he sneers at Remington.

Remington stops mid-stride. "Yeah?" He brushes the dirt from his jacket as he walks back to Cyden. "There's at least one difference between us, though."

Cyden's jaw is tight set when he asks, "What's that?"

"You won't get to kill me."

I choke on a gasp as Remington slams his hand against the man's chest, uttering those words I couldn't bring myself to learn, and watch as Cyden meets the same fate he chose for so many.

He's gone before his body hits the ground with a thud, and I let out a breath.

Remington bows his head, stepping away from Cyden's still form. Slowly, he turns toward me, his eyes shadowed with a heartbreaking mix of grief and guilt.

I launch myself at him, wrapping my arms around his neck and burying my face in his chest as a sob tears through me.

His arms come around me and hold me to him. When I pull back, wiping my cheeks, Adeline and Matthew offer weak smiles.

"I'm so sorry," I tell them, sniffling. "I didn't think . . . It wasn't supposed to happen this way."

Matthew nods before looking at Samuel. "Do we need to keep running? Hiding from the Elders?"

Samuel shakes his head. His voice is deep with exhaustion when he turns to me and says, "You have your amendment, Emery." He looks to what's left of the Elders—Selene and David. "Things are going to be different now."

I lick the dryness from my lips. "Thank you. And I'm sorry about Myra. I know she was on our side."

Samuel nods solemnly.

My stomach is in knots, a confusing mix of anxiety and excitement that is often difficult to differentiate. Once word gets out that dark Wielders are safe from the Elders, I have a feeling we'll be seeing more of them. They won't have to hide anymore, and the new ones will need support just like I did—and once I have a solid grasp on my magic, I want to help them.

Selene and David approach us, and Selene says, "I'll put the word out that the Accords will be amended immediately to include both elemental and dark Wielders."

"I can help," Kit says.

Samuel nods. "I'd appreciate that." There's a brief pause before he adds, "I'd also like you to join us."

Kit's mouth drops open. "What?"

"There are a few openings on the council," he says in a grave voice. "You would be an asset."

"I . . . I would be happy to. So long as I can continue to train new Wielders. I don't want to give that up."

"Deal," Samuel says, shaking Kit's hand.

I offer Kit a watery smile. This will be good for him.

The sound of a phone ringing makes me jump. It's oddly jarring.

Kit reaches into his pocket and pulls out his phone, his eyes going wide. "It's Lydia." He brings the phone to his ear. "How is he?"

My heart in is my throat until I see Kit's breath of relief, then I let myself exhale.

"He's fine," Kit announces to the small group of us, nodding to whatever Lydia is saying. "Okay. Thanks. We'll be there soon." He pockets his phone and says, "The blade didn't hit anything major, and they were able to get him to a hospital fast enough to stop the bleeding."

"Thank god," I breathe, my eyes burning with more tears. I don't know what I would've done if I'd lost Nova too.

"Good," Samuel says. "You should go to him."

Adeline catches my gaze and says, "We're going to go. You have no idea how happy we are to not to have to look over our shoulders in fear anymore, so thank you." She pulls me into a hug. I hug her back and then hug Matthew, and after making them promise to keep in touch, the two of them disappear through the tree line.

Samuel nods toward the clearing. "We will deal with this."

"Not to sound self-centered or anything," Remington says, "but what about me?"

Samuel looks at Selene and David—who nod—before turning his attention to Remington. "You want to keep your magic?

"Uh, preferably."

"Okay then. You have a clean slate with us."

His brows shoot up his forehead, and his posture stiffens. "I . . . Really?"

The corner of Samuel's mouth curves up, and his gaze flicks to me for a brief moment before returning to Remington. "I have a feeling she'll keep you in line."

"Whoa, hey now. Don't put that on me," I cut in, a little grin on my lips.

Remington snakes his arm around my waist and pulls me against his side. "Looks like you're stuck with me now."

I roll my eyes, but make no move to shift away from him.

Kit, Remington, and I walk out of the clearing, heading back toward Nova's property. We climb the stairs onto the porch, and there's a stretch of silence between us.

"Congrats on the promotion," I tell Kit in a teasing tone.

He laughs. "Yeah, thanks." His gaze flicks to where Remington stands off to the side, looking out at the snow-covered front yard. When he clears his throat, Remington turns toward us, and Kit holds his hand toward him. "I know you and I aren't friends, and I will never be able to make up for what happened to Aurelia, but I am sorry." He pauses. "And I'm glad Emery has you."

Remington glances at the outstretched hand and steps forward. I can't help but tense, and my breath catches when Remington takes Kit's hand and shakes it.

"Thank you," he finally says in a rough voice, as if he's struggling to keep the emotion out of his tone.

Kit drops his arm back to his side. "I'm going to clean up before heading to the hospital. I'll see you guys in a bit," he says before walking into the house, leaving Remington and me alone.

He shoots me a grin, making my stomach giddy with butter-flies, and holds his hand out.

I take it without a thought. It feels so natural. As if I've known him my entire life. And maybe there's a part of me that has.

CHAPTER TWENTY-FOUR

Six months later . . .

I'm surrounded by boxes. My clothes are sticking to me, and I'm pretty sure I've consumed enough cold brew to give me a heart attack.

Lana and Jessa have been coming over nearly every day since exams finished two weeks ago to help me pack, but boxing up an entire house isn't a small job.

After everything that went down with Elders, I moved back to Covington and finished high school with my friends. They're both moving to Denver in the fall for school, but I'm staying local to Atlanta. There's a house for Wielders there run by one of Nova's friends who wants to work with dark Wielders.

I'm starting at Georgia State University in the fall, and Remington has agreed to be a mentor to Wielders like Kit was to me. I'll be doing the same on weekends and in between classes —well, once I get a better handle on my magic.

Remington walks into the living room, where I'm packing up

the last of the books. He has an iced coffee in his hand and grins the moment he sees me.

"Where's mine?" I ask, frowning at the coffee.

He arches a brow. "Hello to you too."

I narrow my eyes at him. "You didn't bring me one. I knew it. I knew you were evil."

Remington leans in the doorway, smirking as he points to the ledge on the window where my discarded Starbucks cups sit. "I think you're set, little bird."

"Hey, you don't know those are all from today."

"Tell me they're not and you can have this one."

I open my mouth to respond, but I can't bring myself to lie about it. "Whatever," I grumble, closing the box and taping it shut. "Did you come by to help or just distract me?"

Remington peers around the room as he sips his iced coffee and shrugs. "Looks like you could use a break."

"What I could use is a spell or something to pack the rest of this place for me. And a shower."

"Hmm." His eyes come back to me and stay there, roaming the length of me. "I can help with one of those things."

I chuck the roll of tape at him, and he narrowly dodges it. "Seriously?" I groan. "You are just . . ." My voice trails off as he sets down his drink and saunters toward me.

"Yes?" He kicks the box aside and crowds me against the now-empty bookshelf built into the wall.

I shake my head. "Proving my point," I finally manage to say.

He cocks his head, his eyes flicking between mine as his smirk remains in place. "How so?"

"This." I gesture between us. "I'm trying to focus and you're being all . . . distracting."

"If you think this is distracting," he says, leaning in to brush his lips across mine, "you have no idea what you're in for."

I have no doubt in my mind that Remington is right—and I cannot wait.

THE END

Reviews are everything to an author. If you enjoyed *These Wicked Delights*, please consider leaving a review on Goodreads and your favorite bookseller's website.

ACKNOWLEDGMENTS

This book is special in many ways, mostly because it was an uphill battle right from the beginning until the very end. Now it's done and out in the world, and I'm so excited to share it with readers.

On that note, my greatest thanks to the lovely readers who took a chance on this book. Who are sharing it with their friends and posting reviews online. Word of mouth is so important for authors, and I am greatly appreciative of your support!

To my critique partners and early readers, Allison Alexander, Bethany Atazadeh, and Kim Chance, for your encouraging feedback that helped me whip this story into something I'm thrilled to share with readers!

To Vivien Reis, for your hard work on the stunning cover of this book. I'm so grateful you were willing to work with me and my dozens of changes and tweaks until it was perfect.

To my editor, Cassidy Clarke, for your attention to detail while polishing this book.

To Kirsti Salmi for your incredible friendship.

As always, thank you to my friends and family, for your continued support of my creative passions.

ABOUT THE AUTHOR

Jessi Elliott is a new adult and young adult paranormal and fantasy romance author. She lives in Ontario, Canada with her adorable calico cat, Phoebe.

When she's not working on her next book, she likes to hang out with friends and family, get lost in a steamy romance novel, watch *Friends*, and drink coffee.

Find Jessi at www.jessielliott.com and on social media. You can join her newsletter to stay up to date on book news and upcoming releases, and her Facebook reader lounge for exclusive news, promos, review opportunities, and giveaways!

instagram.com/authorjessielliott

patreon.com/authorjessielliott

amazon.com/Jessi-Elliott/e/B079X3RDSJ

bookbub.com/authors/jessi-elliott

goodreads.com/authorjessielliott

youtube.com/authorjessielliott

twitter.com/AuthorJElliott

facebook.com/authorjessielliott